# WEIRD WILD WEST

## CARTER RYDYR AND ETHAN SOMERVILLE

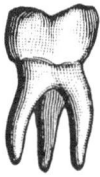

**Bizarro Pulp Press**
an imprint of JournalStone Publishing

Bizarro Pulp Press books may be ordered through booksellers or by contacting:

Bizarro Pulp Press, a JournalStone imprint
     www.BizarroPulpPress.com

The views expressed in this work are solely those of the author and do not necessarily reflect the views of the publisher, and the publisher hereby disclaims any responsibility for them.

ISBN: 978-1-947654-40-2


Printed in the United States of America
JournalStone rev. date: April 20, 2018

     Cover Art: Dave Heinrich

     Interior Illustrations: SCAR—Steve Carter and Antoinette Rydyr

     Interior Formatting: Lori Michelle
          www.theauthorsalley.com

# PART 1

# HELL DORADO

# CHAPTER 1

THE LOPSIDED, SHOT-UP old sign outside the town read "Sunbleached Plains". It should have read "Sunbaked Plains". Or more appropriately, "Sunscorched Plains". Blasted plateau stretched to the horizon where half-melted mesas struggled towards a brilliant, copper-blue sky. What plants did manage to burst through the poisoned flats were twisted and misshapen. A hot yellow sun blazed its deadly rays without fear of soothing cloud or rain. The residents of Sunbleached Plains couldn't remember the last time life-giving water had fallen. What liquid they did have was foul and brown, dug from deep within the toxic earth.

A large carriage, wooden panels held together with brass rivets, was parked out of the front of a Main Street tavern called the Eviscerated Buffalo. It was heavily laden with luggage tied down on the top and at the back, and had four thick iron-shod wheels for rolling through the harsh terrain beyond town. A complicated pulley system ran from the front to its engine, a formidable construction of gears and pistons all held in check within a stout iron shell mounted on four more of those big steel wheels.

At the moment the engine was idling with a low rumble. A tall chimney at the front of the monstrous device puffed the occasional dirty cotton-ball cloud of smoke.

In the front seat of the carriage sat the driver; a man known as Zeke "The Freak" Sarandon. A faded, broad-brimmed hat was pulled low over his eyes, but not so low that it concealed the many stitched-up scars that criss-crossed his craggy face. He muttered under his breath and rocked slowly back and forth as he waited for his gunmen and passengers. Occasionally he would pull something from one pocket of his filthy grey overcoat and gnaw absently upon it. He may not have had many teeth left in his head, but those he did possess had all been filed to points and capped with steel.

He spat out a mouthful of shards onto the dusty ground. They looked like fragments of bone.

From the alley down beside the tavern came a coughing, grinding noise followed by a deep, throaty roar. A large cloud of smoke puffed out from the darkness. A minute or so later a man in a broad hat and rough woollen poncho walked out. He was wearing tall boots and carrying a long rifle at his side. The gun had a scope attached to the top and several dials along the side. There was a lot of wire wrapped around the barrel and the muzzle flared at the end. This individual clambered up into the spare seat beside Zeke and grunted a greeting as he settled with the weapon across his knees.

Zeke lifted a gnarly hand also criss-crossed with scars.

The roaring from the alley grew louder and the object responsible for the racket soon appeared. A tall, narrow mechanical device rolled out, shaped like a horse from the days of old when such creatures had been commonplace. But where the horse's head should have been were the various controls for the engine: crank handle, levers, buttons and gauges to show pressure and fuel levels. Instead of legs the device rode on four enormous disc wheels. The engine was located within the thing's 'belly', a complex system of pistons and drive shafts. Smoke belched from a chimney at the back, where the tail would have been.

Seated astride this bizarre contraption was another individual, similarly clad to the gunman who had climbed up beside Zeke. He too carried a formidable blunderbuss, attached to the back of the saddle behind him.

He manoeuvred his mount up behind the carriage to wait and powered down the engine into idle mode. Its roar softened to a gentle rumble.

Somewhere a clock chimed the hour and the tavern's swing doors were flung wide. Zeke's latest group of customers began to appear from within the bowels of the inn and clamber up into the carriage.

Pat Davison stepped out first. He was a tall, handsome gentleman with a handlebar moustache, aged around forty, well-dressed in a new bowler hat and velvet frock-coat. He had piercing blue eyes the colour of the brilliant sky above. He needed an ebony cane to help him walk as he had an odd, stiff-legged gait like he'd broken his leg. Still, it didn't seem to impair his speed and he scrambled up into the conveyance with considerable agility. Once settled on the plush seat within he poked his head back out and shouted for his companions to "hustle their bustles".

"I have very important business in Kellyville, and I'd dearly like to arrive before my next birthday!"

Marilou-Belle Watkins scurried out next, still struggling to adjust her large, flower-covered bonnet. It would have sat more comfortably had her thick black hair not been so tightly and perfectly coiled on top of her head. She wore a beautiful crinoline covered with beads and ribbons and a lacy shawl around her shoulders. Gemstones glistened in swirling patterns across her cheekbones.

"Awright, awright!" she drawled as she gathered her heavy skirts. "I'm comin'. Don't rush a lady!" Due to the size of her voluminous skirts she clambered up into the carriage with considerably less speed and grace. Pat didn't rise to help her up, but when she was within his reach he did extend a desultory hand to pull her the last few feet.

Some gentleman you are, Marilou thought disdainfully as she sat down, but ever the lady she said politely; "Thank you, kind sir."

Samuel Simkins emerged from the tavern after Marilou. He looked like an undertaker in his long black coat and very tall top hat. He wore a pair of pince-nez and simply sniffed by way of a greeting to Pat and Marilou as he folded himself into a seat. Pat had removed his bowler on making himself comfortable, but Samuel kept his stovepipe hat firmly in place. He smelled very strongly of tabackie smoke, as if he'd just finished a pipe.

Emmett T. Billings followed. He was red-faced and somewhat corpulent, dressed in a brightly coloured coat and matching hat. He greeted everyone as he settled into the carriage, even leaning forward to take Marilou's gloved hand and place a kiss on the back. She blushed and giggled.

The fifth member of the party was Billy Levi, a ten-year old boy. He was also on the plump side, with a head full of angelic curls and a round, surly face. He was dressed in a short coat and knickerbockers. When Marilou called a cheerful "Hello sweetie" to him, he simply grunted and plonked himself in between Marilou and Samuel.

The sixth and last member of their travelling group was Sallianne Veerhoven. Tall and beautiful with long blonde hair piled up high on her head, she wore a very tight, low-cut corset and an enormous frilly bustle. A silk scarf was tied around her throat, but it did little to conceal her very impressive cleavage. "Whoops! Pardon me!" she giggled as she tried to settle in between Pat and Emmet. "Bit of a squash in here, isn't it?"

"It wouldn't be if you ladies didn't wear such gigantic dresses," muttered Samuel. Billy looked up and snorted.

"Well, ah never," declared Marilou. She pulled out a fan and started fluttering it in her face. Fortunately the gale she created was welcome in the close, warm space within the carriage. It may only have been eight o'clock in the morning, but it was already uncomfortably hot.

"Are we all aboard and settled?" yelled Zeke from outside in a distinctive gravelly voice.

"Yes!" called Pat impatiently. A few others echoed their assent.

"Good. We may be takin' the most direct route to Kellyville, but we still 'ave four days of travellin' ahead of us, so we'd best be on our way." Up in his driver's seat Zeke pulled hard on his right-hand rein to bring the carriage engine out of idle-mode. The reins were actually chains, wrapped in leather at the top, used to control the machine from a distance. The engine chugged into life, the chimney spewing out more dirty smoke, and slowly the massive, iron-shod wheels began to turn, crunching on the gravel beneath. The carriage started to roll down the main road of Sunbleached Plains. The gunman on his mechanical horse followed.

The journey to Kellyville had begun.

# CHAPTER 2

A N HOUR LATER the quiet country town of Sunbleached Plains was disturbed once more by the distinctive roar of an approaching mechanical horse. Only this one was far louder, and coughed and spluttered, belching out far more greasy black smoke than it should have. When it finally appeared it revealed itself to be rusty and scratched from thousands of miles of rolling through the wilderness. The wheels were bent in places. Bolts were missing. Coils of rope and wire had been wrapped around sections to hold them together. Showers of sparks flashed from exposed junctions around the head. The horrific machine farted out a particularly nasty sulphuric cloud as it finally shuddered to a stop outside the Eviscerated Buffalo.

Bystanders who had been about to point and laugh at the rickety contraption soon fell silent in fear as the horse's occupant jumped down with an ominous jingle of spurs. Some even retreated back into the safety of their stores and brothels.

The hellfire stench had not come from his engine. It had come from *him*.

The man was tall and very skinny, dressed in a dusty leather riding coat pocked with bullet holes. He wore a battered old cowboy hat pulled down low. With every step he took his spurs clinked. The true purpose of these devices had been long forgotten. These days they were used as weapons in street brawls to stomp opponents into the ground and rip open awful wounds.

As the man moved with a determined, somewhat lopsided gait, his long coat flapped open to reveal the torn, ragged clothes he wore beneath—and the formidable pistol, bristling with dials and levers, holstered at his hip.

The rents in his clothing couldn't quite hide the rents beneath in his flesh.

The gunslinger stomped up a set of wooden stairs and lurched through the swing doors into the Eviscerated Buffalo's dim, smoky interior. Despite the hour there were already a few serious drinkers inside, including the town drunk, who was already halfway through his first bottle of Tonsil Paint. The town sheriff and deputy were also inside, enjoying a couple of nips as part of their weekly bribe. They were a pair of husky, recently appointed young men, puffed up with their own self-importance and pride, dressed in brand new cowboy hats and long leather coats.

All conversation silenced as the newcomer clinked his way up to the bar. The bartender looked up into a visage that was no longer in quite so much shadow. His jaw dropped in horror.

The gunslinger's face was as torn up as his body. One eye was missing completely, a ripped, gaping socket where it used to be. The other was a milky orb that should not have been able to glare so penetratingly through the barkeep's own soul. The lips were shredded, revealing a jaw with several teeth missing.

A maggot crawling along one of the gunslinger's exposed ribs plopped out to wriggle sluggishly on the bar.

"Can someone tell me where I might find Pat Davison?" the gunslinger wheezed in a sibilant tone. He picked up the fat maggot in bony fingers with long, pointed fingernails and popped it back into his mouth. Those crooked teeth mashed it into oblivion. "I know he came here."

The bartender could only mouth silently. By this stage all the other occupants had risen to their feet, even the drunk with his whiskey bottle.

"It's a perfectly reasonable question," rasped the gunslinger. "Just tell me the whereabouts of Pat Davison and I'll be on my way. I don't want no trouble."

"Well, you got trouble, boy," growled the sheriff as he clapped a hand on the gunslinger's bony shoulder. "We don't want your stinking undead kind here!"

The gunslinger spun around and the sheriff gulped at the sight of him up close. The stench of death closed around him like a fist. It wasn't the smell of decay so much as the meaty stink of blood and internals exposed to the air. Behind him his deputy coughed,

struggled to hold on to his guts—and lost the battle in one long, noisy gurgle. Puke sprayed out all over the wooden floor.

"Now git back up on yer junkpile hoss, and ride yer rotting carcass out of our town!" The sheriff pointed a shaking finger at the door.

The gunslinger didn't move. "I'll skedaddle soon as someone tells me where Pat Davison is at."

Suddenly the barkeep rose up behind him and smashed a very large, heavy brewer's bottle over the gunslinger's head, showering him with cheap moonshine. The force of the blow was sufficient to fracture his skull and stagger him, but since he was already dead that didn't bother him overly much.

The gunslinger straightened up as one of the other tavern's occupants swung a punch at his midriff. There was a wet squelch as his fist went in through an old wound due to a broken rib lodged in the gunslinger's chest. The attacker shrieked. The gunslinger shoved the man in the forehead with the flat of his hand. His fist tore from the gunslinger's stomach with another disgusting wet sound as he was sent flying halfway across the room. He crashed into a table and flipped it like a tiddly-wink, falling unconscious on the floor.

"Now it looks like we gotta do this the hard way!" growled the gunslinger. He lifted his hands, curling them into fists. "If it's a fight you want, it's a fight you'll get."

The barman jumped up on the bar and launched himself at the gunslinger. The sheriff dived in at the same time and together they managed to wrestle him down onto the floor. He may have been skinny but he was very wiry, with the formidable strength of the undead behind him. Punches rained down on him, but he found them more annoying than deadly. He managed to throw both the barman and the sheriff off, sending the pair staggering back into more chairs and tables and shattering them to matchwood.

"Gawdammit!" he roared. "Stop wastin' my time! *Where'n hell is Pat Davison?*"

It was at this point the queasy deputy finally managed to get his guts back under control. He joined in the fight by charging the gunslinger at full speed and collected him in the middle of the room. He wrapped his arms around his waist and hurled him towards a window. The gunslinger flew through the glass with a mighty crash and tumbled across the wooden landing to drop onto the street below.

The sheriff straightened up and drew his gun. He pressed a button to cock it. It powered up with a whine and sparks began to sizzle around the barrel. "Let's make sure he can't come back!" he declared as he headed for the Eviscerated Buffalo's doors.

The deputy drew his own gun and followed. The barkeeper raced back around behind his bar to grab his own rifle.

Out in the middle of the dusty street, the gunslinger slowly picked himself up. As he rose unsteadily to his feet he saw the sheriff and his deputy up on the landing, aiming their irons at him. Then the tavern doors banged and the bartender appeared, pointing a rifle with a flared muzzle like a trumpet. Ominous puffs of smoke were coming from deep inside. The gunslinger reached for his own weapon, but he was too late. The others all had the draw on him. Their guns discharged with a mighty roar that echoed through the entire town. Exploding bullets, electrical discharges, plasma blasts and laser beams all ripped through the zombie's body, tearing him limb from limb and scattering his parts across the entire width of the street.

"Dang!" gasped the town drunk at the grisly sight. Hurriedly he quaffed the rest of his whiskey.

The sheriff, deputy and barman lowered their smouldering weapons. They'd dealt with a few zombies in the past. Although some could be stopped by blasting their heads off, the more coherent ones needed to be completely blown to pieces before they would stop.

A wind stirred the dismembered bits on the road . . . only there was no wind. The air was like it always was in Sunbleached Plains— hot and still.

The dismembered bits were moving on their own!

Before the horrified eyes of the onlookers, the shattered pieces of the gunslinger's body crawled towards each other and joined together, reforming limbs, torso and head. What the hell was this? What kind of unholy power did this creature possess? The sheriff and deputy fired off a few more rounds, trying desperately to stop the process, but the creature's inexorable regeneration would not be halted. In fact it increased in speed with each new blast, as though fuelled by some awful, evil purpose that would not be stopped by conventional weaponry.

This was a monster that would not be halted until it had fulfilled its final purpose.

The gunslinger reformed, wearing the exact-same wounds as he'd had before the fight. But now he was naked save for his boots and spurs. Everyone could see the full extent of his ravaged corpse; the gaping cuts in his torso that revealed broken ribs and organs, his distorted head like someone had tried to bash it in, one leg bent at an odd angle. Some of his shrivelled intestines flopped out of his stomach wound as he moved, and he had to stop to shove them back in. Then he bent, plucking something up off the ground. It was his coat, charred, torn to shreds and still smoking. He swore. Flinging it to the ground he turned and started marching towards the four stunned men still standing outside the Eviscerated Buffalo.

The deputy started blubbering like a baby as he pulled off his own coat and held it out with shaking fingers. The gunslinger batted it from his hands into the dust.

"Don't want yours. It's got puke all over it." Fixing the sheriff with his single milky white eye, he said menacingly: "You'll give me yer clothes, yer hat an' yer coat, and maybe I won't burn this entire shit-heel town of yours to the ground."

The sheriff couldn't hand the articles of clothing over fast enough. The gunslinger dressed, covering himself once more, leaving the sheriff standing in his longjohns.

"Now, as I was sayin' 'fore I was so rudely attacked—*where—is—Pat—Davison?*"

His glare swept over the sheriff, deputy and barman. They were all quaking in their boots; they really didn't know!

The gunslinger rolled his white eye in exasperation. "Pat Davison—tall, well dressed fella with blue eyes and a big moustache, aged about forty. Probably dressed in real nice clothes. I heard he came here and was stayin' at the Eviscerated Buffalo. Is he still here?"

"N-not anymore," slurred the town drunk. "Fella o' that exact description left town in a stagecoach at eight o'clock this mornin'!"

"Gawdammit!" snarled the gunslinger. "D'you know where it was headed?"

"No, jus' that it was goin' south!" The drunk pointed a shaky finger."

The gunslinger looked in that direction. "Well, thanks for your help. I'll be outta your hair now." With that he stomped back out into the middle of the street, located his gun and holster and buckled them on. Then he lurched over to his rusty old mechanical horse and climbed up into the saddle. He shifted some gears and a huge black cloud of smoke exploded from the ancient mount's chimney. There was an agonised grind of gears, more sparks and both undead and mechanical monstrosity rolled out of town, heading in the direction the town drunk had indicated.

# CHAPTER 3

**I**T TOOK ZEKE SARANDON several minutes to get his coach up to its top speed of about fifty miles per hour along the broad, straight road heading south out of Sunbleached Plains. The engine roared, its pistons pounding, big wheels spinning. Smoke poured from the chimney, flying in a long streamer above the carriage roof. Zeke may have been a moody eccentric with nervous tics and a habit of muttering to himself, but he was an experienced driver and the only local insane enough to drive the most direct route south to Kellyville. As the carriage neared the mangled mesas on the horizon, he barely slowed his dangerous pace. Fortunately, the mechanical horse behind them had just been serviced and was able to keep up. The gunman seated astride the device was also a veteran rider.

The wide road narrowed to a rocky trail as it wound up into the cooler, higher territory of the mesas. They were known as the Tangled Hills. Tall cliffs were soon speeding by, sometimes on one side, sometimes on the other, occasionally on both. Once the carriage rocketed across a natural stone bridge barely wide enough to accommodate it. One single miscalculation from Zeke would have sent the coach off the edge and crashing into the deep gorge below. Another time he rocketed through a dark tunnel that had been dynamited out a few decades earlier. It was almost pitch black inside, but still Zeke did not slow down.

Centuries of erosion had created this marvellous landscape within the Tangled Hills and uncovered a veritable rainbow of colours twisting through the rock. Occasionally the travellers spotted weird plants growing in patches of sunlight, but due to their speed these always passed in a blur before they could be accurately described. The heavy iron wheels crushed small rocks and knocked them flying. Occasionally a larger stone would send the entire conveyance bouncing up into the air and elicit foul streams of invective from the passengers as they were knocked about like ninepins.

"Well, ah never!" exclaimed Marilou-Belle Watkins as she struggled to flatten her enormous wealth of skirts. The hoop in her underskirt kept flying up and whacking her in the nose. "Is the driver tryin' to kill us all?"

"We'll never make it on time if we don't ride at top speed," answered Pat Davison, irritated. He pulled a watch on a gold chain from inside his expensive frock coat and examined it. It had several faces, one providing him with the time remaining until they reached their destination. Then he slipped it back into his pocket and glared out of his window.

"That sure is a nice watch," Sallianne Veerhoven remarked as she attempted to get back into her cozy spot between Pat and Emmet T. Billings.

Pat simply grunted, obviously in no mood to talk.

Sallianne sighed. She was already bored. "Since we'll be stuck with each other for four days, we really should make an effort to get to know each other a little."

"Ah certainly agree," declared Marilou, and she pulled out her fan to create more much-needed breeze in the carriage. The smell of smoke from Samuel Simkins, the tall thin man in black, was constant and acrid. "Ah shall start. Mah name is Marilou-Belle Watkins of the South Rosewell Watkinses." She deferred back to Sallianne.

"I am Sallianne Veerhoven of the, er . . . Kelly County Veerhovens," she answered with a smile.

"Emmet T Billings," proclaimed the portly, brightly-dressed man on Sallianne's other side. "How about you, little buddy?" He gestured towards Billy Levi.

The boy sustained a very loud, long and particularly impressive burp.

Emmet snickered and quickly covered his mouth.

"Well, ah never!" cried Marilou. "That was quite disgusting!" She fanned herself furiously.

"And smells like old socks and cabbage!" agreed Sallianne. "What did you eat for breakfast, boy?"

Billy giggled and snorted for several seconds until he eventually managed to get himself under control. "I'm B-Billy Levi," he finally answered.

Samuel touched the brim of his stovepipe hat in greeting but did not remove it. He provided his name but said no more. He didn't appear particularly interested in talking either.

No matter. Sallianne was more interested in Pat Davison, who was the handsomest and most finely dressed person in the carriage, certainly cut a swell figure. He was still staring out of his own window.

"You're awfully quiet, Mister . . . ?"

"Eh? Oh—I'm sorry. My name is Pat Davison." He pulled his watch out again and checked it.

"You seem mighty interested in that fine timepiece of yours, Mr Davison," Sallianne declared.

"I had a fine watch like that once," remarked Samuel gloomily, "but I lost it."

Pat stuffed it back into a pocket. "It was my father's," he answered absently, and looked out of his window again. When he saw the same coloured strata passing by outside, he sighed heavily.

"That's not what I meant, Mr Davison," Sallianne insisted. "Why are you so impatient to get to Kellyville? If we go any faster I believe this entire confounded contraption will fly apart at the seams!" She lowered her voice to a seductive purr and ran one hand down his arm. "Is there someone after you?"

Pat quickly turned around. "Miss Veerhoven, you seem like a very interesting and charming woman. Why don't you tell me a little about yourself?"

She beamed a brilliant smile at him. "Why, I thought you'd never ask, Mr Davison! Currently I am a businesswoman."

Across the way, Marilou sniffed. "What kind of business?"

"I run my own bawdy house and armadillo ranch," she proclaimed proudly. Pat raised his eyebrows in surprise. Emmet started coughing. Even Samuel's sullen look was replaced by one of more avid interest.

"A boarding house?" asked Billy innocently.

"They must cost a pretty penny to run," Pat interjected quickly before anyone could correct the boy.

Sallianne flipped a long-fingered hand. "Oh, I've been entertaining the Governor of Kelly County for several years now. He gives me more than enough to keep my businesses out of trouble."

"Goodness gracious!" exclaimed Marilou. "Clearly you have no shame!"

"Shame does not pay the bills, dear." Sallianne started unbuttoning the bodice covering her stomach. "Since you fellows seem to be aficionados of fine watches you simply must take a gander at this."

"Surely you're not going to start entertaining right here?!" spluttered Marilou.

"Certainly not, Miss Watkins. There are children present. Don't worry—I ain't about to show anything personal." She pulled the bodice open, revealing not the bare flesh of her stomach but a very complicated clock installed in her midriff, far fancier and more intricate than Pat's. It had a second-hand and stop-watch and a meter for calculating prices. "What d'you think of this, eh?"

"It . . . it is quite impressive," Pat managed, looking flustered. Samuel, Emmet and Billy all leaned forward for a closer look.

"I had to get the best timepiece money could buy. I've never liked arguments over time or money. I also had to get it installed directly in my person. Less chance of it bein' lost or stolen." Sallianne patted the meter. "It even provides my customers with receipts!"

"Good Lord!" Pat spluttered. He waved a hand at her. "Perhaps you should cover it up now."

"Yes!" Marilou agreed quickly.

Samuel, Emmet and Billy looked disappointed.

"Oh, you people are such croakers." Sallianne buttoned up her bodice and straightened her dress. "One thing's for sure—I'll always have time on my side!" She giggled at her own appalling joke. The others just groaned. "I haven't always had it so good, you know. It took me years to save enough money for my bawdy house and ranch. I used to run with a travelling sideshow."

"Oooh, what kind of sideshow?" asked Billy eagerly.

"The Amazing Dr Barton Bigelow's Travelling Freakshow! He called it his 'Bizarre Bazaar'!" Sallianne proclaimed dramatically. "Full of freaks of nature and hybrids he created himself. He was an extremely clever man and a master of the scientic arts. Oh, he had all the usual sort of weirdos such as a three-legged man, a bearded lady, a fat boy and a rubber man, but he also had a rat-faced boy, an octopus man, a fish girl covered with scales who had webbed hands and feet and a fella with a set of mechanical horse wheels instead of legs. Dr Bigelow created these four freaks himself."

"Good Lord, I find that hard to believe," exclaimed Marilou, pressing a delicate hand against her chest.

"You can see them for yourself. Dr Bigelow now has a permanent home in Kelly County not far from me, and most of his freaks continue to visit me at my ranch. Especially that octopus man. He comes every week. Four arms and four legs make for a very entertaining time!" Sallianne laughed.

Marilou gaped, rendered completely speechless. Then she closed her mouth and fanned herself furiously.

"I met that Dr Bigelow during my travels," declared Emmet. "But I thought he was more of a two-bit huckster than a legitimate scientician!"

"Oh no, Mr Billings. I know exactly what he can do. It was he who put the clock in my belly." Sallianne patted it again.

During the conversation the stage had finally left the mazy Tangled Hills and entered a broad, stony plateau pocked with strange cacti. Some of these plants were large and bulbous, covered with spines, while others were tall and thin, stretching numerous arms towards the blazing sun. A few spread long, sinewy tendrils in a network across the ground to ensnare unsuspecting prey. They were almost obscured in the rocks and dust. Others had thick, round bodies that seemed to pulse with strange colours in the brilliant light.

Pat Davison pulled out his watch and checked the time again.

The zombie gunslinger followed the single road that wound through the Tangled Hills south of town. He cranked his mechanical horse up to its top speed, and it started to fart out truly noxious clouds that took many minutes to disperse behind it. Sparks flew from its exposed wiring and it really did resemble some horrific machine from hell as it thundered along the stony trail.

The gunslinger's stolen coat flapped out behind him like a pair of demonic bat wings.

However, the gunslinger was forced to slow and stop once he burst from the hills and hit the high desert with its bizarre cacti lifeforms. The road he was following split in two. He hit the brakes, bringing his monstrous mount to a stop with an agonised squeal of ancient brakes. He dismounted with a jingle of spurs and walked up to the fork in the road. In the sand and stones he could see the tracks of the coach's thick steel wheels and the similar marks left by its accompanying mechanical horse.

They appeared to be continuing due south. Good. Then that was the way he had to go. He turned, heading back to his own rumbling, puffing mount. He wondered how much longer it would last. Then he caught a glimpse of movement out of the corner of his eye. He turned, spotting something small and sinewy moving low to the ground on about a dozen legs. It was about a foot long. The creature scuttled across a couple of tendrils half-buried in the sand.

The predator plant reacted with frightening speed. Its pseudopods whipped up from the dirt, wrapping the critter up in a tight ball. The plant then rolled off like a tumbleweed, digesting its meal as it headed to a new hunting ground.

The gunslinger grunted as he was reminded of his own endless, undead hunger. He reached into the wound in his middle, pulling out a handful of maggots. He popped them into his mouth and chewed them absently as he returned to his horse. He allowed the flies to breed inside him only until their offspring hatched and could provide him with sustenance. He didn't particularly want them to start feeding on him, forcing him to waste energy on regenerating the additional wounds they caused.

Their tiny bodies popped delightfully between his teeth and filled his mouth with the hot, tangy flavour of flesh. He liked the meat, but it wasn't what he wanted. He craved, most of all, the tiny flare of energy that came from their miniscule brains. Even intelligences that small created flickers of pleasure within him. He could only imagine the power a full-sized human brain would give him— perhaps even enough to heal the injuries that had killed him.

But there was only one human brain he really wanted. Oh, he had devoured a few animal intelligences after his 'resurrection' just because he had been so hungry and out of control at the time. Only his superior willpower stopped him from degenerating into a mindless eating machine like so many of his kind. He had far too much purpose bubbling within for that.

He poked around for a few more maggots—anything to assuage the endless appetite within—and then returned to his horse. But as he was mounting the throbbing apparatus a shadow passed over him. He looked up at the monstrosity that had momentarily blocked out the sun. Even he gaped at the massive creature circling hungrily above. It was a pterosaurolophus; a pterosaur with long curved wings like sabres, a high bony crest soaring from the back of its head and a long snout filled with teeth as sharp as needles. It banked and came in, intending to grab the gunslinger with its fearsomely clawed feet.

The gunslinger wasn't interested in becoming a meal. He drew his pistol and thumbed back the hammer. There was a whine as capacitors charged. He aimed the device at the beast. He could see the whites of its glaring red eyes.

The capacitor reached full power. He fired.

The energy blast sizzled off across the monster's right shoulder, missing it by a fraction of an inch.

"Son of a motherless *whore!*" shouted the gunslinger.

The monster shrieked in indignation. The burn might only have singed its leathery grey flesh, but the pain was sufficient to send it flapping off in terror. The gunslinger lowered his weapon and stared after it, making sure it wasn't coming back. He had no wish to tangle with something like that again. It could tear him limb from limb and maybe scatter his parts too far apart for them to be able to reconnect.

But if he had managed to hit it, it would have made a delicious meal and possibly sate his endless hunger . . . for a little while at least.

He yanked down a lever, putting the old mechanical horse into gear, and roared off.

# CHAPTER 4

"**S**UCH A TALL, handsome and moody stranger—I'm sure you have a very interesting story to tell," purred Sallianne as she gently trailed her fingers down Pat's velvet coat sleeve.

Pat cringed. There was only one way to get this nagging woman off his back. And besides, he couldn't keep checking his watch every five minutes. It was becoming downright tedious. He really did need to do something to take his mind off his situation.

He took a deep breath. "Oh, very well. I was the local dentist in Nova Cyrus."

"Nova Cyrus? Where on Earth's that?" asked Sallianne.

"I know it," put in Emmet. "It's a big town at the base of Boloja Mountain."

"Boloja Mountain? Why, that's where all the mines are!" exclaimed Marilou.

"Er, yes," answered Pat, a little taken aback by her knowledge. But then he remembered that she was a Watkins. The Watkins Corporation owned a lot of the mines in that area. "As well as dentist for the town I was also a part-time prospector."

"And judging by those swell threads of yours, far better than any dentist could afford, you struck it rich!" declared Sallianne triumphantly.

Pat smiled thinly. "I certainly did. In fact, I hit the mother-lode." He pulled off his hat and ran a hand through his thick black curls. It was time to earn some sympathy. "But it came at a price . . . a terrible price."

"What kind of price?" asked Billy worriedly.

"An indian curse. I always wondered why I got the mining rights to my site so cheap. No-one else wanted them. No-one else was even digging anywhere near me. This was because the entire area was actually an old indian sacred site. When I struck it big I disturbed the soul of a long-dead indian chieftain." He paused dramatically before continuing in a hushed tone: "This chieftain is now following me as one of the risen dead. I'm heading south into the warmer climes of the Costa Pica in the hope the heat will decompose this zombie quicker, melting it into a puddle of ooze before it can get me."

"Ewww!" exclaimed Billy, looking a little green.

"You are running from the risen dead? I find that hard to believe!" scoffed Emmet.

"You can believe what you like," snapped Pat. "I witnessed this monstrous creature explode from the ground right before my eyes, beads and feathers in its hair, skeletal body wrapped with old leather. It had blazing red eyes. It was all I could do to grab what I could carry and run. Fortunately, as an undead monster, it was not quick and I was able to outrun it. But it's filled with dark purpose and it doesn't sleep. It will catch up with me eventually. That's why I appear so nervous and keep checking my watch. I must put as much distance between it and myself as I can."

"After what I seen during my travels, zombie indian chieftains ain't so scary," declared Sallianne. "Dr Bigelow had a machine what he called his Electro-Resurrector. Great big wooden thing with glowing columns, winking lights and dials all over it. Throbbed and belched out more smoke and steam than a sleeping dragon. Wires trailed everywhere. He used to cut up dead animals and stitch 'em back together in different ways, like a cat's head on a dog's body with a bird's wings attached, and a rat's tail. Then he'd stick them inside an iron box, shove it into the belly of his machine, and pull a whole sequence of levers to build up charge. There'd be a great screech of power, a clap of thunder and sparks would fly everywhere. I thought I'd descended into the bowels of hell itself. But at the end he'd pull out the box and release the creatures—*alive*. So if a scientician like Dr Bigelow could bring back the dead, I'm sure some old indian curse could do it too."

Emmet flipped a hand. "Sounds like a lot of smoke and mirrors if you ask me!"

"I seen it happen with me own eyes!" cried Sallianne.

"Look, dear—I've travelled the world myself and seen a lot of strange things, but nothing that would compel me to believe in black magic!" Emmet shouted.

"Please! Enough with the fussing!" cried Marilou. "I'm getting a mighty terrible headache!" She clapped a gloved hand against her brow.

Suddenly the coach hit a rock and bounced into the air, sending everyone crashing together and falling over each other. "Dammit!" Pat cursed, and looked out of his window.

They had finally reached the end of the high stony plateau. The edge dropped down in a sheer cliff many, many feet into a valley filled with swirling clouds. The stage was now travelling along a narrow pass running along the cliff's edge. It was known as Sabre-Wing Pass, and switch-backed its way down the cliff for several miles. Zeke had slowed down a little, but they still seemed to be moving dangerously fast along a trail that was barely wide enough to accommodate them. Occasionally the carriage's steel wheels would knock stones off the edge into the void below.

"Holy moly!" gasped Billy. "It's like we've reached the edge of the world! I've never seen anything like it!"

Outside, Zeke kept his eye on the trail. The gunman beside him was more interested in their surroundings. They had been this way before many times and knew the dangers. Thus when he spotted a flicker of movement out of the corner of one eye he was ready, his weapon already whining at full power. He turned in his seat, raising the gun to his shoulder and took aim at a giant, sabre-winged creature. It was swooping down with its huge, fang-filled maw open and salivating, aiming for the tasty human morsel seated astride the mechanical horse rumbling along behind them.

The coachman fired and a one-foot wide laser ball exploded from the massive barrel of his gun. The swirling knot of light smashed into the pterosaurolophus' side, excavating a huge hole in its body, right under its armpit. Ribs charred and organs boiled as the white-hot energy burst from its back and veered off into the sky. Stunned, still not realising that it was already dead, the creature struggled to flap despite the enormous hole in its body and wing. It spun around and crashed into the cliff face up ahead. Screeching in agony it clawed and struggled, its massive talons dislodging a small avalanche of rocks.

"*Look out, Zeke!*" the gunman shouted in alarm.

Zeke saw no other choice. If he braked hard now those boulders would surely come crashing down on the coach. He had to go *faster*. He flung the two rein cables down as hard as he could and the engine surged forward with a mighty blast of smoke. The gunman was thrown back into his seat. "*Hold on!*"

The coach thundered along the narrow trail at a truly horrifying velocity. Several boulders as big as humans bounced down only a few feet behind it. Smaller ones struck the luggage on the roof and clattered against the sides. Zeke was about to heave a sigh of relief when another man-sized rock caught the back of the carriage and knocked its right rear wheel off the edge of the path. There was a sickening crunch as the rear axle hit the cliff's edge and a deafening squeal of steel. Fortunately it held. For now.

The entire coach lurched sideways. Inside, Pat fell against the door and there was an ominous creak. He realised what was about to happen and managed to wrap his arms around the window-frame in the door just as the handle gave way and the door swung open.

Pat Davison found himself flung out over a void of swirling white. The door creaked and groaned beneath his weight, threatening to come off its hinges. He hung on tight and did not look down.

Emmet and Marilou managed to grab onto the opposite door. Marilou reached for Billy and caught hold of the back of his suspenders. Samuel shot to his feet, bracing himself against the ceiling with the top of his hat. Somehow he was able to wedge himself fast within the carriage.

But Sallianne wasn't quite so lucky. She missed the panic bar above her head and started sliding out behind Pat. Emmet tried to grab her but missed, catching nothing but her scarf. She slid out through the open door with a shriek.

Pat could have grabbed her with a free hand as she slid past. He had the strength to hold on with only one arm.

But he didn't.

Sallianne tried to grab onto Pat as she slid out. Her fingers closed around one of his legs and she hung on. The carriage shuddered, the steel axle grinding against the ledge with a shower of sparks as Zeke urged his labouring engine forward towards level ground.

The door Pat was clinging to started to creak and there was a pop as one screw came loose. It couldn't handle the combined weight of Pat and Sallianne.

Sallianne began to slide down Pat's leg. He helped her along with a small kick. The brothel madam fell screaming into the void. Pat dropped his head, pretending sadness. But in reality he was smiling.

That nosy bitch would never pester him with stupid questions again!

The engine strained at full power, smoke pouring from its chimney. Behind the carriage the wounded beast finally peeled away from the cliff face and spiralled down into the clouds below, trailing tendrils of blood and smoke behind it. Then, suddenly, the contraption lurched forward, yanking the stage back up onto the trail. All four wheels slammed back onto the stone with a bone-jarring thud. As the door swung in, Pat scrambled off it and flopped back into his seat. He was white-faced and shaking all over. He could see that the other screw had almost worked its way out of the hinge. Had it broken he was sure the whole door would have come off.

And he would have joined Sallianne in the void.

Zeke pulled on the cables and the coach shuddered to a halt. He popped open the little window that would allow him to talk to the passengers. "Is everyone all right down there?"

"No—we lost Sallianne!" cried Marilou. "That poor madam fell over the cliff! We should stop and look for her!"

"Aw shit," growled Zeke. "That's a sheer bloody drop straight down. There's no possible way she could still be alive!"

"But we must send down a rope or something," cried Marilou. "We can't just go on as though nothing happened!"

Zeke beckoned to the gunman on the mechanical horse. "Take a look—see if you can spot her hanging on or something."

"Yes, Mr Sarandon." The coachman dismounted and walked to the very edge of the trail. He actually lifted his rifle and peered through the scope. "No, nothing," he declared after a few minutes. "She must have fallen through the clouds. If that's the case then she's gone."

Zeke sighed and quickly put away the arm bone he had been gnawing on impatiently. "We can't waste any more time here—I've got a schedule to keep. We continue on." He tugged on the right-hand chain, bringing the engine out of idle-mode. It began to chug forward. The gunman returned to his mechanical horse and clambered back onto it.

Zeke shook the chains and the engine began to speed up once more, rattling down the narrow trail. The wheel that had slid off the edge wobbled erratically but held. Zeke realised with a sinking in his gut that it would need repairing before long. He hoped it would hold until they reached their night time rest stop.

Inside the coach a sombre silence fell. Marilou might not have approved of Sallianne's status but the poor thing certainly had not deserved to die so horribly. She glanced at Pat, but the dentist was examining his watch again.

She scowled and picked at one of the jewels attached to her cheekbone. She was sure that so-called "dentist" could have done more to help Sallianne. The woman had slid right past him. The least he could have done was try to catch hold of her on the way. But he hadn't moved a muscle . . . almost as though he had not cared about her fate at all!

Marilou didn't like the direction her thoughts were taking. Any more such morbid notions and she would surely get the vapours. She produced her fan and started flapping it vigorously.

# CHAPTER 5

**T**HE DAY WORE into afternoon as the carriage finally reached the bottom of Sabre Wing Pass and continued into the wilderness below. Due to the clouds and moist air, a lot more foliage thrived down here than up on the high plateau. Thick bushes known as spikypines grew on either side of the trail. They were large, bushy growths with wizened brown branches that grew out rather than straight up. Instead of leaves the plants grew sharp, pointed spikes between six and twelve inches long.

This area was known simply as Duoquois Country, named after the indian people inhabiting this region. The Duoquois were the only natives hardy—or stupid—enough to live here.

With shaking fingers, Samuel Simkins fished a packet of chewing tabackie out of one pocket. Then, finally, he removed his stove-pipe hat, revealing the reason why he had been able to brace the top of his head so effectively against the ceiling of the carriage. The upper part of his head was actually an iron chimney, attached to his skull with rivets. There was even a little oven door in his forehead. Samuel opened it so he could poke around with a small fire-poker, stirring up the hot coals within. Then he shoved the entire twist of tabackie in and slammed the door. Smoke soon began billowing out the top, filling the entire carriage. "Thought I could last a bit longer, but after what happened to that Veerhoven woman, I needed a little pick me up," Samuel declared in his soft voice.

"Holy moly!" gasped Billy. "So that's why you always smell like you're smoking!"

"I *am* always smoking—now you know," Samuel answered with a thin smile. "I've been smoking since the age of nine because I really like the taste of tabackie. I tried giving up once or twice but it's become too much of a habit now." He rapped his knuckles against the chimney with a dull clanging sound. "So I had this installed."

Billy stared at him in amazement. "That's even better than a clock in the belly!" He turned to Emmet. "I don't suppose you've ever seen anything like that in your travels either?"

"Not a chimney head, but I did know a fella with a clockwork heart," Emmet admitted. "He had to wind it with a key at eight o'clock every morning. One night he got drunk and forgot—his wife found him at around ten the next day, stone cold dead. She tried to revive him by winding the heart but that just made blood come out of his nose."

"Golliwollickers!" gasped Billy.

"Well, ah never!" Marilou fanned away some of Samuel's new smoke.

"Want to see a card trick?" Samuel asked the boy.

Billy turned around. "Sure!"

Samuel pulled out a deck of well used cards and fanned them out with the ease of a practised shark. "All right—pick one and don't show it to me."

Billy pulled out the three of clubs.

"Now put it back."

Billy did. Samuel shuffled the deck and then without looking pulled out a card, holding it face-up to Billy. It was the three of clubs.

"Is this the one you picked?"

"Yes!" Billy clapped his hands in excitement. "How did you do that?"

"It's a marked deck, am I right?" asked Emmet.

"Certainly not!" Samuel declared, even though Emmet was perfectly correct.

"I'm not sure if we should be teaching such an impressionable young man to gamble," declared Marilou.

"Oh, I'm not about to start a game of poker in here!" Samuel flipped a hand. "But I can certainly tell you all about the hardest game of my life!"

Even Pat, who had only partially been paying attention, turned from staring out of the window to listen.

"I was a banker but I've since retired to pursue my true love in life—gambling. I now dabble in some very high stakes draw poker,"

Samuel explained. "My mathematical experience gives me quite an edge."

"That and the marked deck," Emmet muttered under his breath. Pat just snorted.

"When I first saw you I thought you were an undertaker," Billy declared.

"Ah, the hat." Samuel laughed and put the stove-pipe hat back on. It actually had cleverly concealed vent-holes around the top. "I was playing against Black-Ace McCade."

"Black-Ace!" gasped Billy. "Really?"

"Forgive mah ignorance, but who is Black-Ace McCade?" asked Marilou.

"Only one of the nastiest gamblers and outlaws in all of Westerillo!" Emmet replied.

"Yes, he's a cheat, a liar, and a dishonourable man who'll use any excuse to shoot an opponent in the gut!" Pat said.

"Yes, however did you survive?" asked Emmet sceptically.

"Let me tell you. During this particular game I had that four-flusher beat and he knew it. He already held a gun under the table aimed right at my belly. I knew as I slowly laid out my cards that as soon as I revealed my last one I would be shot. So I stopped at three out of five cards—three aces, and asked if I could smoke. McCade agreed. As I put the last ace down I let out such a billow of black smoke from my chimney-head that it filled up the barroom and sent that low-down chiseller coughing and spluttering, practically falling off his chair. It was the perfect cover for me to make good my escape."

Samuel paused to stoke the coals in his chimney's oven. Pat noticed that Samuel's hand had a rather large scar on the back and palm. He wondered how he got it, but decided not to venture to ask for fear that the old blatherskite might never shut up.

"Unfortunately, I had to leave all my money and my watch on the table and my suitcase in my hotel room, but I lived to tell the tale. All I have are the clothes on my back and the few belongings in my carpet-bag. I'm currently on my way back to my sister's. She's been feeling low ever since her business failed, poor thing. I'm hoping to pick up her spirits a little."

"Dang!" Billy clapped his hands. "That is quite a story, Mr Simkins!"

"It's possible I suppose," muttered Emmet, and Pat nodded.

Suddenly, with an ominous creak, the stagecoach lurched again. This time it dropped heavily on one side with a crash, everyone inside tumbling over each other in a very undignified heap. The coach dragged on at speed, gouging great rents out of the earth. The wheel that Zeke had been trying to ignore had finally come off and was bouncing backwards down the trail, heading inexorably towards the mounted gunman who was riding along behind. He tried to manoeuvre out of the way but the mechanical mounts were notoriously hard to turn.

The giant steel wheel crashed into the mechanical horse, knocking it over and sending the gunman flying off the trail. He landed in a huge growth of spikypines. He screamed in horrific agony as the needle-sharp spines pierced his skin all over. Some sliced right through his body, bursting from his chest and stomach. Strangely enough there was no blood on the points that emerged. Then a spike pierced his brain and his shriek died to a gurgle. His eyes rolled back into his head.

Zeke yanked hard on both reins and the engine shrieked as it slowed. He leapt down before the carriage had even slid to a stop to try and help the stricken man. His companion followed close behind.

But as they reached him they realised they were already too late. The coachman, his body pinned in at least a dozen places by the spikes, had already been drained of all fluid and reduced to a dried-up husk. The limb of the plant beneath him had started to thicken and transform from shrivelled brown to glossy red. Both Zeke and the one remaining gunman could see veins of crimson racing towards the plant's bulbous central mass.

Zeke slid a gnarly hand into his pocket and pulled out the arm bone he had been chewing on. "We need to make some repairs 'fore we can continue," he muttered as he turned away to nibble on the bone for a few minutes to calm his nerves.

The coach had halted in the middle of a vast valley. The five remaining travellers managed to scramble from the lopsided vehicle and brush themselves off. "Are we makin' camp here?" asked Marilou.

"Certainly not—far too dangerous. This is just a short rest stop," snapped Zeke. "If you must go off the trail for whatever reason, don't go far. There could be Duoquois creepin' 'round." He declined to mention what had happened to the gunman. He now resembled a weathered skeleton impaled on the spines, his bulging eyes now white, staring orbs. He looked like he had been there for months. In the light of the afternoon sun Zeke noticed other spindly figures outlined; desiccated corpses that could have been killed years earlier . . . or had died the previous day. "And for gawd's sake stay away from the spikypines!" he added as he bit off a very large chunk of bone. He masticated it into small fragments and cursed. "Come on, help me retrieve that wheel," he ordered the last gunman.

Together, Zeke and the coachman managed to heave the heavy steel wheel from the overturned mechanical horse. The battered machine still gurgled and issued the occasional puff of smoke. Zeke knew it probably could be repaired but they simply didn't have the time. Right now he needed to focus on the stage.

He had a schedule to keep.

Zeke and the gunman rolled the massive wheel back towards the coach. He enlisted the help of Pat, Emmet and Samuel to steady the conveyance, then he and the coachman worked on slotting the wheel back into place and installing new bolts to hold it there. As he worked Zeke noticed, with no real surprise, that the plant that had drained the gunman was now sprouting a cluster of new blood-red flowers from its centre. They turned their succulent petals towards the afternoon sun.

"Mista Sarandon: where did the other fella go?" asked Billy worriedly. He pointed to the mechanical horse, still lying on its side. He couldn't see the gunman anywhere, and fortunately for him he couldn't recognise the skeletons caught within the spikypines' deadly embraces.

"His horse was damaged. He's walkin' back to Sunbleached Plains," Zeke answered roughly. He looked up, daring the adults to contradict. Even though some now realised what had happened to the hapless coachman, they all nodded vigorously in agreement with the gruff old driver.

Pat, Emmet, Samuel, Marilou and Billy all moved to wait off on one side of the trail—a safe distance from those nasty-looking plants. Marilou fanned herself distractedly. "Ah can honestly say ah have never been through a journey quite this long or difficult," she declared. "And I have travelled quite a bit during my life time."

"Where are you from?" asked Billy conversationally.

"Ah said before, ah am from South Rosewell," she proclaimed proudly. "But my lineage goes back to the Antlantis Watkinses."

*"The Antlantis Watkinses?"* gasped Billy. The sceptical Emmet raised his bushy eyebrows, but since the start of this bizarre journey he had learned not to instantly voice his incredulity.

"Yes. Mah family may not have been responsible for the discovery of Antlantis, but it was my great-great-great-great-grandpappy who designed and built the giant river-going engines that hauled the submerged pyramid up from the murky depths of The Great Lake. They dragged it across the sea and anchored it off the coast of Excelsior." She smiled with pride.

No-one dared gainsay that! Everyone knew that a Watkins had been responsible for the salvage of that great, mechanologically-advanced wonder.

"It was the Antlanteans' scientic knowledge that enabled us to develop the clockwork we needed to further our own mechanology," Marilou continued proudly. "Mr Billings—that fella you knew with the wind-up heart—a marvellous device like that could never have been created without Antlantean influence."

"Yes, of course," Emmet answered, a little flustered. He had always thought Marilou a distant relation of those illustrious Watkinses, not a direct descendant! But it wasn't long before images of dollar-signs started to nudge through his shock, and he started to wonder how he could turn this knowledge to his advantage.

"Anyway, it was my great-great-grandpappy who first planted a piston seed in a muck of oil and turned it into the thriving squillion-dollar plantation it is today!" Marilou clapped her hands. "Now Daddykins—"

"Daddykins?" spluttered Emmet.

"Big Daddy Watkins, silly!" Marilou cried, as though Emmet was simple. "He uses Antlantean-designed clockwork labourers on our plantation, but there are just so many people out there jealous of our success." She rolled her eyes dramatically. "Those lowlife snakes constantly sabotage our clockworkers by secretly planting explosive devices inside them while they're powered down. So far we had to restock our troop of robot labourers and servants fifty times! *Fifty times!* A very expensive endeavour, don't you agree? Sometimes ah think we should have just hired ordinary humans."

"Er, yes," said Pat quickly.

But Emmet just stared at her. He didn't believe a word!

"On that note, I think I'll take a little walk. Explore the area," declared Samuel as he rose to his feet.

"Are you sure that's wise?" asked Pat. "Those spikypines are deadly. And didn't Mr Sarandon say something about injuns?"

"I can avoid those disgusting things." He lowered his voice. "Besides, I really need to drain the lizard!" Samuel headed off into the foliage to find a nice secluded spot to do his business. Unfortunately, the puffs from his chimney soon gave his position away to Billy, who had followed him into the bushes.

"Mista Simkins? While we're waitin' can you show me some more card tricks?" Billy called as he pushed aside the long grasses to reveal Samuel in the middle of a piss.

"Confound it, you little nuisance!" shouted Samuel as he struggled to button up his fly. He caught some pubic hairs in the process and swore. "Give me a minute here!"

"Sorry! Sorry sorry sorry!" gasped Billy, and he turned around to give Samuel some more privacy. He started into the bushes in front of him as something large and spindly started to rise up out of the green like a weird giant insect. "What the . . . " Billy trailed off in surprise.

It looked like a giant bug, with long, spindly limbs that stretched out like an attacking spider's. But it had a tall green trunk and branches covered with long, thin leaves. At its centre was a huge multicoloured flower with petals that looked like the big rouged lips of a whore. The lips opened wide, dribbling some sort of nectar, and a long, thin stamen started to emerge.

"Look out, Billy!" Samuel shouted, and blew his stack at the plant. A great cloud of thick, dark smoke shot from the vents in Samuel's hat, making him look truly demonic in the mid-afternoon light. The noxious cloud enveloped the weird plant. It began to writhe and the stamen flailed wildly. Billy gaped in horror.

"Let's get back to the carriage!" Samuel grabbed Billy to run with him—just as another of the horrible plants rose up from the foliage right beside him. Its obscene flower opened and the long, thin stamen emerged. Samuel shoved Billy from him just as the needle-sharp protuberance shot out as fast as an arrow, driving right through Samuel's midriff with an awful wet tearing sound. A stream of blood exploded from his back.

"Jumping jellybeans!" Billy gasped. He struggled to scream for help, but his voice deserted him. He could only mouth silently, tears pouring down his pale plump cheeks.

The stamen was covered with spikes that prevented Samuel from sliding off as the plant lifted him in the air. He slumped in shock as those huge gruesome petals parted before him like the mouth of an illicit lover. Billy could not tear his gaze away, rooted to the spot with horror and fascination.

The stamen retracted, yanking Samuel into the depths of that huge, unholy flower. The thick crimson petals closed completely around his body and held it within a giant bulb. There was some throbbing and pulsating within, but Billy doubted it was coming from the retired banker. That barbed shaft had gone through his heart. There was no hope for him. Not now, not ever.

Billy finally found his voice. He screamed and kept on screaming as he turned and raced back to the camp as fast as his fat little legs in their plus-fours could carry him. "*Mista Sarandon, Mista Sarandon!*" he shrieked hysterically.

Zeke the Freak nearly jumped out of his skin at the noise. He and the one remaining gunman had been about to tighten the last rivet in the wheel. "What . . . *what?*"

"It's Mista Simkins, sir! He's been taken by some awful devil plant!" Billy pointed vigorously.

"Consarn it!" Zeke shouted. "I thought I told you all to stay away from the spikypines!"

"This weren't no spikypine, Mista Sarandon!" Billy screamed. "It was some other plant, ugly as homemade sin!"

Zeke gestured to the gunman. "Show us, boy."

Billy darted back into the bushes. Zeke followed, the gunman right behind him with his weapon powering up.

"Right here!" Billy cried and pointed. Both plants had shrunk back down into the foliage, their spidery limbs and giant flowers barely visible within the brush.

But the detritus regurgitated by the one that had eaten Samuel was clearly laid out on the grass below. All that remained of the gambler was a pile of perfectly cleaned grey bones . . . and the chimney from his head, now polished to a shine. The rivets that had attached it to his skull were still smouldering from the deadly acid that had dissolved his flesh.

# CHAPTER 6

**M**ARILOU-BELLE WATKINS really didn't like being stuck so far out in this awful wilderness. She felt lost and out of control. She preferred being within the safety of Daddykins' luxurious mansion, surrounded by walls and servants. All this . . . nature was really starting to make her nervous.

And when she got nervous she sewed. She didn't have any new jewels that she could attach but she did have a new dress. She excused herself from Pat and Emmet just before the hysterical Billy appeared and dragged Zeke and the gunman into the bushes, and retired to the coach to change. She was carrying the new dress in her hand-luggage so during quiet periods of the trip she could work on it. She was determined that this one would be her masterpiece—the one article of clothing that was so perfect she would not want to remove it for many months to come.

It was the dress she was going to wear for her presentation.

She changed into the new outfit, a more modern dress with a large bustle and a tiered skirt of fine lace. It had ruffled sleeves and a draped bodice. It was blue and trimmed with little pink flowers. Jewels glittered all over it. She was a beauty but looked truly stunning in this; almost too perfect to be real. She sat back down on her rock and pulled out her sewing kit.

She started to sew the new dress directly onto her body.

Both Pat and Emmet gaped at her in surprise. They had thought the jewels attached to her face were stuck there with some sort of adhesive. Now they realised they were stitched directly into her skin!

"Wh-why are you doing that?" asked Pat, a little disturbed by the sight of Marilou's needle sliding into the flesh of her shoulders and then the skin rising as the cotton was pulled through.

"What, sewing the dress onto myself? So no-one can steal it, of course. It's nearly priceless, you know." She gestured to the jewels that glistened all over it. "I attach the gems directly to myself so no-one can take them, either." She lifted her hands to her cheeks.

"But doesn't that hurt?" gasped Emmet.

"Oh no. It hardly prickles at all." She smiled. "I must look the best for Lady Florence Barrymore of Kellyville."

"Lady Florence Barrymore? Why?" asked Pat.

"I am soon to be married to Lucius Barrymore of the Southern Fried Barrymores. A true gentleman of noble stock and good bearing. When I reach Kellyville . . . *if* I ever reach Kellyville," she added somewhat dispiritedly, "his great-aunt Florence is going to bestow on me the precious family album of the Barrymore family."

"Oh," said Pat and Emmet together. Emmet quickly quashed his dream of somehow weaselling his way into the Watkins family by marriage. He would just have to think of another way. Maybe he could save Marilou's life somehow and receive a huge reward in response.

Just then Zeke and the gunman appeared, holding a shaking Billy between them. All three were trembling, as white as ghosts.

"What happened?" asked Pat, rising to his feet in concern. Emmet followed.

"Mr Simkins got himself et by a Kissing Orchid," Zeke answered gruffly. "Look after the little fella—he saw the whole thing. We still need to finish reattaching the wheel."

"Damn!" gasped Pat. "Poor Mr Simkins!"

"Come sit by me, Billy." Marilou patted the rock she was sitting on. The boy flopped down. Emmet felt around his person and produced a hip flask of cheap whiskey. "Here, have some of this. It might calm your nerves."

"He's just a little boy!" Marilou protested. "You can't give him hard liquor!"

"Pish-tosh. Alcohol is the main ingredient of most medical remedies these days, anyway. Besides, he's had a terrible shock." He handed the gut-warmer to the boy who took it gratefully, slugging down a good third of it.

"Hey hey hey! Not so much! That's my only booze!" Emmet snatched it off him.

Billy burped out a cloud of alcoholic fumes. "Thanks, Mr Billings."

"We've got the wheel attached properly," Zeke called. "Everyone back aboard! The sooner we get away from this bone orchard of a place, the better!" He gestured impatiently towards the coach.

The four remaining passengers scrambled back into their seats. Now each had a window and enough room to stretch out. Billy immediately lay down on the seat, rested his head on Marilou's lap, and fell asleep. "Look at him, he's all tuckered out, poor lad," she declared and stroked his curly blond hair.

"It does smell a tad better now that smoking freak has gone," muttered Pat as he checked his watch again.

"Mister Davison!" Marilou gasped, pressing a hand against her chest. "That was an absolutely *appalling* thing to say!"

"Come on! He stunk up the joint worse than a skunk in heat! Don't you agree, Billings?"

"What? Oh. Yes, he did reek a bit. Might be a while before I light up a pipe again."

"Well, ah never!" exclaimed Marilou.

Just then Billy farted in his sleep, and the coach stank all over again.

Outside Zeke was soon pushing the engine up to a dangerous pace once more. It bounced and rattled along the bumpy trail. Beside him the one remaining gunman kept his weapon charged up and ready to fire at the first sign of trouble. Zeke had seen a lot of awful things in Duoquois country, but never a Kissing Orchid as big as the one that had taken Samuel. Normally they ate rabbits and foxes, small game. He'd never needed to worry about them before. But it seemed Duoquois country was still full of surprises. Or perhaps new dangers were developing over time.

Up ahead, about thirty feet away from the path on the left, stood a giant dead tree with skeletal limbs that looked like witch fingers. It had a bulbous trunk with a large split down the middle, like it had been hit by lightning or something horrible had burst out of it a long time ago. It looked creepy and Zeke was instantly suspicious.

"That is one ugly tree and I don't like the looks of it at all. Keep an eye on it." Zeke pointed it out.

"Yes, Mr Sarandon," answered the gunman.

As they came level with the dead tree something started to emerge from the crack. It looked like smoke until the gunman made out the bodies of individual insects. The giant swarm appeared to be heading right for them. The coachman cursed and fired, hoping to disintegrate them. The laser-ball fried a good percentage of the creatures, but they just kept pouring out of the tree. And instead of scaring them away, the energy blast made them mad. They swamped the coach, enveloping it in a thick dark cloud. Squinting against the onslaught, Zeke attempted to keep the coach on course without crashing or rolling it. Beside him the gunman dropped his weapon on the floor and tried to shoo the bugs away from Zeke's face.

They were about the size of cicadas, with red and black striped bodies and wings that moved so quickly they were just a blur. Their buzzing was almost deafening. They attempted to bury their needle-sharp stingers in whatever bare flesh they could find. Both the gunman and Zeke's hands were soon peppered with red welts. Fortunately they didn't appear to be fatal, just itchy and annoying.

Bugs now flew into the stage. Pat, Emmet and Marilou started swatting at them furiously. Billy woke up and squealed in horror. Marilou yanked down the shutter on her window so more couldn't fly in. "Close your window, Billy!" she shouted.

Billy grabbed it and yanked it down, plunging the carriage into near-darkness. The passengers could still hear the angry buzzing of bugs as they flew around. Then Marilou shrieked.

"What is it?" shouted Pat.

"One flew right ub by dose!" she squealed. She started to jerk and twitch violently.

"It must have stung her on the inside!" yelled Emmet. He felt one land on his hand and slapped it, feeling its body explode like a ripe blueberry beneath his palm.

"We have to help her!" cried Billy. He grabbed hold of Marilou's arms to try and stop her from shaking.

Then sparks started to fly out of her ears, temporarily illuminating the carriage.

"*Sparks?!*" shrieked Billy, jumping backwards onto the seat between Pat and Emmet.

Marilou's convolutions became even more violent. Her head

shook from side to side. Her entire body trembled and lifted up from the seat. More sparks shot from her eyes and nose.

Then there was a colossal bang and flash of light. Something thudded against the ceiling. Pat, Billy and Emmet were all showered with smouldering cogs, gears, springs, cables and hydraulic fluid. The carriage filled up with smoke, noxious enough to kill the rest of the bugs within.

"*Bejabbers!*" shouted Emmet.

Pat shoved open the window and the full extent of the carnage was revealed.

Marilou-Belle Watkins' chest had exploded, blowing her head right off her shoulders. Her charred, smoking skull was now rolling around on the floor between the three remaining passengers' feet. It continued to issue sparks, and more angry flashes came from the cavernous hollow of Marilou's chest.

Billy screamed.

"Stop the coach!" Pat yelled through the little window to Zeke.

Since they had cleared the plague of insects, Zeke yanked on the chains. "What's up? What was that gawd-awful bang?"

"It was Miss Watkins, Mr Sarandon. She . . . er . . . exploded," Pat explained.

Zeke jumped down, raced around to the door and yanked it open. "Sweet mungknuckle! What a mess. Well, this'll have to be cleaned up 'fore we can continue. Everyone out! Quickly now!" He yanked a broom from the back of the coach as the three dishevelled travellers jumped down and started dusting themselves off. Emmet handed around his flask of Red Eye, not caring if it was finished off. Maybe the crusty old driver had some more on him.

Zeke rolled Marilou-Belle Watkins' body out onto the side of the trail and swept her head and the rest of her parts out after it. Her charred, smoking head bounced off to one side of the trail and rolled behind a boulder.

"Holy moly," whispered Billy, still horrified by what he had seen. "She . . . she looked so real!"

"She certainly did. I'm willing to bet she was real everywhere that counted, too!" Pat gave a crude laugh.

"Wh-what?" asked Billy, still distressed from the ordeal.

"Oh, nothing," Emmet said quickly, and handed him the whiskey bottle. "You finish that up."

The boy took it with shaking hands.

Emmet realised that Marilou's body was still wearing that beautiful jewel-encrusted dress. Apart from some charring around the shoulders, it was still largely intact. He knelt down beside the body and quickly pulled the dress from it. He folded it up and stuffed it into his jacket.

Beneath, Marilou's body was dressed in long frilly pantaloons and camisole. It was so perfectly made it didn't need any corsetry to give it shape. "Mr Sarandon?" Emmet called.

Zeke jumped down from the coach and put the broom back. "What?"

"It might be wrecked but it's still a fine machine. Its parts should fetch a pretty penny in Kellyville." Emmet gestured towards Marilou's body.

"It's still sparkin'," Zeke growled. "It could explode again at any moment. No way in hell." He directed his attention to everyone. "Now get back on board. Time's a-wastin'." He stomped back around to the front of the carriage.

Emmet shrugged. No matter. The dress was worth more than enough. It looked like he would get to make some money out of the illustrious Watkins family after all. He clambered back into the coach. Pat followed him.

Billy was slower to follow. He could only stare at the mess that had been Marilou. A tear trickled down his cheek. She'd had so much personality and had been so nice to him. He couldn't believe that she too had simply been another of Big Daddy Watkins' clockworkers.

# CHAPTER 7

**A** FEW HOURS LATER, as a bloated red sun was skimming across the western horizon, the quiet, deadly wilderness was disturbed by the roar of another mechanical device. The zombie gunslinger, astride his ancient horse, pulled it to a stop on the side of the path. The engine shuddered and coughed, farting out huge black clouds before finally falling silent. He jumped down and walked around it, realising that he probably wouldn't be able to start it up again.

No matter. He had stopped because he had spotted something that would be useful to him. An overturned horse, a bit dented but in much better condition than his old one. He walked over to it and easily heaved it back up onto its wheels. He pressed a hand against its engine. It was still warm—it had only been here a few hours at the most.

But what had happened to its driver?

Looking around the gunslinger noticed the spikypines and their various skeletal victims, impaled on their deadly spikes. At first he didn't think those revolting things were responsible for the driver's death; those corpses looked like they had been there for ages. But then the gunslinger realised otherwise. He had just spotted something else he could really use.

An electric rifle clutched in the frozen claws of the missing driver.

The weapon was a lot bigger and more powerful than his pistol. He licked his ravaged lips. He had to get it. He began to pick his way into the cluster of spikypines. He tried to be careful, but the spur on his heel caught on a vine and he tripped, falling right onto one of the spine-covered branches. He flung out his arms to arrest his fall and the needle-sharp spines pierced his sleeves and drove deep into his flesh. He felt an odd pulling sensation as the spikypine tried to drain

44

the fluid from him—and found nothing within him but dust. What fluid he did have in him came from things he'd eaten.

Beneath him the branch started to shrivel as it struggled to feed on him. He managed to get his feet beneath him and push himself up. The spikes ripped from his skin. As they were new wounds, not the ones that had caused his death, they healed instantly. But the rips in his sleeves remained.

Now, *that* pissed him off. This was a new coat, dammit!

He managed to reach the impaled man, his flesh dry and desiccated like an old creek bed. His withered lips were pulled back from his teeth in his last scream. A particularly large spike had driven deep into the back of his head.

The zombie shivered, wondering what would happen to him if a spike pierced his brain. He didn't think such an injury would kill him, but would it scramble his memories, turning him into one of the mindless living dead?

He yanked the rifle from the dead man's hands, strongly enough to rip one of them off. He had to snap the fingers like dried twigs to remove them from the wooden stock. With a curse he stomped back to the path and powered up the weapon. He wanted to make sure it still worked, and he had a perfect target.

A laser ball one foot wide hit the spikypine right in the middle, at the junction of its branches. It exploded, destroying not only the plant that had tried to claim him, but burning out a circle of destruction twenty feet wide and sending a thick black cloud high into the air. The smell of burning sap filled the air. The gunslinger laughed blackly. "That'll learn ya to try'n eat me, you dumbass!"

At the very edge of the circle of destruction, his blast had seared a couple of plants that reared up out of the foliage like infuriated spiders. They had long, spindly branches like limbs, and large multicoloured flowers that opened like whore mouths to release barbed stamens.

They couldn't reach him, but they were ugly enough to receive another laser ball, right in the middle of those obscene petals. The gunslinger cursed. He hated this place.

Before anything else could menace him, he returned to the new horse to see if it powered up as well. Beneath the chimney at the horse's rear end was the furnace. He opened the door, unfortunately located right beneath the chimney. Obviously whoever invented these devices had a warped sense of humour. The zombie peered inside, and noticed some gleaming coals and a few lumps that hadn't been consumed yet. Should be enough to keep going, he thought as he drew a poker from a slot beside the furnace and poked the coals into life. Then, as the furnace was warming up, he made sure the boiler had enough water. These mounts were well-insulated and extremely efficient, but if the boiler did dry out temperatures could escalate very rapidly. He had heard stories of men getting steamed alive.

The gunslinger returned to his old horse to collect his meagre belongings and transfer them. At his new mount he turned the crank at the head, starting the engine. It rumbled smoothly into life. Good. He would make far better time now—perhaps even catch up with his quarry this very night!

The thought pleased him as he hopped into the saddle and roared off.

However, he hadn't been travelling long before a large bug buzzed angrily into his face. He swore and batted it away. It came around for a second pass and he got a better a look at it.

It looked extremely fat and juicy.

Instead of swatting at it, he managed to catch it in one hand and shove it into his mouth. It crunched delightfully between his teeth, filled with meat and blood and life. It was far more satisfying than the tiny maggots he had been eating. Where had it come from? He looked around, but couldn't see a hive.

A shame. He could have used a few more fat insects like that.

But then he noticed something that made him forget the bug completely.

The near naked, headless body of a woman, sprawled beside the path. It looked fresh and new, like it hadn't been there for long at all!

The zombie braked so hard he nearly flipped his new mount. He jumped down before his horse had slid to a stop and hurried eagerly towards the body. He didn't even wonder how it had come to be here. All he could think about was gorging himself on fresh meat. If his salivary glands still worked he would have been drooling.

But as he knelt down beside the body he realised something was wrong. It didn't smell like meat at all. It had a perfume about it, but beneath he detected the odour of ozone, hot metal and burnt fabric. He touched the corpse and rolled it over. Beneath his fingers he felt not soft flesh but silk over some sort of artificial padding. When he looked into the cavernous hollow of its chest and saw only dark, silent cogs, cables and wires, he realised what it was.

A machine.

He had heard of the mechanical servants of the super-rich, but he had never seen one up close before. His experience was with heavy duty mining equipment. How had such a finely crafted specimen got all the way out here in this gawdforsaken wilderness?

He was disappointed—it looked like he wouldn't be getting a fresh meal tonight—but his curiosity managed to clamber on top of his hunger, pushing it back to its usual, ever-present background ache.

An evening breeze hit him, bringing with it an odd chattering sound, like someone talking softly and really, really fast. The zombie gunslinger turned, searching for the source of the weird sound.

It appeared to be coming from behind a large rock.

He found, lying on the ground, the clockworker's missing head. He picked it up. He could see that it had once been very beautiful, but now its locks and silk skin was gone, burnt off to reveal the tarnished Titezium alloy beneath. Gears and cogs still ground deep within the skull. The jaw clicked and a pair of porcelain eyes, glistening with oil, rolled in the steel sockets. Tiny cameras set into the pupils focussed on the gunslinger's face.

"Well . . . ah never . . . " slurred the head of Marilou-Belle Watkins. "You are as ugly as a burnt boot!"

"You're . . . no picture yourself, ma'am," the gunslinger heard himself say.

"Ah . . . daresay Lucius . . . Barrymore won't want me now I'm just a head . . . he'll have to make do . . . with one of my sisters! I have . . . a dozen all like me, all ready to go . . . they just need to be wound up and given a little education . . . " Her chattering trailed off for a second, and her eyes rolled back into her head. But then her gears continued to grind and she focussed on him once more. "Ah am sorry, sir . . . didn't mean to malign your appearance . . . you did stop and come to my aid . . . although I fear I am . . . at this stage

BASED ON AN ILLUSTRATION BY TANYA NICHOLLS

beyond help. But you can do me one favour . . . There is a switch at the back of my head . . . be so good as to push it in for me? It will turn me off. Ah don't fancy . . . lying here and muttering to myself . . . until mah clock runs out in about a year's time."

She may only have been a machine, but suddenly the gunslinger felt sorry for her. After all, he'd had extensive experience dealing with complicated mechanical devices that seemed to have a life of their own. Right now, just a severed head in his hands, she seemed far more human than half the people he had encountered over the years. "Oh, certainly I can do that for you, ma'am. But I was wonderin' how you came to be here, in such a sorry state."

She gave a wry laugh. "A most undignified way to go, sir. A big bug flew up mah nose, down my throat . . . and lodged in mah workings."

"Surely a little insect couldn't have made you explode like that! I saw the rest of yer body back on the road. You were a very fine machine."

She gave another laugh. "You are right, sir. In the time I've been lying here I've come up with another theory. The bug didn't make me explode . . . it simply activated prematurely the bomb that had been planted inside me. Obviously I was sabotaged before I was wound up . . . probably rigged to blow on my wedding night and kill Lucius Barrymore."

"Hell's bells! That would have been one bang he'd never forget!" The gunslinger laughed, then remembered he was talking to a lady. "I'm sorry, ma'am. I didn't mean to be so crude. Did you, perchance, happen to see a carriage come past a couple of hours ago?"

"Yes, ah was on that carriage, sir."

The zombie clutched Marilou's head tightly in excitement. "And was there also a man named Pat Davison on board?"

"Yes, sir. That cad was there."

"Yes! Thank you, ma'am! You've been most helpful. But how did ya know he was a cad?"

"Well, when we were travelling down that awful cliff back yonder . . . a rock struck the carriage and nearly sent it over the edge. It was leaning at a dreadful angle and one door flew open . . . Pat would have slid out, but he managed to hang on. Another passenger . . . a madam named Sallianne, fell out. He could have grabbed her with one hand as she slipped past him. He could have saved her . . . but he just let her fall." Marilou rolled her porcelain eyes and tears of transparent oil slid down her steel cheeks.

"That sounds like Pat Davison all right," growled the zombie. Even now he wanted to help her. He wished he had the knowledge to reattach her head to her body, but he was just a simple man, with only a rudimentary education. "Would you like to see justice served? Instead of switchin' you off I could take you with me."

"Accompany you as just a head mounted on the pommel of your horse? Oh no, sir . . . that's no way for a lady to travel. Just turn me off. I'll feel no more."

The gunslinger didn't want to send her into darkness. He had been there once already and really didn't want to go back. But he could see how that would be preferable to being a disembodied head without any way of moving around. "All right, ma'am." He turned her around and found the switch that she had mentioned. It was located at the base of her skull and normally would have been hidden under her hair. "Are you sure about this?"

"Yes, sir. Just push it in hard and hold it. I'll switch off. You needn't worry."

"All right." He pressed his thumb against the switch and held it. He heard the clockwork within her skull grind to a halt. He turned the head back around in time to see her eyes roll back into her head. Her chattering jaw ceased its movement and she fell silent forever.

The gunslinger felt an odd sensation, like a cold hand was closing around his stomach. It was something he hadn't experienced since he was alive. His tear ducts burned, but there was no liquid inside him to form tears.

Even though Pat Davison had not been responsible for the clockworker's demise, the zombie still felt a deep, dark need to avenge her destruction. He decided to take his anger out on the one he was after.

Gently he put the clockworker's head back down behind the boulder where he had found it, and returned to his idling horse. He hopped aboard, and yanked on the right hand lever.

# CHAPTER 8

THE COACH RATTLED on into the late afternoon. Emmet T. Billings upended his empty whiskey bottle and patted the bottom in the hope he could dislodge any precious liquid that just might have stuck inside. Nothing came out.

No longer worried about offending the ladies, Emmet swore. Then he knocked on the little door separating the passengers from the driver.

"What?" growled Zeke the Freak, in no mood to be disturbed.

"Um, Mr Sarandon? You wouldn't happen to have any whiskey on you, would you?"

"Nope—stone cold dry," Zeke answered quickly. "Don't drink while I'm drivin'."

Emmet swore again and flopped back into his seat. He peered out of his window at the slowly descending sun. "Gadsbudlikins. Won't this gawddamn day ever *end?*" He pitched the empty bottle out of the window and watched it fly end over end into the fading light. Eventually it smashed into a thousand shards on a distant rock. They glittered like sparks in the afternoon sunshine.

"I heard somewhere that the days have been getting longer and longer," drawled Pat Davison. He'd managed to quaff a significant portion of Emmet's tornado juice and was actually feeling quite happy. He didn't drink often and even a small amount could calm him. A fact of which he was quite glad, since he was now not quite so worried about his pursuer. They had come through so much already—any one of the dangers they had already faced could have slowed the undead spirit down. And he doubted the creature could match their breakneck speed.

"Well, it certainly damn well feels like it," growled Emmet. He turned to Billy, who was also happy from the booze and zoning out on his seat. At the moment all the horrible things that had happened seemed blurry and distant. "So, what's your story, kid? Why are you here all by yourself? Where are your folks?"

Billy looked up and his expression grew solemn. "My folks are dead, Mr Billings, sir. I'm an orphan."

"I'm an orphan, too, but you don't see me bragging about it!" declared Pat. Then, on seeing that Billy didn't get the joke, he ruffled the lad's hair. "Sorry, boy. Didn't mean to be so unkind. Why don't you start by telling us where you come from?"

"All right, sir. I'm from Spitdiddle."

Both Pat and Emmet raised their eyebrows. Even the well-travelled Mr Billings had never heard of this place.

"It's not much more than a wide place in the road, sir. A one-horse hick town. It was so small you had to step outside to change your mind!" Billy giggled. He didn't really understand the reference, but he had heard it many times and thought it sounded funny.

Both Pat and Emmet snickered.

"It was so small that on weekdays the church doubled as the schoolhouse." Billy explained. "Our local minister was also the teacher. His name was Preacher Farrow and he reared salmon in a deep well back o' the church house."

"Salmon? In a well?" exclaimed Emmet. "Don't they need whole streams and lakes to breed in?"

"Probably, sir. I don't know much about that sort of thing. But these salmons they had more eyes than any normal fish should have had, and their scales were all the colours of the rainbow. They had fangs and clawed feet instead of fins and they could climb up and down inside the well. Preacher Farrow had to put a steel grate over the top to keep them from escaping. I still remember the time one got loose and he had to chase it down Main Street with a net!" Billy started to snicker. But then his expression grew solemn again. "Anyway, Preacher Farrow made salmon mousse out of 'em and sold it to raise funds for the church-and-school. Everyone used to rave about it. Said it was really tasty."

Billy paused to take a deep breath. "My folks were never big fish eaters, 'cause the only fish we could catch in our local stream were these horrible spiky things they called cow fish on account o' their black and white spots. They tasted awful and the only way they could be cooked proper was real slow in a big oven. But one day my folks decided to buy some of Preacher Farrow's salmon mousse. They offered it to me, but I knew what those salmons looked like. I was too sick in the guts to try it. But my folks gobbled it all up and said it was delicious, like nothin' they had ever tasted before. Manna from Heaven, they said, whatever that means." Billy paused again and mopped his brow. All the whiskey he had drunk on an empty stomach was starting to make him nauseous. He took a deep breath to calm his rumbling guts.

"But then something weird happened. They both started burping, which at first I thought was real funny, 'cause grown ups never burp. But then they started to swell up and turn red. Their bellies became like big balloons and their faces looked like tomatoes. I jumped up to fetch Doctor Cassidy, but then they both exploded into flame! They went up like bloody roman candles!" Billy started to cry.

"Criminy," gasped Emmet. Awkwardly he slipped an arm around Billy's shaking shoulders. "You poor little urchin! That must've been horrible!"

"I raced down to our well for water," Billy sniffed, "but by the time I was able to put them out they was both charred to skeletons and quite dead!"

Even Pat gave Billy a comforting hug.

"Now I'm on the way to my grandmother's house in Kellyville," Billy finished with a loud sniffle. Emmet dug around for a handkerchief and eventually handed over the scarf he had pulled from Sallianne. Billy took it and loudly blew his nose into it. Then he cuddled into it and curled up beside Emmet.

"Poor little fella," said Emmet after Billy had fallen asleep. "Those must have been some seriously inbred salmon."

"Either that or he set his own parents on fire," drawled Pat.

Emmet glared at him, but didn't say anything. He was also beginning to have serious suspicious about Mr Davison. After all the tragedies that had happened, Pat still looked cool and in control. In fact he hardly looked ruffled at all, his bowler hat still firmly planted on his head and his dark expensive suit impeccable.

The only thing that seemed to really annoy him was how long their journey was taking. Then again, it was getting on Emmet's nerves, too.

The sun was skimming the south western horizon as the coach approached the beginning of the salt flats. It was almost black inside the carriage when Zeke finally brought it to a stop. Billy was still sleeping, and Emmet gently laid him down on the seat so he could leave the carriage without disturbing him. Pat followed him out, quietly closing the door behind him.

Zeke had also jumped down and was standing nearby, staring moodily out across the flats. In the dying light they looked flat and grey, featureless almost to the horizon where a few hills rose to hide the vanishing sun. "We're gonna camp here tonight," Zeke declared.

"Here?" scoffed Pat. "But those plains look so smooth—I'm sure we could keep going for a few more hours at least!" He tapped the face of his elaborate watch. In the half-light the numbers were glowing.

"No, we're campin' here," growled Zeke. He gestured to the coachman, and he started pulling bundles of tents from the back of the coach.

"Come on Mr Sarandon, how much will it take for us to continue on for a few more hours?" asked Emmet. He slipped one hand into his pocket and drew out a large wad of bank-notes. "We might be able to reach Kellyville a day early if we do."

Zeke glared at him. "No amount of money you have will compel me to cross the Demon Flats!" he shouted. Then he turned and joined the gunman in unwrapping the tents and setting them up. He was growling and swearing under his breath.

Emmet heaved a sigh and turned to Pat. "Demon Flats?"

Pat shrugged and walked over to a twisted, ancient log to sit down. Emmet joined him.

"Shall we help 'em set up camp?" asked Emmet.

"Nope," answered Pat. "I'm quite happy to sit and watch. Besides, they look like they have everything under control."

Zeke and the gunman only took a few minutes to set up two tents. Then they collected some dried wood and constructed a fire. Soon a can of beans was heating up in the flames. Since no-one had eaten since a very greasy bacon and egg breakfast back at the Eviscerated Buffalo, they were all looking forward to some food, no matter what it was. Zeke unpacked some bread and cheese and handed out battered tin plates and tarnished eating irons.

For a few minutes the little camp was silent save for the sound of the crackling fire, and the scrape of forks and knives across the metal plates. Zeke set aside a small serving for Billy to eat when he woke and covered it up.

"So, why did you call those plains the Demon Flats?" asked Pat, gesturing towards the deceptively still, featureless terrain, now barely visible in the dusk. Millions of brilliant stars shone down from the clear dark sky. There was a faint glow on the eastern horizon, heralding the rise of a full moon.

"What you fellas assume is a plain, ain't," growled Zeke with his mouth full of beans. "It's really a giant lake one day's ride across."

"A lake?" asked Emmet sceptically. "I didn't see any water."

"By day it is a lake of salt that covers black mud underneath. It is hazardous to cross 'cause you can sink into it and get bogged. Fortunately I know the best way over. But at night, during the full moon, the water rises to create a lake o' deadly quicksand."

Both Pat and Emmet cast their glances east, where the full moon was preparing to rise.

"Many people, machines and animals have been lost in the lake," Zeke continued as he mopped up the sauce on his plate with a piece of bread. "When you cross by day while the water level is down you can see some of these poor drowned carcasses start to poke out, forming weird sculptures. The salt and heat make short work o' the iron and steel engines, but the humans and beasts are dried out into hard, leathery creatures what look like zombies rising from the grave. Their bodies are all twisted from their last death agonies, tryin' to escape to the surface for air."

Pat couldn't stop a gasp of horror from escaping at the description and especially the word *zombie*. Zeke gave a nasty laugh.

"Now you know why I didn't want to continue on durin' the night." He got up and collected everyone's empty plates. He walked back over to the fire and poured some boiling water over them to clean them. "Make sure if you've gotta take a piss or a shit, you don't go too far."

"Yes, Mr Sarandon," both Pat and Emmet said together.

Zeke spat into the fire and headed off to his tent. The gunman joined him a few minutes later.

Pat and Emmet took the second tent where bedrolls had been

laid out for them. After the long, harrowing day it didn't take them long to fall asleep.

And for a few hours the camp was silent. A brilliant yellow moon soon rose above the horizon and began its long, slow climb into the sky. Nearby grasses shone beneath its light, but the flats remained inky black in colour. Slowly the coach's door creaked open and Billy Levi jumped out, rubbing his eyes. He'd had a good nap, but eventually his growling stomach and full bladder had woken him.

He relieved himself behind the carriage and then approached the fire, able to see perfectly clearly by the light of the moon. He found the plate of food Zeke had left for him, covered by a second overturned dish. He wolfed everything down in five minutes and burped. He knew he ought to go back to the carriage to sleep, but he didn't feel tired anymore. The sleep had cleared his head and the food had refreshed him.

He wanted to explore.

Every instinct told him to stay put—after all, this awful wilderness had already claimed several members of his party. But then he reasoned in the manner of a curious ten-year-old that Sallianne's death had been a terrible accident, Samuel's had been caused by a horrible plant that didn't grow anywhere around here, and Marilou would never have exploded had she been human. A few of those bugs had stung him, and apart from a couple of itchy welts, he was fine.

How bad could this area be? Zeke hadn't even set any watches.

Thus Billy set out from the carriage towards the edge of those dark, still plains, wondering what he would find.

Zeke and the gunman rose with the sun. While the coachman ignited the carriage and horse engines to give the boilers time to heat up, Zeke prepared a breakfast of fried camp apples, johnnycakes and more beans. Zeke found the plate Billy had cleaned and assumed the boy had gone back into the coach to sleep. When the food was almost ready he poked his head into the passengers' tent and bellowed for them to rise and shine.

Then he knocked on the side of the carriage. "Wake up, little buddy! Time's a-wasting!" He didn't receive an answer, so he knocked again.

Still nothing.

He opened the door and looked inside.

The coach was empty; only Sallianne's scarf lay on the seat where Billy had been sleeping. Zeke's stomach fell in dismay. "Oh no, don't tell me!"

"What's going on?" asked Emmet as he crawled out of the tent wearing nothing but a pair of grubby long-johns.

"The kid's gone!" Zeke turned from the carriage. He cupped both hands around his mouth and shouted: "Billy! *Billy Levi!*"

The coachman and Emmet joined him, hollering the boy's name.

"What's the bet he's hiding somewhere, waiting for the right time to jump out and shout 'boo'!" Emmet declared.

"Maybe, maybe not. *Billy!*" Zeke yelled again.

"If that little shit delays us, I'm going to kill him," muttered Pat as he scrambled out of the tent, already fully dressed and ready to leave. But he joined the others in calling for Billy.

The only answer they received was the sound of the early morning breeze rustling through the grasses at the edge of the salt flats.

Zeke's shoulders slumped. "We can't afford to waste any more time here. We have to get moving." He returned to the fireplace to gobble down his breakfast. While Emmet and Pat ate their food at a more sedate pace, Zeke and the coachman raced to dismantle the camp.

Pat also ate the serving that had been set out for Billy.

"Where on earth could that blasted kid have gone?" wondered Emmet. "He knew it was dangerous to wander around!"

"Did he?" asked Pat softly as he dabbed his moustache with a napkin. "As I recall he was asleep when Mr Sarandon told his story."

Emmet stared at the handsome prospector. His jaw dropped. "You . . . you don't think he fell in that quicksand?"

"Who knows?" Pat shrugged, once again completely unruffled.

A sick feeling churning in his stomach, Emmet turned away. He prided himself on being a cool customer, but Pat Davison took the biscuit! Emmet knew he had done some terrible things, so what in the world could Pat have done to become so cold-hearted? It must have been something truly awful.

In only a few minutes Zeke and his companion had the bedrolls and tents packed and tied onto the back of the stage. Zeke kicked some dirt over the fire pit and turned to the two men. "All aboard. It'll take us a whole day to cross the Demon Flats."

Emmet and Pat climbed into the coach's suddenly roomy interior. Each man now had an entire seat to himself. But only Pat sighed with relief as he stretched his legs out. Emmet continued to shake his head.

Zeke steered the coach out onto the salt flats. The hardened crust crunched beneath the heavy steel wheels. Every time the surface crumbled beneath them and the entire conveyance lurched into a hole, Zeke drew in a nervous breath, convinced they were about to plunge to their doom into the thick, dark mud beneath.

But the mud was only a foot deep and they were able to continue on. Bizarre, twisted things were already starting to protrude from the salt. Some were the badly corroded bodies of mechanical horses, others the mummified remains of large bullocks with three horns and tusks. They did indeed resemble zombie monsters, only a thin layer of skin covering their skeletons.

Then Zeke spotted him. It was a wonder he had made it this far. But then again, he was only small and would have been able to walk quite a distance across the mud before finally falling through its thin veneer.

Unlike the other creatures his body was still fresh, not yet mummified into an emaciated husk by the salt and the years and elements. However, the sodium chloride had already hardened around him, freezing him solid into the last position of his life. Now that the mud had receded the agonised body of Billy Levi was revealed. He stood with his hands raised above his head and hooked into claws, mouth open in a silent scream, eyes wide and staring into oblivion.

Zeke "The Freak" Sarandon swore and muttered and pulled out a fresh human bone to nervously gnaw upon.

# CHAPTER 9

THE ZOMBIE GUNSLINGER didn't need to sleep and could travel through the night. On his new mount he was able to close the distance between himself and the coach, and knew he would reach it in only a few hours.

He also wasn't worried about the night. As an undead creature he could see in the dark. Everything was a washed-out shade of grey, but since that was how he normally saw the world, he didn't worry. Only the fresh internals of a body had any colour.

It was still far more than he'd been able to see during his life.

He just had to slow his horse down to half-speed, as distances through his weird night vision could be confusing and he didn't want to misjudge the size of a rock and send himself flying. But his revenge was so close he could almost taste it! He licked his torn lips in anticipation.

A few hours after sunrise he arrived at the edge of an enormous grey plateau. It was completely smooth save for various oddly shaped lumps rising out of it. Some looked like trapped machines, others like animals. A few even resembled humans, frozen in their last agonies until the end of time.

The gunslinger stopped to survey his surroundings. He didn't trust those strange flats and wanted to make sure his quarry had gone that way. He checked the area and found that the coach had stopped for the night to make camp. But the black muddy tracks continued on into the plateau. He could see cracks in the surface and a few yards distant a large hole where one wheel had become momentarily stuck.

The zombie squinted into the distance. He realised that if he had a spyglass he just might be able to spot them. Well, if that was the way they had gone, then he had to follow. It looked dangerous but he had no other choice. He wanted his revenge.

He accelerated his mechanical mount onto the plateau. The salty silt crunched beneath his wheels and cracks spread out around him as he continued forward. He realised that the coach, with its wider profile spread over a larger area, had been able to pass over areas that were too unstable for his narrow mount. Even though his machine was far lighter than the carriage, it still cut through the crust like a knife. He managed to keep going for a couple of hours, then the surface split beneath him like thin ice. His mount tipped over and he fell onto the salt. The surface held beneath him but his heavy horse was bogged in about a foot of the dark, stinking stuff. He had the strength to lift it out, but mud had already seeped into the furnace and doused the fire. The things could ride through rain, but not standing water.

He swore. It would take time to clean and relight—time he didn't have right now. And he didn't want to think about how much of that foul black liquid had worked its way into the engine. He had no idea how to flush that out.

With a sinking feeling in his mangled guts he realised that he would have to abandon his mount and walk. On this unstable terrain he had only been moving at half-speed anyway.

Collecting one leather saddlebag, he packed some spare clothes into it, then wrapped up his guns and a small silver cigar case as tightly as possible. He hoped the bag would hold should he end up falling into the mud himself. Slinging it over one shoulder he started walking, his boots crunching into the thin salty surface. It looked like the stage would draw ahead of him again.

No matter. He had endless patience. All the patience in the world. He would catch up with it eventually.

Focussing on those misty, distant mountains on the horizon, he walked. And walked. And walked. To amuse himself he started singing a song that had been one of his favourites when he'd been alive. It was 'Clementine'. He'd even made up some verses of his own.

The sun beat down on his stolen hat as it crawled slowly across the pristine blue sky. The grey salt seemed to stretch on forever. Only the weird, twisted sculptures of abandoned machines and dead creatures broke the monotony. The gunslinger spotted something that could have been a locomotive with enormous treads instead of wheels, lying on its side. The builders of such a contraption must have thought it could handle the unpredictable surface. Then, an hour or so later he saw an entire frozen maracleptops bullock-train. Desiccated and withered, it could have been there for one year, or a hundred.

The gunslinger didn't bother looking for booty. Anything useful would have long been corroded. All he could do was plod on, warbling his endless song.

And then, finally, the sun set behind him, taking the heat of the day with it. Even though he didn't feel much heat or cold anymore, he appreciated the departure of the blinding sun reflecting off the endless grey. He paused for a moment to remove his hat and mop his hand across his skull, smoothing back the few wispy white strands of hair he still had. He squinted at the horizon ahead and fancied he saw it.

A tiny, pin-prick sized flare of light. A *fire!*

Was he looking at the very coach he was after? Did Pat Davison sit beside it, eating his dinner?

The zombie skinned his ruined lips back from his fang-like teeth in a snarl. He was hungry, so damned hungry. Out here on these salty plains there was no life. Even the flies had departed, and there were no new maggots breeding inside him. The salt had purified his desiccated body.

The gunslinger picked up his pace into the dusk, now moving at a steady jog. His boots pounded into the crystalline surface. The salt crunched beneath him. His spurs jingled. Was it his imagination, or was that distant glow getting brighter? Had he still been alive, his heart would have been racing with anticipation instead of banging against his ribs like a pendulum.

He was so excited he didn't notice the change in the sound his boots made as they thudded into the salt. From a dry crunching noise it changed to a wet squelching. Only when he was pulling his feet out of mud did he realise that something was happening.

Where had all this moisture come from? The salt had been so dry and crunchy before! The gunslinger stopped to take stock of the situation. There was a wetness around his ankles that hadn't been there before. A wetness that was quickly moving up his legs. He looked down, realising that he was standing in thick, dark mud.

He hadn't even felt the surface break beneath him! But as he looked up he realised the mud was stretching as far as his keen undead eye could see. It was extending all the way to the horizon, where a large yellow moon was slowly beginning its climb.

As the wetness began to creep up his legs he realised he was sinking fast. He hauled his foot up out of the mire with an obscene sucking sound and put it down, only to descend into the mud up to his knee.

"Damn!" he swore. "Quicksand!"

The gunslinger hauled his back leg out . . . and his front leg dropped another few inches. He was now stuck up to his thigh. Another curse escaped his ravaged lips. That winking light on the horizon was taunting him. How would he ever reach it now? He was caught in this awful lake-sized midden!

His quarry was only a few hundred yards away. A few hundred yards! But he was stuck out here in the middle of nowhere, in a giant lake of salty quicksand! He could feel it pulling at him, dragging him down. Now it was up to his hips and rising fast. He struggled to wade forward, and tipped face-first into the muck.

*SPLAT!*

Lucky I don't need to breathe, the gunslinger thought miserably as he slowly sank into the mire. He flung up an arm, managing to grab onto his hat before it was left behind on the surface. Even now he didn't want to lose it.

The inky wetness closed over his head and he disappeared from sight. Soon the surface of the mud-lake was smooth and flat once more, as though there had never been any disruption.

And as the moon climbed higher, so did the liquid, growing thinner and more fluid.

Oh well, the gunslinger thought as he descended ever faster into the darkness—a blackness that even he couldn't see through. At least it won't kill me. But when will I be able to resurface to continue my quest? Some of those trapped creatures looked like they had been caught centuries ago . . .

Pat might be long dead by the time I emerge . . .

As the sun neared the western horizon once more, the two remaining travellers finally saw the end of the long, boring journey across the salt flats in sight. A line of grass, shifting in the afternoon breeze, greeted their tired eyes. Emmet actually heaved a very loud sigh of relief. "I don't know about you, Pat, but all that grey going on and on was really starting to shit me off."

"I don't know," said Pat. "Some of the things coming out of the salt looked quite interesting. Did you see that locomotive? Obviously someone thought they could get one across these plains."

Emmet shuddered, wondering how anyone could think any of those death-sculptures were actually interesting. "Well, it's over now and I sure could use something to eat. And drink," he added mournfully.

As soon as there was solid soil instead of crunchy salt beneath the carriage's heavy steel wheels, Zeke pulled the contraption to a stop. "We're campin' here!" he yelled as he jumped down. The gunman followed him and they began setting up the tents and camp fire.

Emmet and Pat climbed down from the coach and stretched their legs in the cool afternoon breeze. Emmet went for a short walk but Pat simply stared out across the flats. He felt even more confident than before. I doubt you could possibly follow me across that, he thought. I'm surprised that we actually made it.

At the fire, Zeke was already heating up some pease porridge and skirlie. Nearby, the coachman hammered in the last few tent pegs and straightened up with a grunt.

"Food's ready," growled Zeke as he held out two plates of questionable beef slop. But it smelled good and the passengers fell on it like starving dogs. It was filling too, and made them feel deliciously contented. The events of the previous day began to recede.

After retiring into some nearby bushes for a much-needed crap, Emmet returned to the carriage to collect a briefcase from the luggage-rack. After all that had happened, he wanted to check that his prize possession was still intact.

"What's that?" Pat asked conversationally as Emmet brought the case over into the light of the campfire. The case glittered in the half-light, made from a strange, particularly lumpy leather.

"A case made from the finest devil-toad skin," Emmet proclaimed. He ran one hand over the case's surface. "They can get all sorts of drugs from the warts of those things, can't they?"

"Oh yes," agreed Pat. "Sleeping draughts, pain-killers, anaesthetics, hallucinogens . . . Devil-toads are incredibly useful. But you need the right distilling equipment, not available to just any snake-oil alchemist. So what's inside?"

"My prize collection." Emmet popped the clasps. The inside of the case was covered with red velvet and had rows of small indentations pressed into it.

In each nestled a human eyeball.

As soon as he realised what they were, Pat leaned forward in interest. "Are those real eyes?"

"Oh yes." Emmet popped one out and held it up in the firelight so Pat could examine it. This one was a brilliant shade of blue, so bright it almost seemed to glow with its own inner light. Pat expected it to be soft and squishy like a normal eyeball, but it was as hard as a rock.

"They solidify after they're removed," Emmet explained. "They're like gemstones—just as precious and rare. These are the finest ones out of all the ones I was able to gather, and I'm sure to make a real fortune from them." He pulled out another. This one was ruby-red and reflected the glow of the flames.

"Removed? From where?" asked Pat.

Emmet grinned. "As you may have already gathered, I'm a travelling salesman. But a salesman of what, I hear you ask? Well, there is a very exclusive, but substantial market in second-hand body parts." He swept his hand across the eyeball display. "These might look like jewels, but they are still perfectly formed, perfectly functional eyes. Should you lose an eye in a shootout or go blind from cataracts, one of these inserted into your skull, replacing your old eye, will enable you to see perfectly once more. That's why they're so valuable."

"Zounds, but you still haven't told me where you got them from."

"These are the last dozen eyeballs I personally collected from the Blemmyae."

"The *who?*"

"Also known as the Black Rock native indian tribe."

"What's so special about the Black Rock indians?"

"Their faces are in their torsos and their chests are studded with eyes."

"What in the world? How in hell did they grow faces in their chests?"

"The story is that many thousands of years ago a chief named Lonely Crow was betrayed by his brother Prowling Cougar and exiled from his tribe. Starving in the wilderness, he begged the sky spirits for help. They instructed him to go on a vision quest. So he ate some mescala worms and went off to the spirit world. He saw a giant eye in the sky, looking down at him. When he woke he found one eye in his chest, growing right above his heart. He could see out of it, but he had no idea how it would help. He decided to return to his tribe to find out.

"When he saw his brother Prowling Cougar with his wife Wind Song, Lonely Crow realised what his new eye could do. It could see into men's hearts. He saw Prowling Cougar tell everyone that Lonely Crow had been the betrayer. He saw everyone believe him, even his own wife. He saw Prowling Cougar take over the whole tribe.

"Infuriated, Lonely Crow charged into the camp and speared his brother in the chest, in the heart, killing him and taking back the leadership," Emmet continued. "Lonely Crow's children were all born with eyes in their chests. The Black Rock indians changed over time, and now their entire faces are in their stomachs, and their hair grows right out of the tops of their necks. They also have a whole cluster of eyes in their chests, not just one or two."

"Nice story, but I doubt it's the truth!" Pat scoffed.

Emmet shrugged. Usually he was the sceptical one. "Stranger things have happened. Like your tale about the zombie indian shaman followin' you," he added pointedly.

Pat winced.

"Anyway, after last year's massacre at Black Rock Pass, I personally carved all the eyes out of the dead Blemmyae's chests. I managed to sell all bar these dozen. I'm hoping to get a pretty penny for them in Kellyville where all those rich folks live."

Pat gave a long, low whistle. "Mr Billings, if there isn't a dead indian shaman also pursuing you, I'll eat my hat!"

Emmet flipped a hand. "I don't fear any indian zombie coming after me. I never killed any of those redskins. I just took advantage of all the unguarded dead bodies lying around. That's my job. To seize whatever opportunity I can." He closed the case and took it back to the carriage.

An hour or two after dawn, after the sun had climbed over the eastern horizon, the thin crust that had started to form on the salt lake as its muddy waters descended oozed and bubbled and burst apart to release a filthy figure. With the dark substance pouring from it, it marched from the mire up onto the grass.

When it reached solid ground it fell to its hands and knees, vomiting out several pints of mud. More thick wads oozed from the open wounds in its chest and belly.

When the zombie gunslinger was about fifteen pounds lighter he clambered to his feet, yanked off his coat, and shook another three pounds of muck from it. Then he upended his boots and poured out more goo.

As soon as the mud cleared from his voice box, he started swearing. Still cursing he pulled out a handful of guts and squeezed another pint of mud out of them through various holes. "Son of a bitch!" he yelled.

So what if he was undead? He *never* wanted to go through something like that again!

He might not have needed to breathe. He might have been able to sink to the bottom of the lake and, by carefully putting one foot in front of the other, use his superior strength to simply continue walking along. But he hadn't been able to see a thing, his body had filled up with mud, and he had completely lost track of time.

He hadn't even been able to sing his song to pass the time!

He bashed both his hat and coat against a withered tree, shaking as much loose mud off the articles as he could. As it dried to salt he hoped it would simply flake off.

He checked his bag. It was ruined and mud had seeped inside. But the guns and case he had wrapped so carefully appeared to have survived. He shoved the cigar case into one pocket, holstered the pistol and took the rifle in one hand.

Then he checked his surroundings for some sign of the coach. During his long slog through the mud the night had ended and it was now midmorning. It had taken him almost eight hours to walk a couple of hundred yards.

At least he hoped it had only taken him eight hours. It could have taken him thirty-two hours, or longer!

But his decision to carefully place one foot in front of the other had been a wise one. It had kept him going in a straight line. Only a few yards from where he had emerged he found an abandoned campsite, sand kicked over the fireplace and a few turds already attracting flies. The stage's tracks cut through the grass, heading off due south.

He had only missed them by a few hours!

"*Bastards!*" the zombie gunslinger snarled.

# CHAPTER 10

THE COACH TRAVELLED up out of the plains and back into more high country. Pat relaxed to see grassy hills studded with relatively normal-looking trees and the occasional rocky outcropping made from some dark basalt-like stone. However, the further they travelled the more nervous Emmet became: fidgeting and casting increasing glances out of his window.

"What's the matter, Emmet?" asked Pat. "I'm thinking we've finally reached a relatively safe area, but instead you're jumping around like a cat on hot bricks!" Truthfully, Emmet was starting to irritate him and he wanted to tell him to settle down. Pat didn't like anyone else fussing bar him.

"Dang it," growled Emmet. "I was hoping we'd ride around this, but obviously the fastest route is right through the middle."

"Right through the middle of *what?*" demanded Pat.

Emmet glared at him. "You think we're safe, but we're not. These are the Black Rock Hills!" He gestured towards the dark boulders that had given the area its name.

Pat gaped. "Where those Blemmya chest-eye injuns live?"

"Yes!"

Emmet T. Billings was correct. Behind those grassy, rocky hills and spreading green tress lurked tall, copper-skinned natives with long, shiny black hair decorated with beads, bones and feathers. Some wore bracelets and rings, others belts made of leather and hair. But all were headless and bare-chested. Their faces were indeed located in their chests, and in between their well-chiselled pectorals nestled clusters of eyes. The scouts in hiding were on foot, but behind them the warriors approached on the backs of large, piston driven horses. These were old, rusty mounts, scavenged from battle-sites and repaired with homemade glue and strips of leather.

But although they rumbled ominously and belched out foul-smelling smoke from their crooked chimneys, they were still perfectly functional, restored to full working order by the tribal shamans.

The shamans had managed to get in contact with the abandoned horses' machine spirits and spark them back into life, coercing them to work above and beyond normal system parameters. Only too happy to hear from someone who could really communicate with them instead of bully them into compliance, the spirits agreed. Now these clapped-out old machines, looking ready to fly apart at the seams, actually functioned at peak efficiency on the absolute minimum amount of maintenance and fuel.

The Blemmyae carried stolen guns, strange spears made from wood with bits of cut steel embedded into them, and other weaponry including spring-loaded grappling hooks made from sabre teeth.

Normally they didn't travel in such large, battle-ready groups, but they were on a mission to find who had violated their dead after the Black Rock Pass Massacre. A scout had informed the current chieftain, Winking Lizard, that the culprit was possibly an unscrupulous body-part salesman who had been seen skulking around the area before the battle.

So the group had been prowling their surroundings for months, searching for more clues as to the whereabouts of this salesman. They had been considering disbanding and returning to camp when one of their long-range scouts arrived with the news that the man was once again on his way south, hoping to unload the last of his ill-gotten gains in Kellyville.

The large, battered carriage rattling along the narrow trail below was the first such transport the indians had seen for weeks. Only a few dared to pass right through their territory. Did it contain the one they sought? There was only one way to find out.

Chief Winking Lizard, resplendent in his massive eagle-feather headdress and glittering war paint, raised his enormous spear with its deadly serrated blade. Unleashing a deafening war cry, he led the charge down the hill towards the coach.

On hearing his shout, another party came from the other side to catch the carriage in a pincer movement. Zeke Sarandon cursed and shook the metal reins to urge the engine on faster. Maybe he could

outrun those heathen bastards on their dilapidated mounts. Beside him the gunman rose in his seat, lifting his rifle to his shoulder.

"Aim for the bloody leader!" shouted Zeke. "There are too many of them, but if you can hit him the others might back off!"

"That's what I'm trying to do!" The gunman fired and his laser ball shot off, heading up the hill towards Winking Lizard and his closest warriors. But it missed him and struck a mechanical horse a few yards behind him, blowing the ancient contraption—and its rider—to smithereens. The ensuing blast took out half-a-dozen warriors, knocking them from their mounts and toppling their horses. But since there were over fifty of the warriors, that didn't make much difference to the attacking horde. And with flames licking at his heels, the leader was still coming!

As the wild-haired indians with the maniacal, shrieking faces in their bellies approached they began to rise up in their stirrups, lifting their spears onto their shoulders. The coachman cursed and raised his weapon, waiting for it to recharge. But just as he was about to fire, a spear slammed into his throat, nearly decapitating him. He toppled from his seat beside Zeke and tumbled onto the road. His gun spun from his fingers and exploded against a rock, excavating a large, charred hole. Zeke cursed again, hunching into his shoulders in the hope he now made a smaller target. A spear clanged into the side of the coach's engine, mere feet from where he was sitting. More of the murderous implements clattered against the sides of the coach.

Zeke hazarded a glance over his shoulder.

The Blemmyae, the numerous eyes in their chests blazing blood-red with battle-lust, were keeping pace on either side of the stage. Crikey, how the hell can those beat-up old horses move so damn *fast?* Zeke thought.

One of the indians, standing in his saddle, reached the stage-coach door, the one that was really only hanging on by one hinge, and yanked it open. He peered inside and gave a whoop of excitement. He screamed something and reached for an object at his waist.

It was the sabre-tooth grapnel.

Need to go faster, Zeke thought, shaking the reins. Come on, come *on,* you piece of junk!

But the engine was straining at top speed already, oily black smoke pouring from its chimney. The steel wheels sent sparks flying from the stony ground. And the indians were actually starting to draw ahead! A warrior turned in his saddle, aiming a spear at Zeke.

"Shit!" Zeke cursed. He tried to dodge—the spear slammed into his shoulder, pinning him to the seat behind him. His curse ended in a shriek of pain.

Incapacitated, he couldn't turn to see what was happening behind him.

The open door banged against the side of the stage, one hinge now completely broken. The Black Rock indian warrior riding alongside, still balanced on his saddle, whirled his home-made grappling hook above his head like a lasso. Inside the coach Emmet and Pat could only stare in horror. Neither had immediate access to any weapons.

The indian flung the grapnel and it shot in through the open door of the carriage. There was nowhere for Emmet or Pat to hide.

The grappling hook, sabre-blades folded in close, sliced into Emmet's jaw like a knife. He lifted a hand to pull it out just as the indian jerked on the rope.

The three blades sprang out, shattering Emmet's jaw and dislodging it from his body. The indian yanked on the rope again, and the grapnel lodged around Emmet's neck, yanking him from the coach.

Not much fazed Pat Davison, but the sight of Emmet being dragged out like a skewered sidewinder was far too disturbing for him to handle. He reacted on instinct, trying to grab Emmet's body as he was pulled from the coach.

But despite his efforts he wasn't quick enough. He sprawled on the coach's wooden floor as Emmet was hauled out and slung across the back of the mechanical horse directly outside.

The indian astride the ancient beast gave him a little wave, and then fell back out of sight. Pat could only stare in horror at the landscape blurring past. How the hell did those pagan bastards know we were coming through here? he wondered miserably as the open door continued to bang in the wind.

Draped across the mechanical mount like a kill, Emmet felt only agony surging through his jaw. His blood poured down the side of the mount. He could smell its hot metallic tang mixing with the smoke from the engine and the brassy stench of overheated metal. No coherent thought entered his mind. His pain was as large as he was.

Having acquired their quarry the Blemmyae headed back to their camp, several miles from the white man trail that had cut through their hunting grounds. Up here the entire landscape was dominated by dark stony outcroppings. They looked like watching statues, tall and gaunt against the fading light of the afternoon sun. The Black Rock indians called them the Sentinels. They were the physical embodiment of their sky spirits and watched over them.

Their lengthening shadows fell like grasping fingers over a large pile of decomposing bodies of Blemmyae laid on a huge pyre of faggots. They had been covered in salt to preserve them, and although this had withered them to fleshless, desiccated skeletons, there was no mistaking the rough cut-marks on their chests—gouges where their eye-clusters should have been.

Emmet realised that he was looking at the corpses of the indian bodies he had desecrated. Horror began to nudge through his agony.

The man who had captured him brought his mount to a halt and jumped down. He gestured to Emmet and said something that sent his fellows into a frenzy of cheering and clapping.

Then another mechanical horse drew up, in better condition than the others and decorated with paint, beads and feathers. The clouds of smoke that puffed from its chimney combined all the colours of the rainbow.

Chief Winking Lizard jumped down and clapped the warrior who had captured Emmet on the back, congratulating him. Then he stopped in front of the prisoner and spoke to him in his heathen tongue. Emmet did not understand a word spitting from that giant stomach-mouth and wished someone would come and drive a tomahawk into his brain. Maybe then the pain would go away.

The chieftain reached into a belt-pouch and brought out a handful of white powder. He waved a hand over it, intoning some foreign words, and then blew it in Emmet's face. Emmet's eyes watered; he wanted to sneeze but knew the slightest movement would send more agony through his wounded jaw. His eyes started watering.

"Tie him up!" shouted Winking Lizard.

Emmet blinked in surprise. Why did they want him to be able to understand them? What did they have in store for him?

The Blemmya who had captured him and another brave with tattoos all over him hauled him down from the back of the horse. The agony in his jaw was blinding and he blacked out, for the next thing he knew he was bound to a wooden stake next to the warriors' pyre.

He had no idea how long he had been out for, but it must have been a considerable while. The sun had set and the night sky was studded with stars.

He wanted to ask what was going on, but the indians seemed to anticipate his question. Could they see into his heart with those weird chest eyes of theirs?

"We cannot burn our braves until retribution is paid for the removal of their eyes," the chieftain declared, gesturing towards the preserved dead. He snapped his fingers at the man who had captured Emmet, and he drew a shiny steel blade from a pouch at his side. He smiled as he approached the salesman, lifting his knife high.

Emmet began to quake against his bonds. No, not more pain! he thought frantically.

"Hold him!" shouted Winking Lizard.

Another indian clapped his calloused hands around Emmet's skull, keeping his head steady. Emmet's captor held his blade up in front of Emmet's face.

It was the last thing he saw.

The indian poked out both of Emmett's bloody eyeballs and offered them to the funeral pyre of dead, preserved indians. Reverently, he placed Emmet's eyes on the pile of corpses, then removed the shocked, trembling blind man from his stake.

"Now, you too, are a fallen warrior!" declared Winking Lizard. With that they bound Emmet's arms and legs secure and then swung him up on top of the pyre. He landed with a sickening crunch on dry, dead bodies that creaked and settled beneath his weight, filling his nostrils with the sickly stench of decay.

Emmet could no longer see but he could smell the scent of smoke as another brave approached with a lit torch. Then a far stronger stench of burning flesh filled his nostrils as the bodies beneath were set on fire.

Hungry flames ate up the dry faggots beneath the corpses and built up a formidable heat. They licked the bodies despite the salt that had been rubbed into them. Their dry, desiccated state only helped the cleansing fire to soar higher and higher, rising towards the one living man at the top of the heap, roaring incoherently because he no longer had a jaw, and struggling ineffectually at his ropes. His flesh began to blacken, char and melt from his bones.

The bright yellow flames climbed higher and higher into the sky and Emmet T. Billings was burned alive.

Despite the spear in Zeke the Freak's shoulder, impaling him to the seat behind him, he continued on down the pass through the Black Rock Hills until he was sure he was out of Black Rock indian country. Then, only when gentle grassed hills were surrounding him and the sun hung low in the western sky, did he pull on the reins to slow the engine to a stop. For a few minutes in the dusk he sat breathing heavily, building up his courage. Slowly he managed to manoeuvre his left hand around and dip it into his right-side pocket, bringing out a precious flask of the finest whiskey. He had been carrying it with him since Sunbleached Plains, saving it for an emergency. An emergency such as now. With his left hand he lifted out the precious flask. Every movement sent jolts of agony through his right shoulder. But he could do this. All he had to do was be strong.

He lifted the flask to his lips and started to drink. He didn't stop until the entire flask was three-quarters empty, and a delicious warmth was spreading from his middle out to his extremities. Alcohol always had a wonderful effect on him, driving all pain and infirmity away. When he felt the whiskey had deadened him sufficiently, he tested out his right arm, making sure he could still move it without knocking himself unconscious.

He was able to lift it to the spear jammed in his shoulder and curl his fingers around it. He joined it with his left hand, and gritting his teeth, he yanked the jagged shaft out. A fountain of blood splattered down the front of his shirt. He cursed at the sudden, unexpected jolt of pain. It had been a while since he'd had a wound this severe.

Behind him the coach door slowly creaked open, and Pat cautiously stepped out in time to see Zeke yank the bloody spear out of his body.

"Jabberin' jabberwock!" Pat cursed, his guts rolling at the sight. "You should have hollered—I could have helped.

"I can do this," growled Zeke. "Done it before. You can make yourself useful and start settin' up the camp. It's only us now, and I'm in no condition to work at the moment."

Pat pulled a face, but realised that if he wanted to make it to Kellyville he had to do this. He turned and stomped around to the back of the stage where all the tents and cooking utensils were packed.

Still in his seat, Zeke pulled open his shirt to reveal the ugly, jagged wound. It was still bleeding freely. He upended his whiskey bottle again, pouring alcohol directly onto the injury. He hissed at the white-hot stinging of his own flesh. Come on, you can do this, Zeke, he thought. Compared to what you've been through, this is nothing! He rummaged through his pockets for his sewing kit, and with shaking fingers, threaded a needle.

While Pat bustled and clattered and swore as he made a dog's breakfast of setting up the campsite, Zeke proceeded to stitch up the wound in his shoulder. Then slowly he climbed down from his seat.

Pat had managed to erect one lopsided tent and get the fire started. He had filled a can with water and was boiling it. "I'll need your help to stitch the wound in my back," Zeke told him.

Pat looked up. "What?"

Zeke pointed over his shoulder. "Spear went right through me and came out the back. I can't stitch it myself. You'll have to do it."

Pat's jaw dropped. His eyes widened. Slowly he turned green. "Ummm."

"It needs to be closed otherwise it'll keep bleedin', and tomorrow I'll be in no condition to drive!" Zeke snapped. "So long as I get stitched up, I can continue." He peeled off his coat and blood-soaked shirt to reveal a torso that was criss-crossed and pocked with dozens of scars.

"Mother of mercy . . . " Pat whispered. He gulped. How hard could it be? It couldn't possibly be any worse than what he had done back at Nova Cyrus!

"It's one of the reasons why they call me 'The Freak'." Zeke handed Pat his sewing kit and then sat down on the ground in front of him. He handed him his bottle of whiskey, which still contained a little liquid at the bottom. There were more scars on his back, including the spear's ragged exit-wound.

He pulled a bone from one pocket of his jeans and started chewing on it.

As Pat lifted the whiskey bottle to his lips Zeke snapped; "It's not for you, idjit—pour it on the hole to clean it!"

"Oh shit, sorry." With shaking hands, Pat poured the liquor on the ugly, torn wound. His stomach performed another lazy roll. He gulped, licked his lips and tried unsuccessfully to thread the needle. Eventually, Zeke had to snatch it from him and do it. He even tied a knot at the end of the black cotton.

"No need to be a seamstress about it—just make sure it's closed. It'll heal pretty quickly once the ends are joined."

"A-all right." Pat pinched the edges of the wound together and poked the tip of the needle into Zeke's pallid flesh. It was at that point he lost control of his stomach on the ground next to Zeke in a noisy splatter.

"Oh, jumpin' jiminetty!" the Freak swore. He moved over a few feet to get away from the smell.

"Sorry, Mr Sarandon!" Pat wiped his mouth on a handkerchief. "I'll be all right now—I can do this!" He crouched back down behind Zeke and pulled the wound closed again. He pushed the needle in and tugged the cotton through. He expected Zeke to flinch and hiss, but the old driver didn't say a word. He just continued to crunch on his bone. Pat wondered what sort of bones they were. He seemed to carry an awful lot of them.

Sweating, struggling to keep his guts under control, Pat quickly stitched the cut closed, creating a vaguely flower-shaped pattern on Zeke's flesh. He knotted the cotton and snapped it off. "I'm . . . I'm done," he whispered. He got up and staggered off a few feet away to puke some more. But there was nothing left to come out but bile. He straightened, taking long, deep breaths to calm himself. He could poke around inside someone's stinking, diseased mouth until the cows came home, but actually stitching closed a ragged, open wound on someone's back was completely different.

After all that had happened, he wasn't sure he would be able to return to his old life as a dentist. Even before the start of his journey he had lost his appetite for the medical work.

"Thanks." Zeke got up without a wince and walked over to the fire. He collected the water canister and proceeded to wash. Pat couldn't help but stare; a few minutes ago this man had hardly been able to move. Could he really heal so fast?

Pat had only been able to accomplish such a miracle of healing through the use of drugs. Lots of weird, expensive and highly illegal drugs. And even then his own operation had not been entirely successful. He limped back over to the fire to remove the boiling water.

Zeke joined him and they prepared a dinner of dried bread, skunk eggs, beans and salt hare. Pat made some tea, but it was a weak, tasteless belly wash of a brew. Still, Zeke didn't complain and drank it all down.

"So where'd you get all those scars from?" Pat asked conversationally.

Zeke grunted. "I used to be a soldier. I been through a few wars. Including the War with tha Subterraneans of 1802. I was practically cleaved in half in that one. I was lyin' on a stretcher with me guts hangin' out and one leg nearly off. The sawbones was gonna pull the blanket over me face, but then I opened me eyes and said 'Doc, I'm still alive here! Just shove me innards back in, straighten up me leg, give me some booze and stitch me closed. I'll live'. The old bugger couldn't believe his eyes, but did as I asked, and I was walkin' around by the end of the day. The Doc said it was a miracle."

Pat could only stare in surprise. That was the longest speech that Zeke had ever given. Of course he didn't believe a word of it. Even deducting ten years due to The Lost Decade that would still make Zeke over eighty years of age. He couldn't possibly be that old, could he?

"I fought all over this dang country." Zeke continued. "After the incident at Little Big Cactus, I decided I'd had enough of bein' the army's cannon fodder. Too old to be soakin' up bullets."

Pat raised a quizzical eyebrow. "Little Big Cactus, eh? That was a total massacre, wasn't it?"

Zeke went all sullen and quiet. He stared off into the distance, avoiding Pat's stare.

Pat recognised that he'd struck a nerve and didn't press it. "And now you drive a stage." Pat said, changing the subject.

"Yessiree." Zeke perked up. "Of course it's not easy driving this route. I'm the only one dumb enough to take the most direct path. Everyone else goes around these particular badlands, adding almost a week to the journey."

"Crikey, I can see why!" Pat exclaimed. He finished his corned beef and popped the last onion into his mouth.

"I must admit this trip's been harder than most. Don't usually lose this many people. Normally only one or two at the most, and that's mainly 'cause they don't do as they're told and wander off." Zeke mopped his plate clean with his bread and then collected Pat's plate. He packed away all the food and utensils and returned to the coach. He rummaged through the belongings for several minutes, rearranging things and depositing bags that were no longer required. Pat wondered what he was up to. But then he returned with a big, toothless grin on his craggy face—an expression Pat had never seen before. "Mr Davison, look what I found!" He produced several bottles of whiskey and twists of tabackie.

Pat's eyes nearly came out on stalks. "Where was that hidden?"

"In Samuel Simkins' carpet-bag. I think we earned this, don't you?" He handed one of the bottles to Pat.

"I certainly do!"

As the sun disappeared beneath the horizon, Zeke the Freak and Pat Davison proceeded to have a party. Pat almost poured his story out to the crotchety old driver. Almost.

But the pair didn't get so drunk that they missed the other glow on the horizon, the flickering one to the north of their little encampment.

It belonged to Emmet T. Billings' funeral pyre.

# CHAPTER 11

THE RISING MOON shone full and bright down on the zombie gunslinger as he trudged along the stony trail that wound through the Black Rock Hills. His coat, hat and clothes were dusty with salt that hadn't yet flaked off and he was uncomfortable, miserable and hungry.

He smelled the carnage before he actually saw it: the coppery scent of dried blood, the stink of burnt flesh, smoke from damaged machinery. And then, as he came around a corner, he saw the battle site.

Immediately his mood improved.

What the hell happened here? he wondered as he stopped and surveyed the area.

His stomach growled.

Sprawled on the road directly in front was the body of a man, almost decapitated by a spear through the throat. A large puddle of blood had collected beneath it. Flies were already buzzing around it. Since he hadn't eaten for a while, the zombie grabbed a few and popped them into his mouth.

A few yards away up a hill lay more bodies, some charred and burnt beyond recognition. But a couple were still recognisable as the headless corpses of Black Rock indians. The eyes in their chests glinted in the moonlight.

So, the coach was attacked by indians, the zombie realised. I wonder who they were after? I hope it wasn't Pat.

That bastard is *mine*.

The gunslinger reached into the pocket of his dusty leather coat and drew out the silver box he had managed to save. He removed a cigar and lit it from one of the still-smouldering mechanical horses. All I can do is continue on, he thought as he blew out a cone of smoke into the cool night air. More smoke wafted out from the gashes in his chest and stomach.

He checked the fallen horses for one that wasn't too badly damaged and could possibly still be used. He found an overturned mount beside the body of a brave who had broken his back when he'd fallen. He pushed it up onto its wheels and checked its engine.

It was still warm. But would it work? It looked even older and more dilapidated than the antiquated mount he'd ridden into Sunbleached Plains. It had been extensively repaired with strange-smelling animal glue, tightly-wrapped vines and leather straps. It was painted all over with weird tribal designs, and had bones and feathers attached to the handles and dials that made up its 'head'. It even had a few unburnt coals still smouldering inside, and the boiler appeared to be full.

The gunslinger prodded the coals into life with the poker and then threw his cigar-stub inside. When the boiler eventually heated to boiling point, he pulled out the switch to start the engine.

He expected lots of jolting, spluttering and shuddering. Instead the engine started with a purr, like it had just rolled out of one of those massive east-coast manufactories. He climbed up into the saddle and it felt soft and comfortable beneath his bony undead butt. He pulled on the right-side handle and the horse rolled smoothly down the hill, coasting to a gentle stop beside the body of the dead coachman.

The gunslinger jumped down and scooped up the body, slinging it across the back of the horse. He tied it down with some of the indians' home-made twine and continued on his way.

He felt a little exposed and didn't want any indians who might still be lurking around the area to see what he was about to do. He was sure one of their shamans would be able to exorcise his spirit and reduce him to his constituent bones.

A few miles further down the trail he noticed some ancient ruins capping a hill, forming an evil-looking outline against the starry sky. A thick copse of trees lay beneath, forming a perfect area of dark shadows. He drove up the hill and parked his mount within the safety of the trees. From his vantage point he could see down onto the plains below.

But he was confident that no-one could see him.

The zombie gunslinger climbed down from his horse and untied the body he had brought with him. He laid the corpse out on the grass and stripped the torn, bloodstained clothing from its body. It had been dead for a few hours now and was already cooling and stiffening.

But the meat was still fresh and in sufficient quantity to sate his unholy undead hunger. At least for a little while. He broke the skull from the few scraps of skin that still attached it to the spine and used a rock to crack it open like a coconut. He peeled the fragments of bone away and scooped out the still warm brain from within. He brought it to his nose and savoured the smell first. Then he took a delicate nibble. It was salty and nutty and delicious! He began to cram chunks into his mouth, faster and faster. He discovered sparks of activity within—brief flashes of life that sent him quivering all over with delight. He could feel new energy flowing through him, invigorating him. He couldn't stop a groan of pleasure from escaping.

However, the hunger remained.

In fact now that the hunger realised that something was being done to sate it, it rose to consume him with an all-encompassing need for more. He finished cleaning out the skull and tossed it aside like an empty cup. Then with his long, sharp zombie fingernails he cut open the chest and hooked both hands in between the two halves of the rib-cage. He cracked the ribs open like a pair of stubborn saloon doors. Within lay a veritable smorgasbord of lukewarm organs steeped in a soup of blood. He dipped his hands in, bringing out a mouthful to his ravaged lips. It smelled almost as good as the brains had. He began gorging himself on the internals. The heart was chewy but full of blood and the lungs soft and light and airy. The liver was thick and juicy. Even the intestines served to satisfy. When nothing remained in the empty cavity he started stripping the flesh from the bones with his clawlike nails and teeth. For a while all he could think about was eating.

He had not had a feast like this since . . . ever. How the hell had he managed to survive so long on scrawny animals, insects and maggots? Truly his willpower was phenomenal.

Only when he had nearly skeletonised the corpse and just a few pieces of ragged flesh and sinew remained did he sit back on his haunches and stare out through the trees at the moonlit plateau. He noticed a strange glow on the horizon. It looked like a fire, but if so, it was a damn big one. Thick grey smoke billowed into the night sky.

The zombie fancied he could smell what was burning.

It was meat.

*Human* meat.

He rose to his feet and inhaled deeply. He was still hungry. And in more ways than one.

He looked down in surprise, realising he was sporting a massive undead hard-on.

He couldn't remember the last time he'd had one of those. It must have been years before his 'death'.

Still convinced that his midnight feast would be discovered by the mysterious indians who roamed these parts, the zombie carefully hid the remains of the coachman he'd devoured under some rocks and brush. It was early morning by the time he fired up his horse and rode back down the hillside to the trail. He followed it along as the sun slowly rose on his left, and reached a recently abandoned campsite.

He had managed to close the distance between himself and the man he sought, but he was still too far behind. Once again all he found were the remains of a fire, a pile of sticks, a dried up puddle of puke and the campers' lavatory. He cursed his decision to stay so long up on that hill, filling his undead belly with human flesh. He could have caught up with them hours earlier, surprised them while they were still in their undergarments . . . and exacted his horrible, bloody plan of revenge. Pulling his mangled lips back from his teeth in a furious snarl, he kicked dirt over the fireplace, scattering the sticks in all directions.

*Dammit!*

Well, there was nothing for it but to continue following their trail, which was still continuing almost due south. The gunslinger climbed back onto his horse and chugged off.

The path continued on through the hilly, deceptively ordinary country. Only occasionally did a cluster of strange old ruins break the monotony. The gunslinger wondered where those broken buildings had come from. Did the redskins build them, or had they been erected long before by an even older culture? He didn't often ponder matters of such a philosophical nature. Normally he was a simpler, more down to earth 'soul'. But since his resurrection he'd had time to think. Lots and lots of time in the saddle, just thinking.

And occasionally singing his own 110-verse version of Clementine.

Almost too late he realised that such rumination would probably be the death of him.

A spear whizzed past his right ear, missing him by a fraction of an inch. He cursed as he turned, looking for the source.

A group of indians were charging towards him on foot, aiming bows and spears. Behind them a second party hung back. They appeared to be guarding something.

They all looked perfectly normal: long black hair dressed with feathers, war-paint, tassels on their trousers and jerkins.

Their heads were located where they should have been—growing out of their necks. The trouble was that they all had *two* of them. Both were screaming bloody murder in some pagan tongue.

An arrow nearly knocked his hat off.

Now that annoyed him. It was a new hat, dammit! He had been about to accelerate away, leaving the weird two-headed heathens in his dust, but if it was a fight they wanted—well, a fight they would get.

The zombie couldn't get to his rifle; it was in the saddle bag behind him. But he did yank the pistol from his belt. With his thumb he powered it up and aimed it at the rapidly approaching horde. He hoped that after its dunking in the salt lake it still worked.

He fired and a laser blast hit the closest indian in the face at point-blank range. It vaporised one of his heads, blowing corpse-dust in the faces of a redskin behind him, blinding him. As the now single-headed indian dropped to his knees screaming, and the second indian cursed and spluttered, the gunslinger lowered his gun and reached into his boot with the other hand.

The two-headed indians attacked. A pair tried to grab him and pull him from his horse. One swung a tomahawk and it cracked into his spine with bone-crushing force. Unfortunately, the broken back the brave was hoping for didn't eventuate, and the zombie turned, burying a knife in between one set of very surprised eyes. He yanked it out with a fountain of blood just as another indian jammed a spear into his thigh. Then the two men who had hold of him managed to haul him from the mount. He slammed into the ground on his back, his hat falling from his head to reveal his ravaged face. His gun slipped out of his fingers, but he managed to retain his grip on his knife.

Immediately, the indians gasped and started to back off, making protective signs across their chests.

The zombie snarled in fury and lurched to his feet, holding his knife high. With his free hand he yanked the spear from his leg. He lunged forward, stabbing one man in the chest with his dagger. At the same time he jammed the spear into the guts of another. Due to his superior strength, the knife went in up to the hilt, and the spear sliced right through the man's middle.

That was enough for the rest of the indians, who screamed and scattered like crows. Even the ones who had lost heads staggered off. Only the ones he'd crippled with savage wounds to their bodies remained, lying on the ground moaning.

Swearing, the gunslinger flung the spear to the ground. Then he went back for his hat and gun. What the hell caused those weird two-headed redskins to attack me like that? he wondered as he slapped his hat back on his head. He turned to head back to his horse when he noticed what the other group had been guarding. When the first party had run off they had fled too, leaving behind a small group of frightened-looking people, all tied together with rough homemade rope.

What the hell?

He powered up his gun and cautiously approached them.

As he drew closer he saw that they were all filthy and covered in cuts and bruises. They were dressed in rags, although some of their garments looked like they had been quite expensive. The rough rope had been bound tightly around their wrists and linked one to another in a human chain.

They were slaves. Some white, some brown, some copper-skinned. There was even a Black Rock indian with his face in his stomach, half his chest-eyes blackened and bruised. Those two-headed indians had not discriminated.

As soon as the slaves saw the gunslinger's torn face they started to back away, gibbering in fear. Then someone tripped and the whole bunch fell over in a tangle of arms and legs. It would have been comical if it wasn't so pathetic. "Oh for pity's sake, I'm not gonna hurt you!" the zombie growled. He holstered his gun and drew his knife.

He started cutting through their bonds. "Yer free to go."

Some thanked him quickly before running off, others fled as soon as their ropes were severed. Only one person remained, a tall, slender woman with curly blonde hair. She didn't look as if she had been a slave long. Her gown was ripped and stained, but still in relatively good condition.

She was the only person who hadn't baulked at his mangled face.

"I must thank you for savin' me, sir," she declared.

"How come you didn't run?" he exclaimed.

"Oh, I've had far weirder zombies than you at my bawdy house, sir. One fella used to come in who was only a head. He liked to spend the entire day beneath my skirts. In the end I had a special truss made for him so I could still go about my other business." She giggled.

The gunslinger gaped. "Just who are you, ma'am?"

"Sallianne Veerhoven, at your service." She beamed a brilliant smile at him.

# CHAPTER 12

"MIGHT I KNOW your name, sir?" Sallianne asked.

"Er . . . " the zombie had been alone and focussed on revenge for so long he had almost forgotten it. "Steel . . . Steel Hawl."

"Pleased to meet you, Mr Hawl." She stuck out a hand to him.

He knew a gentleman was supposed to kiss her hand, but since he was no longer a gentleman, or even a man of any kind, he simply took her fingertips and shook them gingerly. "Well . . . I might as well be on my way now." He turned to leave.

"What?" She planted her hands on her hips. "And leave me out here in this awful wilderness all alone? Surely there's also room for me on the back of that fine injun hoss of yours?"

She wanted to ride with him? "Ma'am—I don't think you'll be wantin' to come with me. I'm chasin' down a man, and when I find him . . . well, it won't be purdy."

"A dark gunslinger on a bloody trail of revenge!" Sallianne clasped her hands together. "That sounds like fun! Are you sure I can't come with you? These wilds are really no place for a poor unescorted lass like me."

He sighed. "All right—you seem like you've been around a bit. Come on." He trudged over to his horse and moved his saddlebag back so she could sit behind him.

She paused beside the mount. "So, who is it you're after? A rogue cowboy? An evil sheriff? A vicious outlaw?"

"A dentist."

"A *dentist?*"

"Name of Pat Davison. Now get on if you're comin'. I don't wanna dawdle around here all day." He gestured towards the seat he had made for her.

Sallianne gaped at him in horror. Then to his surprise she spat at him! It hit him right in the empty eye-socket.

"What the hell was that for?" He wiped it off with one hand.

"How dare you pursue such a brave and courageous man!" She planted her hands on her hips again.

"Brave and courageous? *Brave and courageous?* The man is a lying, cheating, murdering cur!" Steel shouted at her. "He took my find, took my money and then he took my *life!* Don't you *dare* tell me he's brave and courageous!" He pointed a quivering finger in the direction most of the fleeing captives had taken. "You run along after the rest of your slave buddies before I forget myself and hit a lady! Or whatever the hell you are!"

Sallianne clapped a hand to her chest in shock. "I—I'm sorry sir— I had no idea what Mr Davison did! Perhaps—perhaps while we ride you can tell me your story?" She gave him a shaky smile.

He glared at her through his one milky white eye. "Very well. But if you try to stop me in any way, I'll toss your ass right off the back."

"Oh no, Mr Hawl. I wouldn't dream of it." Sallianne scrambled up onto the indian mount and carefully arranged her torn skirts around her legs. The zombie gunslinger muttered something and climbed up in front of her. She slipped her arms around his narrow waist and he pulled on the right lever to send the horse moving forward.

"I was on the coach with Mr Davison, sir," Sallianne explained once they were on the trail again, leaving behind the site of the skirmish with the strange two-headed indians. "That's how I know him. But a few days ago we were travelling along a narrow mountain pass and something knocked a giant boulder from the cliff. It hit us and nearly set us plummeting off the edge. One door flew open and Mr Davison fell out. He managed to grab onto the door but I slid out after him. I caught hold of his legs and tried to hang on, but I couldn't . . . " She tailed off as memories of the horrible incident returned. It had been traumatic but not nearly as bad as what had followed, the far worse events that had practically blocked it out.

Now, with the clarity of hindsight, she remembered Pat kicking his legs to dislodge her. He had *wanted* her to fall!

No, surely not. But hadn't Steel said he was a lying, cheating, murdering cur? But wasn't Steel also a hideous mangled zombie?

Oh, now she was all tangled up! Who the hell did she believe?

"What happened next?" Steel asked softly. "How did you survive, ma'am? That cliff is hundreds of feet high."

"It was a miracle. After I fell through the clouds I slid through a few bushes. They hurt a lot but I guess they slowed me down enough so I could catch hold of a branch. I've always been very athletic!" She forced a laugh. "Anyway it was then I realised I was dangling only about ten feet above a path. Had I missed those bushes and that branch, I would have hit it hard enough to break every bone in my body. But I was able to drop and land quite lightly. I thought some mysterious entity had saved me for a reason, that I was destined for something great. But as it turned out, I was just really, really lucky." She sighed. "Scarcely had I started walking when these two-headed injuns who lived at the base of the cliff came charging out and grabbed me."

"They lived in amongst all those demon plants?"

"Yes. They knew how to avoid them. They scavenged all sorts of things from the plants' victims, but what they wanted most of all were live slaves. They traded them with whomever would buy off 'em."

"What's with the two heads?"

"I don't know, sir. But because they had two heads they could keep going a lot longer than normal people. One head slept while the other watched. They tied me up with a bunch of other slaves, and made us walk. And walk. And walk. We were only allowed to stop and sleep for a few hours at a time."

"Did they feed you?"

"Just a few scraps of dried, rancid meat. It was horrid. I've had some awful things in my mouth during my years, but that was by far the worst!" She spat off to one side. "I'm so glad you came along when you did, Mr Hawl. I wasn't sure how much longer I could have kept going. We'd already lost half-a-dozen to exhaustion. The indians cut them up and made us carry various body parts for eating. Perhaps I have been saved by a higher power after all."

Steel grunted. "I doubt it. It wouldn't have sent someone like me to be his servant." As though on cue, his stomach growled. Sallianne's comment about the body parts had set it off. Now he'd finally tasted fresh human flesh he wanted more. He remembered the indians they had left behind and wished that he'd thought to cut off a few chunks to take with him.

That bloody hard-on was back, too. He grumbled in irritation.

"Mr Hawl, why don't you tell me your tale now? Why are you after Mr Davison? He said he was being chased by some decaying indian shaman zombie."

"I ain't indian, and I ain't decaying," Steel growled. "I heal everything except the wounds that killed me . . . the wounds he caused." He sighed. "All right. Gotta tell someone, so I might as well tell you."

Steel Hawl had been a prospector all his life. As a youth he panned for gold in the rivers and streams around Mt Boloja, and as he started to make a small, modest living from his finds he moved up into the hills to start digging for gold and other precious metals. He continued to find tiny deposits, always just enough to fund his next expedition. An eternal optimist, he believed his big fortune was just around the corner. "One day soon I'll strike it big," he would tell his friends down in Nova Cyrus. "I'll find the motherlode and I'll be able to retire in the lap of luxury on some tropical island, surrounded by gold and naked strumpets who'll do my every bidding."

"What's a tropical island?"

"I don't rightly know, ma'am, but I seen it once on a postcard and it sure looked mighty purdy."

But the seams always petered out, leaving him with only enough money to grimly continue looking. At one stage he managed to scrape together enough to buy the rights to forage for minerals in a large cave on the East side of Boloja Mountain. He also had acquired enough to hire a machine called a Gripper. This massive device, developed by the Watkins Corporation, was powered by coal and had the brain of a clockworker installed. It had a giant drill head that could bore into the earth and four thick steel wheels underneath. As it drilled a hole it stretched out two hydraulic arms to grip the walls of the cave and slowly pull itself forward. At the same time it laid a rail track out the back of it so it could reverse out or travel back into the cave. The track remained for carting minerals out of the mine.

And so the years wore on. Steel worked alone with only the mining machine for company. He talked to it and called it Grip. It couldn't speak back but it learned to understand him and knew exactly what he wanted it to do. Unfortunately, it couldn't tell him where all the precious minerals and metals lay. Promising leads continued to peter away into nothing, leaving him with just enough money to keep on searching.

He grew old and grey and bent. He continued to sing and prattle to Grip and trundle his trolleys of rubble out of his mine to sift down at the sluicing area. Sometimes he travelled down to Nova Cyrus to drink and whore and pass out in the corners of various taverns. Other people who mined the area and made their modest fortunes began to feel sorry for the mad old geezer who just kept on going when really he should have given up years earlier.

Then, when he was fifty-eight years old, Grip struck a gas pocket and there was an almighty explosion. The machine's bulk protected Steel from the majority of the blast, but the flames still seared his eyes, burning one from his skull completely. When the bandages finally came off, he had one charred, ruined socket and barely ten percent sight left in his other eye.

Locals were convinced that the indomitable Steel Hawl would finally retire and return to town to live out the rest of his days there. But Steel refused to leave the mine. Grip hadn't suffered from the explosion and could continue digging. Steel continued on, squinting at the walls from mere inches away with his good eye, searching for the fortune he was convinced lay just a few more feet . . . just a few more feet . . .

Then, just after his sixty-fifth birthday, it finally happened. With his one good eye, Steel discovered a thin seam of Titezium, a very rare and extremely hard precious metal. In its pure form it was ten times stronger than steel. Big Daddy Watkins used a very small percentage of Titezium in the alloy that made up the chassis of all his clockworkers. Even an ounce was worth hundreds of dollars. And Steel was gaping in total and utter disbelief at pounds of the stuff. Grip drilled it all out and Steel poured it into a rucksack to take it to the bank.

By this stage everyone in Nova Cyrus knew the eccentric, mostly blind old prospector Steel Hawl, including the dentist, Pat Davison.

It was Pat who spotted Steel first, trudging down the main street with a big grin on his face, leaning heavily on his cane, bent almost double beneath the weight of his bag. "I can help you with that," Pat called from the door of his surgery. "I have a wagon around the back you can use!"

Steel had no reason not to take Pat at his word, and brought his heavy backpack around to the alley behind the shop—where Pat was lying in wait for him with a shovel.

Because of Steel's blindness, he didn't see him raise the shovel above his head.

He bashed the old man's skull in and that was the last thing Steel remembered about being alive.

"He killed me and took my Titezium," Steel muttered. "All the wounds you see on me he did—my shattered skull, my ripped up face—Pat did that. The first blow killed me; he could have left me. But no, he bludgeoned me to a pulp. I got broken ribs, gashes in my chest and stomach, a smashed up leg. He wanted to make *sure* I was a goner."

"Oh no," whispered Sallianne. "That's awful. But how'd you come back? Was it magic or some sort of machine? My friend Dr Bigelow can bring back the dead with his marvellous Electro-Resurrector device."

"It wasn't magic and it wasn't no machine. I dunno what the hell it was," Steel answered. "All I know is Davison took my remains and buried me in Beggars' Cemetery down near the foundry. He didn't even give me a grave marker. That was where I clawed my way out of the earth. I remember it was raining. Really pissing down. Like the sky had burst. Maybe that was what did it."

"A cloud burst?" Sallianne mused sceptically. "Wait, did you say the pauper cemetery was next to a foundry?"

"Yeah. It was where the metals and minerals from the mines were melted down. All the slag was poured into a huge pile behind it, and whenever there was a storm the poisons ran down across the Beggars' Cemetery . . . " He tailed off in understanding. "That must have been it! Something in that vile slagheap must have brought me back so I could have my revenge!"

Sallianne nodded understandingly. She had suspected something like that all along, but put the idea into Steel's head. Having been a prostitute all her life, she had learned at a very early age to disguise her intelligence and let her clients believe they had come up with ideas on their own. "Such a terrible story, Mr Hawl. I'm so sorry I ever called Mr Davison brave and courageous and spat in your . . . er, eye. I'll never do so again."

Steel grunted. "'S all right. You didn't know any better. I'm sorry I . . . I ever thought you were anything but a lady."

Sallianne raised her eyebrows in surprise. It was fortunate Steel was facing the other way and was unable to see her shock.

No man had ever apologised to her like that before. She lifted a hand to wipe a tear from her eye. It was funny how, after the many and varied customers she'd had over the years, that a zombie gunslinger was the only man who'd ever referred to her as a *lady*. She had always been a woman, a madam, a strumpet, or a two-bit harlot. Even her current lover, the governor of Kelly County, quite happily called her his whore.

It took Sallianne several minutes to get herself back under control. "So Mr Hawl," she continued without trying to sniff and give her emotions away, "what happened after you crawled out of the earth?"

"Uh . . . don't remember a lot. All I recall was how hungry I was. There were some rats fossicking around the graveyard and I grabbed a couple and et 'em, bones and all . . . " He trailed off, realising he probably shouldn't be quite so descriptive.

But Sallianne prompted him to go on. She knew all about zombie eating habits.

"Anyway, the fresh meat cleared my head a bit and I was able to start thinkin'," Steel continued. "I looked down at my busted-up body and realised what had happened to me. That snake Davison had killed me. But it was then someone else spotted me and took a shot at me. I was forced to run and hide, and I took refuge in someone's barn. As a zombie I had no right to be walkin' around, and the townsfolk were on the lookout. I needed to get out, but I had nothin' but the clothes on my back. And after gawd only knows how many months in the dirt they were rags.

"So I went back up to my mine. No-one had been up there yet, and I still had a few things up there—clothes, a bit of money I'd managed to stash away, and Grip. I didn't want to leave him behind, but how could I take him with me? He was made to dig out mines not travel the countryside. His top speed wasn't much more than five miles per hour and he burned through coal like crazy. Anyway, I figure the Watkins Corporation will come and get him eventually, after they realise they're not gettin' anymore rent for him."

Sallianne gulped, moved to hear him talking about an inanimate device like that. He must have been so lonely up there in the mine. And then, just after he'd dug out the greatest fortune of his life, he had to lose it to a greedy dentist!

Well, that just made her fit to be tied!

"I started walkin', headin' for the next town where no-one knew me," Steel continued. "I wrapped a scarf around my face and with my last few Lincoln skins I managed to buy a clapped out old nag on its last wheels. Then I began my search for Pat. Been lookin' for him ever since."

"I will help you to catch up with Mr Davison, Mr Hawl," Sallianne promised. "I know exactly where that stage-coach is headed. It's on its way to Kellyville."

"Kellyville eh? I never knew that. Thank you, ma'am. Thank you, very much."

# CHAPTER 13

**D**ESPITE THE DREADFUL wound Zeke had sustained the previous evening, he rose with the sun the next morning like he always did and stoked the coach engine. When Pat crawled from the tent he found a hot, greasy breakfast ready and waiting.

"Unbelievable!" the hungover dentist exclaimed. "Yesterday you had a spear right through your body!"

"Time's a-wasting, Mr Davison," Zeke drawled. "I'll be needin' to pack up that tent now." He shooed Pat away from it and started pulling the poles out. "You eat yer vittles and we'll be on our way."

Pat could only shake his head as he sat down next to the fire to eat his ranch pickles and raccoon pie. His head still ached from all the whiskey and tabackie he'd consumed the night before.

As soon as they were back on the road Zeke yanked on the right-hand rein to send the engine moving forward and they took off along the stony trail. Soon they were flying along at a reasonable speed, making good time. While Pat nursed his enlarged head in the back, Zeke sat in his seat muttering and gnawing on a bone and tugging on the cables in his rough, gnarly hands.

After a few hours Pat stretched out on the rear bench seat to catch up on some more sleep, and for a while the bumps and rattles of the coach lulled him into unconsciousness. It was only when the stage actually stopped during the mid-afternoon that he finally woke up. He blinked and stared out of the window to see only flat, featureless prairie stretching in all directions. There was a lot of dust hanging in the air as up ahead large animals thundered off towards the east, though all he could see was their furry humped backs moving like waves across the plain.

Pat opened the little window separating him from Zeke. "What's going on out there, Mr Sarandon? What's the hold-up?"

"A herd of maracleptops, Mr Davison. This could take a while. They can go on for upwards of a hundred miles."

"A herd of *what?*"

"Well, look at 'em, Mr Davison. What'n hell would you call 'em?" the driver retorted.

Pat squinted out into the dust, examining the creatures at the edge of the herd. Having grown up all his life in the northern mountain town of Nova Cyrus, he didn't have a lot of experience with all the weird new hybrid herd animals of the lower plains.

It had a big, furry hump on its back, just like a bison. But it was at least twice the size of that extinct herd animal of old, and had the three horns and the frill of a triceratops. Part reptile and part mammal, it had one cyclopean eye and the snout of a giant warthog with long, curving tusks. Its hooves were the size of silver serving trays. The musky smell from their big hairy bodies joined the dust those massive feet kicked up.

Pat gaped for almost five minutes at the sight. He whistled. "That sure is a lot of meat!"

"Each one weighs upwards of three thousand pounds," Zeke answered. "They're being sent to feed all the big city folk on the east coast."

"How's such an enormous herd controlled?"

"Look to yer right."

Since they weren't going anywhere, Pat climbed out of the stage and jumped down. The thundering maracleptops didn't even notice as they continued on their way. Zeke was pointing out a distant figure, seated astride a very large mechanical mount with oversized wheels and two chimneys at the back instead of one. "Those mechanized cowpokes know what they're doing. There's one riding every half mile or so, on alternate sides of the mob."

The cowboy lifted what looked like a baton and brought it down on the rump of a creature that had been straying a bit too far from the main line. There was a bright flash and shower of sparks. The creature squealed like a very large pig and bolted forward back into the herd.

"Electro-batons. Nasty. The blast from one of those could cook a man's insides dry. But it's just like a kick in the ass to one of those monsters." Zeke chuckled. "I suggest we stop here and make camp."

He manoeuvred the stage off the road to one side, where a very large, gnarly looking billius tree stood, stretching its numerous bright green branches in all directions like questing fingers. Its thick leaves provided ample shade for the camp. Zeke cut the engine and jumped down to start pulling the supplies from the back.

Pat wandered around behind the tree to take a piss, and then watched the monsters lumber past, occasionally snorting and squealing. Before long he joined Zeke by the fire. Despite last night's binge there was plenty of whiskey and tabackie left for a repeat performance.

This suited Pat fine. He wasn't normally a big drinker, but the fact they had to wait here for that humungous herd to pass was very concerning. Out here on the wide open plains, there was no cover. The massive tree and coach beneath could be seen for miles.

He swallowed a mouthful of alcohol and its warmth began to spread through his insides, easing his churning guts sufficiently for him to be able to gut down another of Zeke's greasy meals.

He had to tell the driver what was really going on.

Right from the very beginning of the journey, Zeke had sensed that something big was eating Pat. He thought Pat would have come out with it last night, but he'd been too drunk to be coherent. He knew his passengers' private lives weren't any of his business, but since only the two of them were left, he no longer cared. So he just came right out with it, "So, what's really buggin' you, Mr Davison?"

Pat gulped down another mouthful of whiskey. "All right—I'll tell you. It's quite a tale. You see, many years ago my entire family was cursed by an old gypsy witch."

Years earlier, before the great manufactories had spread up and down the east, and the influx of refugees from the Old Country during The Great Calamity had clogged the city slums, Pat's family lived in a small east coast town called Providence Falls. His great-grandfather was the mayor and owned a large tabackie plantation outside of town. His lands were quite extensive, and a travelling circus asked if it could set up on his property. At first he agreed, but after a few belongings disappeared from his house, he blamed the performers and ordered the circus to leave. The circus' fortune teller, a crusty old gypsy woman who must have been at least two hundred years old, denied that they had stolen anything.

But the mayor was adamant. He had his overseers and servants run the circus off his fields.

The woman spat at him from the back of her caravan and made a gesture with her fingers, condemning the male line of his family. But when she named the disease she did it in some strange foreign tongue, so no-one would know what she was talking about.

Of course the mayor simply laughed it off and quickly forgot about the incident. Later, the stolen belongings were discovered in the house of a local, a well-known compulsive gambler. He was strung up from a tree outside his house.

The mayor was a fit, young man but after he reached the age of forty he began to suffer strange aches and pains in his limbs. He started to fall and break bones. These were splinted and set, but they refused to heal. Soon he was bedridden, wracked with the most excruciating agony. Eventually he couldn't even lift his arms without snapping bones. His fingers broke when he tried to use them. He died not long after when he tried to turn his head and his skull broke apart like an egg and spilled his brains out all over the bed.

When his distraught family tried to gather him up for burial, all the bones in his body disintegrated. His wet, rubbery flesh had to be poured into a barrel.

His son, Pat's grandfather, simply thought he'd died from one of the many horrible new diseases that were always being brought into the region by greenhorns from the old Country, transients, vagabonds and blow-ins. But then he reached the age of forty and began to suffer similar aches and pains in his bones. He realised with horror what was going on, that the gypsy's curse really had worked and would claim him in a matter of agonising months. He tried everything he could to allay the disease's awful progress. He sought help from the best doctors, and when they couldn't help him, he tried quack medicines. Finally he resorted to black magic. Unfortunately one of the spells he tried backfired and he exploded in a fiery ball that burnt half the family house down.

At least he was spared his father's horrible, painful death.

Pat's father and his uncle tried to track down the gypsy who had cursed the family, but they couldn't find any trace of the mysterious travelling circus. They both lived in fear of what would happen to them as soon as they turned forty. Pat's uncle committed suicide at the age of thirty-nine. Pat's father tried various doctors and remedies like his father had before him, hoping that a cure might have surfaced during the intervening period.

Then he turned forty, and it started all over again. Unable to face the dreadful progress of the bone-wasting disease, he put a pistol to his head and blew his brains out.

"And now my tale," Pat told Zeke. By this stage they were both very drunk, and the sun hung low on the horizon. He burped out a large cloud of alcoholic fumes. The herd of maracleptops were still thundering along, their massive humped bodies silhouetted against the dusty orange sky. Occasionally a cowboy would rumble past on one of his oversized mounts, thwacking slower-moving beasts on their titanic backsides with his electro-baton.

"Sweet Mother of Pearl," Zeke agreed. "How old are you?"

"I turned forty, three months ago."

"And you're still alive?" Zeke gasped. "How?"

Pat gave a thin smile. "I realised the only way to thwart the curse was to replace every single bone in my body."

Zeke gaped. "With what?"

"I thought about it for a while and realised there was only one material I could use. The hardest and most expensive metal known to man—Titezium."

Zeke's bloodshot eyes went wide. "You . . . you have a *metal skeleton?*"

"Yes. It makes me stronger than a normal man, and quite a bit heavier, but I'm also slower and not as agile."

"Yeah, I noticed the limp. So how the *hell* did you manage to give yourself a metal skeleton?" Zeke exploded.

"Well, it wasn't easy, let me tell you! But I had help from my trusty indian nurse, Running Deer. She's a deersquaw." He smiled and his blue eyes gleamed in the light of the fire.

"Ah, one of those half human, half deer females."

"Yes. A very clever woman. It took months to do the whole operation. First I had to melt all the Titezium down and pour it into bone-moulds I'd created from a skeleton model that was roughly the same size as me. Then came the hard part. There was no way I could replace all the bones myself while I was awake and conscious, so I had to get Running Deer to do it. Fortunately for me, being a dentist, it wasn't hard to get hold of all the drugs I'd need to perform such an operation. First I got Running Deer to inject me with a tranquiliser made from devil-toad venom. Not only did it knock me out but it also slowed my vitals right down into a form of suspended animation. A relatively new anaesthetic that's currently being used in eastern hospitals right now."

"Dang!" Zeke exclaimed in amazement. "So then what happened?"

"I had to trust in Running Deer. With me out cold on my makeshift operating table, she could have grabbed the Titezium and run off. But she didn't. She was a very reliable assistant who had been with me for years. She started the operation by carefully cutting me open right down my back. Then she pulled out my spine joint by joint, and slowly replaced it with the Titezium one. The first operation took several hours, and at the end she injected me with a new-fangled fast regeneration drug called Regro. Very expensive stuff—one quart cost me half my original Titezium stash—but it healed everything in seconds, reconnecting and restoring all my nerves to working order. Then she brought me out of the suspended animation. I woke up, stiff and groggy, but with a completely new spine. I spent a few days getting used to it, then I got her to perform the next stage of the operation. My skull."

Zeke whistled.

"How'n hell did you manage to do that?"

"That was even trickier than the spine. Running Deer jabbed me with more devil-toad sedative and peeled the skin away from my skull. She actually had to do my head in sections; cutting it into segments with a bone saw and pulling out the fragments one by one so she could replace them with the new Titezium ones. I have bolts holding everything together." He rubbed his jaw. "Some of the pieces didn't quite fit right. My head's a different shape compared to what it used to be. But the Regro made sure everything healed up properly. I'm taller than what I used to be, and my head's not as round."

"Jeepers creepers!" Zeke drank more whiskey.

"After the spine and head the other bones were easy. Ribs came a few days after my skull, bolted directly to my spine. Joint by joint, Running Deer replaced my skeleton with Titezium. The whole operation was completed within a month. I don't have any old bones anymore." He flexed his fingers. "The Regro healed everything. Well . . . practically everything."

"Why d'you say that?"

Pat sighed. "I shouldn't be limping, but I seem to be getting stiffer and stiffer, and I can't feel parts of my legs properly. Running Deer was clever, but she was no doctor. All she learned about human bodies came from *The Anatomy Book* by the renowned neurosurgeon, Doctor Grissellwelt. I'm starting to need a cane to walk. I have an awful suspicion that the Regro did not replace all the nerves in my spinal cord. I sent Running Deer ahead to work and learn from Doctor Grissellwelt while I tidied my affairs in Nova Cyrus. I'm on my way to Kellyville to meet up with Running Deer and to see Doctor Grissellwelt."

"Well, Mr Davison—I'm not sure I believe you have an entire Titezium skeleton, but your family's tale is certainly a sad one." He reached into one pocket and pulled out a fresh finger-bone. "Here, have a gnaw on this."

Somewhat dubiously Pat took the bone. He really didn't want to, but Zeke was looking at him expectantly. So he took a little nibble on the end. Zeke slapped him across the shoulder so hard he nearly ended up face-first in the fire. Then he upended the last of the whiskey bottle into his mouth. "On that note, it's time to hit the hay! G'night Mr Davison." Zeke staggered off to take a leak behind the billius tree.

Pat looked up at the herd still streaming off into the east. He finished his bottle, belched and rose unsteadily to his feet. He watched Zeke crawl into the tent and then returned to the coach to go through his belongings. He found his revolver and loaded it.

He remembered back to the time a terrified Nova Cyrus local had told him that he had seen something burst out of a grave in the Beggars' Cemetery. He'd shot at it, but it had managed to run off and hide. Pat hadn't bothered going down to the graveyard to make sure it was the right zombie. He knew. Located behind the foundry's slagheap that cemetery was notorious for sprouting undead creatures. Every few months or so one would rise and shamble mindlessly around the town until someone blew its head off.

But after what Pat had done, Steel's zombie would be different. It wouldn't be mindless at all, but a nearly indestructible killing machine hell-bent on revenge. It was fortunate Pat had just finished his Titezium operation and was getting ready to visit Dr Grissellwelt. The incident gave him the impetus to buy a gun, pack his bag and jump on the first stage out of Nova Cyrus.

He probably shouldn't have buried Steel in the Beggars' Cemetery, but really it was the only place to dispose of a body that wouldn't arouse suspicion.

Now Pat took his gun back to the tent with him and tucked it into his shirt. He knew Steel was out there. He could feel his unholy presence drawing closer.

# CHAPTER 14

**T**HE MOON SHONE down from overhead as Steel and Sallianne approached the stage-coach parked beneath the billius tree. The maracleptops herd continued to rumble past, the beasts moving slowly with their heads hanging low. So long as they didn't have to change direction, they could sleep and walk at the same time. With their electro-prods hanging across their laps, the cowboys also appeared to be sleeping in their saddles, but being clockworkers they had no need for sleep.

"There they are," whispered Steel with real excitement in his soft, raspy voice.

Sallianne caught his arm. "But why only one tent? Surely they can't all be sleeping in there together? That would be a tad cosy, even on a cool night like this."

"Perhaps there aren't that many of them left," Steel mused. "I do hope Pat's one of them though." He licked his torn lips. He remembered the ravaged corpse impaled on the spikypine, the clockworker's head and the preserved, screaming body of Billy Levi rising from the salt-lake. He reached into his holster, slowly drawing his pistol.

Sallianne tightened her grip on his arm. "They're not goin' anywhere, Steel. Listen to that thunderous snoring, loud enough to wake the dead. We can move in at any time."

"I'm already awake," Steel growled, turning to look down at her.

"Oh, very funny. Let's take a moment here." She ran her other hand down his torn, ragged shirt.

Steel couldn't believe his enhanced, undead senses. No woman had ever paid attention to him in the past . . . unless he had offered her a considerable sum of money, of course. Now here he was, a rotten walking corpse, and a beautiful brothel madam was coming on to him for free in the middle of bloody nowhere! "Wha-what are you doing?" he spluttered.

"Don't you know?" Her wandering hand reached the crotch of his jeans, where his throbbing, undead erection refused to settle. She rubbed it and it pulsed even more insistently.

"Dagnabbit, woman—we're on a mission here! A mission to avenge my death!"

"A mission that can wait at least a minute."

He glared at her through his milky white eye. "Are you sayin' that I can only last one minute?"

"Oh no, Mr Hawl, I *never* said that," she purred, and tugged him down behind the coach. "It was just a figure of speech. I'm sure like most of your kind you could keep goin' for hours." She lay down in between the tree's thick roots and lifted her torn, ragged skirts to expose her long, shapely legs. She also opened her blouse to reveal the clock in her midriff.

He glanced towards the tent, from which that awful, sonorous rumbling was coming. There was no way the composer of that dreadful sound was moving any time soon. Surely he could spend a few minutes indulging in a pleasure that he had only partaken in a few times during his . . . life. And Sallianne was far prettier than any skinny, consumptive Nova Cyrus whore. Even in her torn garb, her face scratched and bruised and her hair messy and filled with twigs . . . she was beautiful.

He could feel the unholy energy that passed for blood in his body throb relentlessly. Sallianne fell to her knees in front of him and pulled open his fly to allow his huge throbbing pecker to finally spring out and be free. He stared at it. Had it been that big before? He couldn't remember. It felt like it was about to burst out of its skin.

"Oooh, that is a fine one," Sallianne marvelled, curling her skilled hands around it. Suddenly her warm, moist lips were surrounding him and moving up and down with considerable experience. He groaned. He couldn't remember a whore's mouth ever feeling so hot! Was he really so cold and dead inside? Her searing tongue seemed to coil around him like a snake. His pleasure soared. Then, just when he thought he would explode, she lifted her head. "You don't need much more of that." She leaned back against the carriage wheel, hitching her skirts up to reveal the fine blonde curls between her thighs. At once the wonderful smell of her life wafted over Steel and his stomach growled. He buried his face in between her legs. He wanted to devour every inch of her.

"No biting, now. I can't heal like you can."

He lifted his face. "But you smell so hot and salty and *alive.*"

She wagged a finger at him. "You can lick and suck and gobble all you want down there, but no actual eating."

"Aww, you're no fun, ma'am." But he did as she'd asked, and only tasted her. Her folds were so warm and wet and wonderful—she was soon groaning and writhing in such paroxysms of pleasure that he couldn't hold himself back anymore. He plunged his aching member into her. She gasped at how cold and hard it was, like an iron rod thrusting deep into the core of her being. She knew zombies could keep going and going, just like clockworkers, but Steel was different. He seemed to have more control than the average undead creature. He was so sensitive that he almost seemed alive.

But he was also governed by his endless hunger. She felt so good surrounding him, so soft and warm. He started slowly at first, respectful of her mortality, but he soon lost himself in sensation. She started to moan beneath him and that drove him harder. She even clawed up the back of his coat. He began pounding away at her, and felt his own ecstasy surging higher and higher, towards some distant plateau he had never, ever traversed before. He might have done this before when he was alive, but it had never felt like this. It had never been so all-encompassing, like his entire body was taking part instead of just one very insistent section. When he came his orgasm filled his entire being, and he knew if he kept on it would just keep going and going and going . . .

But he couldn't do that. He would kill Sallianne. So he pulled out of her and sat back with a gasp. She was still groaning and quivering from the multiple throes of her own pleasure. "Why-why did you stop?" she croaked.

"If I didn't stop then—I'd never have stopped." He tried to tuck himself away. It was too hard. Literally. "I'd . . . I'd have put a hole right through you.

She pushed herself up on her elbows. "Ohhh," she answered, both relieved and disappointed. But she understood all too well. Back at her brothel, when she thought a zombie had had enough and wanted him to get off her, she would throw him some bloody meat. Generally his other hunger would then take over.

Steel turned from her, struggling to get himself under control. It was time to finish what he'd come here for. He drew his pistol and cautiously approached the tent and its snoring occupants. "You stay back behind the coach. This is gonna get messy."

All the alcohol in Pat's system enabled him to fall into an uneasy slumber despite his bad case of nerves. He was having a rather nice dream about two people having some very noisy sex when something that felt like a crane-hook clamped down on the top of his head, digging claws into his skull, and began hauling him out of the tent.

Pat clapped both hands to his chest, scrabbling for the gun he had been holding, and managed to catch it before it slid out of the bottom of his shirt. Whatever had a hold of him hauled him up and dangled him in the air.

By now it was pre-dawn, and a soft light bathed the area. The maracleptops herd was still passing, but it was thinner than before, finally nearing its tail end.

Pat Davison found himself staring into a pale, torn face with a gaping eye socket and a single milky-white eye glaring back. There was a gaping wound in the creature's cheek, and teeth could be seen bared in a snarl through ravaged lips.

"Where the hell is my Titezium, you thieving dog?" Steel snarled.

Pat realised the zombie was holding a gun, but at the moment it was pointed at the ground. The creature's eye was on his face, not his chest. He managed to pull his pistol free and fire.

The explosion was almost deafening in the quiet early morning. The force of the .45 bullet hitting Steel at such close range was sufficient to cause him to lose his grip and drop Pat. He staggered back and fell on his backside. Pat started to run, but he had no idea where he was going. He thought only of escape.

And to make matters worse the noise of the gunshot had startled the maracleptops. They bellowed in terror and started to bolt from the main line, stampeding in all directions. Within seconds everything was chaos.

Sallianne saw them coming and clambered desperately onto the top of the coach. But one of the beasts slammed into the carriage and its weight was sufficient to knock the conveyance onto its side. Sallianne was sent flying. She tumbled into the midst of the thundering animals.

The noise had also awakened Zeke, who shot from the tent like a jackrabbit just before one of the beasts trampled it flat. Zeke headed for the billius tree and managed to scramble into it. Desperately, he climbed as high as he could into the bright green branches with their thick leaves. He looked down, but could see nothing below but humped backs and dust.

All he could do was hang on and wait.

Suddenly all the hair rose on the back of his neck and he twisted his head just in time to see something moving in through the leaves above, something with long, spindly green legs that he'd previously thought were the billius tree's branches. It was bigger than he was, and lunging towards him with its giant pincers open wide.

It was some sort of enormous arachnid.

He could have dropped, but then he wound have fallen to his death in the stampeding herd. If he tried to dodge he would fall. This was not Zeke's natural environment.

Zeke always slept fully clothed; had done so since his soldiering days. He was even wearing his boots. Thus he was able to reach inside one with his free hand and yank out a dagger.

He swiped at the giant spider as it lunged at him. The dagger's point squealed across a hard, shiny carapace. The creature flinched back and glared at him through its many eyes. Zeke realised that if he wanted to hurt it he would have to stab it between its armoured plates.

Realising that he hadn't killed it, the arachnid came in again, snapping its mandibles. It lunged and Zeke stabbed at it, trying to get under its chin.

It managed to nip him on the off arm.

Almost immediately an icy coldness filled his flesh. *Venom!* Zeke cursed and stabbed at it again, managing to stick his knife in between its head and neck. The dreadful cold raced up his arm and surged into his body. Suddenly he could no longer move that limb. It was paralysed, stiff and solid.

I'd rather take my chances with the stampede, he thought, and jumped backwards off the branch he had been precariously balanced on.

But the enormous creature was faster than he was and caught him in its four front legs before he could drop. Suddenly, Zeke found himself hauled up into the middle of the tree, where the spider had its nest. He tried to struggle, but the paralysis had already spread to the rest of his body. Stiff and solid, he could only gape in horror at the large mass of silk below, still with old bones, scraps of clothing and bits of flesh stuck in it.

Zeke's surroundings disappeared into a blur as the creature started to spin him around and around, cocooning him in silk. Soon he could no longer see. He wanted to be sick, but his guts were paralysed as well.

But he felt, all too keenly, the needle-sharp proboscis that lanced into his chest and began draining all the blood from his heart.

# CHAPTER 15

**A** MARACLEPTOPS BOWLED Steel over and stepped on his chest and stomach, but all that did was piss him off. He scrambled back onto his feet, pulled his smashed rib cage back together and stuffed his guts back in through the hole in his belly. He tried to spot Pat through the milling bodies, but couldn't see him anywhere. Then another beast butted him, sending him flying. He swore as he scrambled up, straining to see through the dust. Was it his imagination, or was the herd thinning out? Was the stampede over at last?

The thunder of massive hooves slowly died away, and the dust settled to reveal the smashed remains of the campsite. The tent was gone, probably dragged off by one of the animals, and Steel's horse had also been knocked over and stomped on. Water from its ruptured boiler had spread in a puddle beneath it. He certainly wouldn't be riding it out of here. The carriage was on its side, possessions strewn everywhere, but its engine still appeared to be intact.

Then Steel spotted a crumpled shape on the ground. Was that Pat? He hurried towards it, reaching for his gun. But the weapon wasn't in his holster. Then he remembered that he'd already had it out, and must have dropped it during the melee. He looked around, but couldn't see it anywhere. "Gawdammit," he swore.

He stopped at the fallen figure. It wasn't Pat. It was Sallianne Veerhoven. She was quite dead, her neck bent at a strange angle and one arm smashed from a massive hoof. The dress had been torn from her body, leaving her midriff exposed to the sky.

The clock in her stomach was crushed. The hands had stopped at a quarter to six.

Steel's lips peeled back from his crooked teeth in a furious snarl.

Pat had fired the shot that had caused the stampede! Sallianne's death was his fault! He rose to his feet—suddenly a fountain of dark blood and guts exploded from his chest, spraying several yards. He whirled around to see Pat Davison standing behind him, pointing a revolver. The dentist's face was black with fury. "I don't *have* your Titezium any more, you stinking corpse!"

He shot Steel again in the shoulder, nearly blowing his arm off. He staggered back a few steps. "I used it all! It's *gone!* Get that through your dead, rotting brain!"

Pat shot Steel again, this time in the belly. The blast went right through his middle and out of his spine, making a hole large enough to see through. He fell to his hands and knees. A fifth shot went through his brain and out the back of his skull, knocking his hat off.

Steel's thoughts scrambled for a few seconds and he didn't feel the final shot that hit him in the throat, blowing his head from his shoulders. He crumpled onto the dusty ground on his belly, his head rolling a few feet away. That horrible milky white eye glared up at Pat. The dentist stepped back, breathing heavily. Was it over? He fumbled through his pockets for more rounds and started reloading his weapon. His fingers started to shake as he realised Steel's head was rolling back towards his body.

"Shit, shit, *shit!*" Pat cursed. He dropped one of the rounds in the dirt.

Steel's head attached itself to his body. He pushed himself up onto his hands and knees. Slowly he turned his head, cracking the neck joints.

How was this even possible? Pat had shot his bloody head clean off! Wasn't that supposed to stop a zombie? Pat pointed his gun at him, but his hands were shaking so badly that his first shot missed completely.

Steel grabbed his hat and slapped it back onto his head. Then he rose to his feet. Some of his intestines had flopped out of his belly. He shoved them back in.

Pat fired again. The hammer clicked on the chamber he hadn't been able to fill.

Steel lurched towards him. One hand reached out, grabbing Pat's gun arm just as he fired again. This bullet blew right through his chest. Steel slapped the gun out of his hand, sending it spinning away. "If I can't have my Titezium, I'll just have to take what it's worth out of your corpse," Steel said grimly.

Pat snarled and swung a punch with his other hand. Steel caught his fist and twisted it away. Pat seemed a lot stronger than a normal human—it actually took Steel some effort.

Pat may have had a metal skeleton that could take additional punishment, but his flesh was all too human. When Steel squeezed the fist he was holding, mashing Pat's fingers together, the dentist howled in pain. Steel clamped his other hand around Pat's wrist and twisted the limb around, locking it in its socket. Pat screamed as he doubled over. Still holding onto Pat's arm, Steel slammed a booted foot down on Pat's back, knocking him to the ground.

Pat's arm tore loose from its socket. His bones may have been Titezium, but the muscles and sinews holding them together were all too natural.

Pat shrieked as blood started to gush from the wound in long, thin streams.

Steel was about to throw the arm away when he noticed something gleaming inside. What the hell? He tore some of the flesh away from the arm with his teeth, stripping it from the bone.

The blood-streaked bone gleamed in the early morning sunlight. Steel stared at it in wonder, realising that he was looking at his Titezium.

Somehow Pat managed to get his feet under him. Clutching at his gushing shoulder, he started to stumble away. But shock had stolen his strength and his legs were stiffer than ever. Steel hardly had to run to catch up with him.

Steel clubbed Pat over the back of the head with his own severed limb.

Seeing stars, the dentist collapsed onto his hand and knees. Steel grabbed him by the scruff of the neck and flipped him over, slamming him down on his back so hard all the air shot from his lungs. While Pat was struggling for breath Steel lifted one boot and raked the razor-sharp spur down his chest, tearing him open from neck to navel. A delicious smell of hot, living meat immediately wafted out.

Steel squatted down beside Pat and thrust his hands into the hole he had made, gripping the edges of Pat's rib cage. It took considerably more effort, but he was still able to pull the Titezium bones apart to reveal the delicious smorgasbord of organs beneath.

Pat's deep blue eyes fixed onto the zombie.

His last vision was of Steel Hawl tearing his still-beating heart out of his chest and taking a huge bite out of it. With blood pouring down his chin, Steel grinned down at him.

Late afternoon the next day, a battered stage-coach rolled into Kellyville and pulled to a stop outside the bank. It was dusty, dented and badly scratched, and the few belongings that were still attached were lopsided and badly packed with things hanging out. A man jumped down from the driver's seat. He was wearing a dusty broad-brimmed hat and a long leather coat that was pocked with bullet-holes. He held a smouldering cigar in one hand. As he jumped down from the seat he pulled a blood-stained hessian bag down after him. His spurs jingled as he sauntered into the bank.

The teller was a young, nervous fellow who'd only been working a few weeks. He looked up as the man approached, into a pair of the most piercing blue eyes he had ever seen. "Um—er—can I help you, sir?" he stammered.

The man lifted his bag and upended it on the counter. The banker's eyes nearly came out on stalks as several pieces of a Titezium skull clattered out, along with a spine and numerous bones of various shapes and sizes.

"I'd like to make a deposit," said Steel Hawl.

# PART 2

# THE GOOD, THE BAD AND THE ZOMBIE

# CHAPTER 16

STEEL HAWL SAT in an ornate claw-footed bath tub with his bony knees protruding from the lukewarm water. His wispy white hair was covered with soap. A large fire roared in the grate nearby, illuminating an ornately decorated room with lacy curtains on the windows and one enormous four-poster bed with shiny white satin sheets. Other light came from the electric candles in the crystal chandelier dangling above.

Steel tipped his head forward and Sallianne Veerhoven poured a warm jug of water over his hair to rinse away the soap suds. She was wearing a lightly laced leather corset and suspenders. Nothing else. Her thick blonde curls had been piled high on her head, not a single lock out of place. She sang softly as she lovingly sponged Steel down all over. It was his favourite song from Mt Boloja, "Clementine". She knew all the verses, even the ones he'd made up. But he sat hunched forward with his head down, unresponsive to the attention.

The bedroom door swung inwards and another Sallianne entered, carrying a large pile of fresh towels in her arms. She was also dressed in a corset and suspenders, but her outfit was red instead of black. She placed the towels on a chair just as a third Sallianne, dressed in white, entered and started straightening up the messy bed; plumping the expensive goose-down pillows and drawing down the sheet.

Steel Hawl had used his wealth of Titezium to set up his own bordello and armadillo ranch in honour of his one and only love, Sallianne Veerhoven. He even had enough money to order these custom-made clockwork Salliannes from the Watkins manufactory on the east coast.

They looked like her, talked like her. Hell, they even *smelled* like her. He wasn't sure how the Watkins corporation had managed to copy her unique perfume. But no matter how hard he pretended, they weren't her and never would be. They had porcelain eyes with little cameras fitted inside. Their hair was made from dyed horse hair and their skin from painted silk. Beneath lay cloth padding tightly wrapped around a Titezium alloy skeleton powered by a cleverly constructed clockwork brain.

Even so, he could have lived with that.

Initially, when he ordered the Salliannes, he'd naively assumed they would have fully developed personalities like the Marilou-Belle Watkins clockworker had had. He had certainly described her well enough. But only after the Salliannes arrived and started work did Steel learn that Marilou had been a special case, an individually programmed machine designed for all intents and purposes to be human. Apparently it had taken years to write all of Marilou's punch-cards and set her numerous internal switches so she would know how to think and react in every conceivable situation. That kind of programming was priceless—well beyond the range of even the fabulously wealthy Steel Hawl. It was reserved for the Watkinses—and other ridiculously powerful families.

The Salliannes' bright blue eyes may have moved like normal human eyes, but they remained cold and lifeless. Their faces were designed to mimic human expressions, but these consisted of basic smiles and frowns. Thus Steel was surrounded by beautiful dolls, and now he felt lonelier than ever before.

It was slowly eating him up inside, driving him ever deeper into depression. They were supposed to be his dream come true, but instead he felt like he had slipped into hell, constantly reminded of the one true love of his life that he had lost.

Steel's bordello and armadillo ranch was a good little earner, providing quality service that Mt Boloja's yokels, hicks, farmers and miners appreciated. But for Steel Hawl each day quickly merged into the next and he began to wish he were dead. *Really* dead.

But he couldn't die, not completely.

Not long after he realised his clockworker Salliannes weren't anywhere near as good as the real thing, he fell into boozing, barroom brawling and duelling. No matter how many times he got shot up or beaten he simply stitched back together again. His body would always reconstitute itself back into its zombie state as though nothing had happened.

Then, as the "black dog" really began to nip at his heels, he tried to commit suicide. He hurled himself in front of a trackless train steaming ahead at full speed, hoping the massive locomotive would tear him apart so badly his pieces would not draw back together. No such luck. He reformed in its wake—much to the horror of the passengers who had witnessed him jump. Then he wandered into a mine during a blasting. Surely being blown to smithereens would work? No—he even reformed after that. He couldn't believe it. Why was he so powerful? Surely after exacting his horrible bloody revenge against Pat Davison, he would be allowed to leave this world.

Why was he still here, gawddammit?'

His mind simply wouldn't let him forget. And the more he tried the more the past nagged him. Sallianne had gotten well and truly into his undead synapses and she refused to budge.

At his wits' end, Steel tried burying himself in the beggar's cemetery, but even deep in the black womb of the earth he could see her radiant face floating in front of him.

Was she trying to tell him something? Why didn't she want him to go?

Resigning himself to his desultory existence, Steel scrambled out of his grave, dusted himself off and returned to the land of the living. He tried a few different jobs to take his mind off things, such as working long hours on a fandangled chairlift up and across the Mt Boloja mountain range. A pair of east coast entrepreneurs, with more money than sense, thought they could install an exciting new contraption to exploit the picturesque mountain range but ended up losing the shirts off their backs when their scheme failed to attract tourists and their company went belly-up.

Next he moved on to the local cotton mill and even tried prospecting again, but now that he'd made his fortune it didn't hold his interest any more. Not even his old companion Grip could bring him out of his funk. And because the machine couldn't talk it was lonely work and gave him far too much time to think.

Nothing satisfied, nothing worked. He was glum and weary, and weary of being glum. Sallianne had lit a spark in his dead heart, and now she was gone that cold, dead organ hurt like hell.

One day he collected his hat, coat and guns, and walked out of the bordello to check on the armadillos. But after making sure the animals were safe he kept on going down the dusty road out of the ranch. He continued putting one foot in front of the other. Not once did he look back.

# CHAPTER 17

**A**FTER HE'D DEVOURED Pat Davison, Steel buried his clothes and a few body parts he couldn't be bothered finishing. For the first time in his undead existence he was satisfied. Not just less hungry, but actually full. He had time to lovingly inter Sallianne's broken body beneath the billius tree.

Now, a few years later he returned to the same site to keep vigil by her side. Maybe he could even bury himself beside her. Then they could be together forever, and maybe her lovely image would stop haunting his thoughts.

The maracleptops herds continued to be sent past this place every fall. Their constant movement had carved out a flat grey trail where nothing grew. Even though the area was still and quiet, the dust from their hooves refused to settle and the air still stank of their musk and dung. The only sound came from the wind rustling through the thick green branches of the great old tree. It was a still, peaceful place—Steel could see himself lying here forever. Maybe one day the powers that be would let him go quietly into the darkness he had once feared, but now craved with every fibre of his being.

Tentatively, he approached the tree, kicking some steel fragments laying in the dirt. He bent over to inspect them; they looked like small metal cones. He threw them back on the ground and continued to the spot where he'd laid Sallianne down but realised something was wrong. The gentle mound he remembered was gone. Had it flattened out naturally? Steel had to make sure. He dropped to his knees and started digging furiously, his long zombie fingernails quickly scooping away the soft earth to reveal . . . nothing.

Sallianne was gone!

Steel's lips peeled away from his teeth in a snarl. Who could have done such a horrible thing? The dead heart that had burned from loss now seethed with anger.

"Werecoyotes?" he muttered out loud. He had brought his guns with him—he could quite happily go up into the hills and hunt a few of those loathsome varmints down. They were becoming increasingly troublesome lately. Back in Nova Cyrus he had helped the sheriff cull a few pesky packs.

"Weren't no werecoyotes," a voice called down from the billius tree. "Was the Duoquois, them two-headed injuns."

"What the hell?" Steel rose to his feet and looked up, straining to see through the tree's dense branches and foliage. The voice had sounded human, but with a deep, raspy quality—almost like his own.

The leaves overhead rustled. "Them two-headed injuns deal in slaves and body parts, dead or alive," the voice continued. "Their two heads have given them quite a nose for corpses. They sniffed that one out quite a while back and dug it up with a view to tradin' it."

Steel remembered his dealings with those indians, how they had attacked him on his horse, pulling him down. He'd killed a few, sending them scattering in terror, and freed the slaves they had been escorting. Sallianne had been among them.

"Who the hell's hidin' up there?" he growled as he drew his pistol and pointed it up at the shifting branches. "Show yerself!"

"Now, there's no need to be gettin' ornery! I'm comin', I'm comin'." The branches parted and one of the strangest creatures Steel had ever seen started lowering itself down on a thin but very strong thread of silk. It was some sort of human-spider composite critter, about as big as a horse. It had four long, spindly back legs that looked like a cross between a spider's and a human's. Its two front arms split off at the elbow, becoming two forearms each. It had human-shaped hands, but with longer, thinner fingers, each ending in a vicious talon. On top of the torso, instead of a spider's head was the head of a man. His features were hard and gnarly, dark from the sun and criss-crossed with scars. He had long wispy grey hair that shifted in the afternoon breeze and a thin, scruffy beard poking out of the end of his chin. His body was the colour of human skin, but splotched with black and shiny. He wore a battered felt hat, a sleeveless jerkin and a cloth bag slung over one shoulder.

"They call me Zeke "The Freak" Sarandon," he said.

Steel lowered his pistol in surprise. "Well bugger me—you are so ugly you could make a freight train take a dirt road!"

The giant arachnizoid stared at him for a few seconds, then burst out laughing. In fact he laughed so hard he nearly fell out of the tree. "Consarn it! I guess I've *really* earned my nickname now!"

Steel wasn't sure he could trust this bizarre creature so he kept his gun out, muzzle pointed down. "So what were you sayin' about Sallianne?"

Zeke stared at him. "Was that who was buried down there? Sallianne Veerhoven?"

"Yeah."

"How'n hell did she get herself planted all the way down here? Last I heard she fell outta my carriage way up north on Sabre-Wing Pass!" Zeke pointed a claw in that direction.

Steel opened his mouth to explain, but all the words jumbled together and got stuck. Finally he said; "It's a long story. Can ya tell me what happened to her?"

Zeke the Freak clambered down to stand on the ground beneath the billius tree. He plucked a bone from a strand of web and started chewing on it. "All right. But it's a long story, too."

Steel looked bleakly around at the empty plains. "Got all the time in the world."

"Well, I was the driver of the coach Sallianne was on, but by the time we got here only me and Mr Davison was left."

Steel scowled at the mention of Pat's name, but Zeke didn't notice as he crunched on his fragment of femur. "We had a bit of a drink and a smoke and went to bed to the sound of a maracleptops herd rumblin' past. At around dawn I woke to the sound of a gunshot. I barely had time to scramble outta my tent afore the cattle stampeded. I have no idea where the shot came from—I can only assume Pat fired it. Anyway I scrambled up this big ol' tree here," he patted its trunk, "'cause it looked like the safest place. Boy, was I wrong!" He gave a dark laugh. "There was this giant spider thing livin' in it, and it was hell-bent on havin' me for dinner. I tried to fight it but it paralysed me and trussed me up like a Thanksgiving turkey. I couldn't move a muscle. It started suckin' the blood from my heart and I honestly thought I was a goner. Everything went all

dull and grey for a while, but I was still aware. Like I was sleepin'. Slowly I came back to myself. I was here—inside the spider. A part of it. Got me a new set of chompers in the process, too." Zeke grinned to reveal a gleaming set of pearly whites. "The metal caps on me teeth popped right off." Now Steel understood what the strange metal cones were on the ground.

"How'n hell is that possible?" Steel asked.

Zeke chomped his bone into fragments and swallowed it. "I have a really fast healing ability. Been blowed apart and stitched back together more times than I can remember. Maybe it was my healin' power that caused me to merge with the spider somehow, making me into even more of a freak!"

"Nothin' wrong with bein' a freak!"

Zeke stared intently at him. "You look perfectly fine to me, Mr . . . "

"The name's Steel Hawl. And buddy, you have no idea how freaky I really am! Anyway, go on with yer story."

"Right. Anyway, I was hangin' in the tree, just comin' to terms with me new form, when I heard voices and some digging noises. I looked down to see those two-headed Duoquois injuns pullin' a body from the ground. My night-sight had improved, but it was still too dark for me to see who they really were. I was also starvin', so I jumped down on top of one of 'em. The rest scattered like spooked polecats, but they managed to take the body with 'em. They vamoosed, probably back into the Black Rock Hill country." He pointed.

Steel followed the line created by his long, bony finger. He could feel his undead heart burn with a new mission: to retrieve Sallianne's body and return her to her final resting place. He had to find her before it was too late and she was gone forever. He would not stop until she was resting in peace.

"Well, thank you for your tale, Mr Sarandon, but I really must be on my way now." Steel turned to leave.

Zeke grabbed him by a shoulder. "Must you go so soon, Mr Hawl? Kinda bored hanging round this dang tree all day long. Take me with you!"

Steel turned to look at the huge spider-creature. "Well I dunno. I usually like doing things my own way."

Zeke flipped a clawed hand. "I got my own way too, but I really don't wanna stay here much longer. I feel like I've been here for years."

"You *have* been here for years."

Zeke raised his scanty grey eyebrows. "Really? Dad-sizzle! I guess that means it really *is* time I got on my way." He stared at Steel. "You walk all the way here?"

"Er, yeah."

"Well," Zeke scuttled a circle around him, "If you like you can ride on my back. I'm pretty fast—I chased down a lone maracleptops once. Golly! I ate like a king for a whole month! Well, it *felt* like a month!" He scratched his head. "I always had a bit of a problem with time. I'm fine with days, but months and years tend to get away from me."

Steel hadn't been concerned before, but if he wanted to track down Sallianne's body he had to move quickly. After all this time she probably had already been cut up for parts and disposed of. But right now he couldn't afford to think like that. He had to hope she was still intact and buried somewhere.

At walking pace he hardly ate up the miles. Besides, this scarred old codger looked like he'd seen a lot during his years . . . probably even more than Steel had during his lifetime grubbing around in the mines.

"All right—why not. I guess I could use some company."

Somewhat awkwardly Steel clambered onto Zeke's back. Steel felt weird, perched on the strange creature's large round abdomen, but his weight didn't seem to worry Zeke, and he started scuttling off across the flat grassy plain, heading north towards the Black Rock Hills.

"Wow, yer kinda light! I thought a fella as tall as you would be a mite heavier."

"I am pretty skinny."

"Well, yer like a bag o' bones! Not that I'm complainin', mind you," Zeke added quickly.

Steel just grunted and hooked his hands around the narrow joint in Zeke's body, where his abdomen started. He had to admit—the strange arachnizoid could move pretty damn quickly, his spindly legs scuttling rapidly over the flat, grassy ground at about forty miles per hour. When he looked over his shoulder, the billius tree had already receded to a tiny green mound, outlined against the dusty horizon. Now Sallianne no longer rested there, he didn't care whether he saw it again. Although, as they continued to move away, he did wonder if those Duoquois Indians had also sniffed out the bits of Pat he'd buried. Would they be worth anything to those body-snatching redskins?

Running along with the wind blowing his wispy grey hair back, Zeke Sarandon couldn't believe his good fortune. With a rider on his back he was finally back to doing what he loved: ferrying passengers across the wastelands. Of a sorts.

# CHAPTER 18

THEY RODE FOR the rest of the afternoon, continuing until the sun was hugging the horizon. Zeke's long, thin legs took them up into the cooler hills of the Black Rock indian country. Ominous basalt sentinels seemed to glower down at them from every hilltop. Steel spotted the ancient ruins, beneath which he had once devoured an entire body.

"That looks like a good spot," Zeke suggested.

"All right," Steel agreed, realising the chances of anything incriminating remaining would be pretty small. Zeke scurried up the hill and into the copse of trees at the base. Steel noticed with horror that there were still some old bones scattered around. But the bizarre spider-man exclaimed with delight at the sight and immediately gathered them all up, stuffing them into the crude hand-stitched bag he carried over one shoulder.

Steel's stomach growled mournfully. He suddenly remembered how good consuming that body had made him feel. It had been his first meal of human flesh.

Zeke paused. "Want one?" He handed a human femur to Steel.

Somewhat dubiously he took one. "Not much to be gained from bones."

"I've always found bones good at keepin' the hunger pangs at bay." Zeke started chomping vigorously on a rib with his sharp, powerful teeth. He lowered his voice conspiratorially, "It's a bit of a habit of mine!"

Steel took an experimental nibble. He was right—there wasn't much nourishment in bones. But chomping on them did keep him from thinking too much about his growling guts. He couldn't remember the last time he had been so hungry. Back at the ranch, surrounded by his clockworker Salliannes and fresh, dripping meat, he had hardly thought about food at all. He had been far too depressed.

But this new adventure had pushed his unhappiness back a tad. Now he had a job, a goal he could work towards, and a weird companion he could talk to; his old undead hungers were returning.

Steel watched in amazement as Zeke sprang from tree to tree, using his spinnerets to fashion a fine tent of silk. Soon the glistening, finely interwoven strands formed a shelter thick enough to slumber under without being disturbed by bugs, birds or rain. Steel poked at the shining white covering with a long pointy fingernail, finding it as light and strong as fine cotton.

"That's mighty fine," he declared.

Zeke grinned. "Yeah, I'm a weaver all right. Just don't light a smoke up too close!" He felt around inside his crude shoulder-bag. "Here—took this offa drunk hobo who camped under my tree some time back." He held out a hip-flask. "Usually I save it for when I get injured, but I thought we could share a few nips tonight."

Steel couldn't remember the last time he'd had a drink. Probably just before he'd jumped in front of that train. Did the stuff even still affect him? He recalled how he still smoked the occasional cigar. Perhaps he ought to give it a try. He took the flat steel bottle and gulped down a couple of mouthfuls. A delightful warmth immediately filled his undead innards.

Zeke took some too. "Oh, it's Kandaho sheep dip all right, but it hits the spot!" He belched noisily.

"Yeah," Steel coughed, "it could take the paint off the walls!"

Zeke put the bottle back into his bag and settled down on the bed of leaves he had made. Steel sat with his back to one of the trees that held up their strange little shelter. "Today's started me really thinkin' about where my strange healin' ability might have come from," he began conversationally. "Oh, I always mended fast—cuts, wounds, sprains all healed up quicker than normal." He pulled a face that the zombie Steel could clearly see in the strange light of night. "Even when I was a little fella I was always up and about faster than my brothers and sisters. Ailments that knocked them head over heels never laid me up for long. But it never became anything really weird until around the time of the Subterranean Uprising. That was only my second war but I've served in quite a few battles in my time." He held up two of his four hands and started counting on his fingers. "Let's see now . . . there was the Subterranean Uprising, the Tutherside Schism, the Amazebra Revolt, the Battle of Little Big Cactus, the Transdimensional War against the Vkyings—"

"The Transdimensional War against the Vkyings?!" Steel interrupted. "I don't know much about that sorta thing, Mr Sarandon, but I do know one thing, that Vyking War was back in 1808! That was seventy-two years ago! You ain't that old!"

Zeke stared at him in confusion. "I ain't?"

"You can't be more'n sixty!"

"I *told* ya I always had a bit of a problem with losin' time."

"Yeah, but *seventy-two years?*"

Zeke looked away, scratching the back of his head.

Steel stared at him. "I can't gainsay it, Mr Sarandon. I spent my whole life down a hole. Didn't get to see a lot of the world."

Zeke grunted. "You might as well call me Zeke. After all, we just shared a drink from the same bottle."

"Sure thing," Steel agreed. "You might as well tell me the rest of ya story."

Zeke gave a gap-toothed smile, the argument instantly forgotten. "Well, I'd been fighting hard in the war against Tutherside when I got myself blowed half-way to hell by one o' those new-fangled Gatling lasers. I was practically in bits on the ground, convinced I was a goner. But then the camp doctor appeared. He was something else, let me tell you! A true scientician! His name was Dr Bartholomew Gratton. He gathered me up and stitched me back together as expertly as a seamstress. Then, just when I thought I was gonna pass out and meet my maker, he made me drink some fancy new elixir of his. It tasted like shit, but my gawd—it filled my wounded limbs with such fire—even though I'd only been sewn up that day, I was walkin' around that very night, quaffin' whiskey and showin' everyone my scars. I was back on the battlefield faster than a jack rabbit. Anyhow, I'd earned myself some liberty leave so I hiked east to New Haven fer some *relaxing*, if you get my drift.

"I still remember it clear as day. Those Vyking bastards sailing into New Haven harbour in their steam-powered longship hovercrafts and marching ashore in their armoured suits, smoke puffin' from the horns on their helmets . . . they looked like demons that had marched right outta the mouth of hell itself! I was right there, dammit!"

"Bejabbers!" declared Steel.

"During the battle I got cut up agin but this time my wounds just healed right up quick, lickety-split. All I was left with were some scars to remind me.

"Now I reckon it was 'cause of the doc's strange brew that my naturally fast healin' ability sped up to become almost supernatural. Every time after that I was shot up or cut or mangled, all it took was some settin' of my bones, some stuffin' back of my guts, some stitchin' and some whiskey, and I was good as new." He rubbed his ravaged face. "Save maybe for a scar or two. I survived two more wars after that. The Mississipp Secession and the Clockworker Rebellion."

Steel recalled his own phenomenal healing ability. Compared to it, Zeke's was nothing. But the spider-creature still had the advantage. He was *alive*. And if he so wanted, he could die. Steel simply grunted and gnawed on the bone he had been given.

"Yer awful quiet."

"Sorry—lot on my mind right now."

Zeke burped again. "Well, I don't wanna be a croaker, but I gotta hit the hay. Travelled a long way today, and I'm not used to such journeys anymore." He curled his spindly spider legs under his arachnizoid body. As his bulging abdomen settled onto the ground, he let his head droop forward. It wasn't long before a snore escaped.

Steel was envious. He wished he could sleep and leave the real world for a while. But he could only spend the long, quiet night time hours in motionless solitude. He closed his eyes and leaned back against the tree at his back. He could occupy himself, but he doubted Zeke wanted to be woken by him singing Clementine in his raspy, off-key voice. He hoped the spider wouldn't be slumbering for long. He hated waiting while others slept.

Fortunately, as a giant spider, Zeke only needed four hours to wake refreshed. He carefully disconnected the tent he had made and gobbled up all the silk, absorbing it back into his body. "Took a lot of energy to make it. Can't let it go to waste," he explained with a grin. Then he grimaced. "Tastes bloody awful though!"

The strange new companions, Zeke Sarandon and Steel Hawl,

continued deeper into the Black Rock Mountains, following the path north that Zeke used during the old days. Zeke noticed, with no real surprise, that it was cracked and overgrown. Obviously no-one had come this way for a while. At around midday, as they were travelling along a narrow pass between two nearly sheer cliff-faces Zeke got the unsettling feeling that they were being observed and shadowed.

"Normally they wouldn't bother me," he muttered to Steel. "But normally I'm riding high in a coach with two heavily armed gunmen watchin' over me!"

He explained to Steel that high up on the rocky hills were narrow trails running parallel to the main path down below. Various indian tribes used these routes to stalk and ambush their quarries. "I think my spider senses tell me that there are indians up in the rocks right now."

"Whatta you suggest we do?" asked Steel.

"We gotta draw 'em out." Zeke continued along until he came to a rocky outcropping. There he directed Steel to jump down and stay out in the open as a decoy.

"A decoy?" Steel hissed.

"Relax! I know what I'm doin'." Zeke scuttled up the cliff face for a bit of a look around. Steel remained below with his rifle ready to shoot the first thing he saw moving towards him. But nothing appeared and a few minutes later Zeke came running back down. "I didn't spot anyone but if someone was after us, we'll soon know about it."

"What-" Steel began, but was interrupted by a loud bleating and thrashing noise coming from the trail overhead.

"Golly that was quick! Get on my back and let's check it out!" Zeke suggested to Steel.

Steel clambered back aboard and Zeke scaled the sheer cliff face once more. Steel hung on tight as he was pulled into the vertical.

"I spun us a web," Zeke declared proudly. "I kept it in the shadows so the slant of the sun wouldn't reveal it. I think it might have caught us some prey."

Steel's stomach growled again in anticipation. "I sure hope it's somethin' we can eat."

They followed the sound of the desperate bleating and struggling, and there was Zeke's cleverly constructed web stretched out across the overhead path. Stuck fast in the sticky web was another bizarre creature that Steel had never seen the likes of.

It appeared to be half human female and half deer. The female portion was copper-skinned with long beautiful black hair decorated with beads, ribbons and feathers. She was wearing a sleeveless jerkin made from some sort of pale leather—probably not buckskin, considering her nature—and a necklace of teeth and a beaded bag slung over one shoulder. Her deer portion was golden-brown and speckled with white on the hind-quarters. Despite her precarious position, her furious struggles had almost enabled her to kick her way free of Zeke's web.

"She does look mighty tasty," Steel declared, his blue eyes glistening with his rediscovered hunger.

The creature's keen senses had enabled her to hear. She snarled and kicked. "Please don't eat me!" she shrieked. "I have money!" She patted the bag she was carrying over one shoulder.

Zeke's interest was piqued and he scuttled forward to cut her free. Steel gave a hiss of disappointment, but swallowed his need for food and joined in helping the strange creature loose.

"Who are you, ma'am?" asked Zeke once the deersquaw was free and brushing the silken threads from her body.

"My name is Running Deer," she answered breathlessly.

# CHAPTER 19

S TEEL DREW IN a shocked breath and stopped what he was doing. *He knew that name!* The dentist, Pat Davison, had had an assistant named Running Deer. He had never seen her, but he had heard all about her during his various forays into Nova Cyrus; a very beautiful, intelligent indian woman who had helped him with his work.

It was funny how no-one had ever mentioned that she had actually been a deersquaw! He curled his hands into fists, a red mist clouding his vision. He wanted to leap upon her to devour her, but he couldn't—Zeke was cleaning the last strands of web from her so he could speak to her!

But the spider-man wasn't letting her go easily. "Why are you followin' us?" he demanded.

Running Deer brushed her long black hair from her eyes. She had a broad-cheeked face with big dark eyes and full lips. She was gorgeous. But Steel still wanted to tear her head off and crack her skull open. He could only stand back and quiver from a mixture of rage and hunger.

"I'm looking for the dentist Pat Davison," she explained to Zeke breathlessly. "He boarded the coach at Sunbleached Plains and was supposed to meet me in Kellyville to visit Dr Grissellwelt. The coach showed up, but he didn't. I've been searching for him ever since." She blinked at Zeke. "I'm trying to track down anyone who might have been on the coach with him. I've travelled this path many times looking for clues. You two were following the route that coach used to take, so I thought I'd follow you."

Zeke stared back. "Well ma'am—you're in luck. I was the driver of that coach, but I had a little . . . accident on the way." He spread his hands to encompass his spider body. "It showed up in Kellyville you say?" He glanced over his shoulder at Steel. "I was wonderin' what happened to it."

Steel took a deep breath to calm himself. "I drove it into Kellyville and stopped it outside the bank," he answered softly.

"So you two know what happened to Dr Davison?" Running Deer demanded.

Zeke and Steel exchanged glances. Steel dropped his gaze first, and his hat shadowed his face. Zeke frowned. He realised that his new-found friend knew more than he was letting on. But years of driving tight-lipped customers across the country had honed his diplomatic skills. He knew better than to pry right now.

"Perhaps you ought to tell us a bit more about yourself, little lady," Zeke suggested diplomatically.

Running Deer winced at the patronising term, "little lady", but she drew herself up, brushed the last of the spider silk from her body, and began her tale.

The deep backwoods of Kentessee were famous for their weird half-human, half-animal tribes as well as their good hunting. About twenty years earlier, Pat Davison was an adventurous young man who loved roughing it and bringing home big game. He was out to bag himself a six-pointer for his wall, but after a fruitless day of searching he was ready to pack it in. It was then he overheard a mournful bleating coming from a secluded clearing. Prowling closer he pushed some leaves aside to see Running Deer, a five-year-old girl with the hind-quarters of a fawn, clutching the dead body of her mother. Another hunter had shot her in the head.

Pat had heard about the deer centaur tribe. It was rumoured it started when members of a dying indian tribe, struggling to shore up its numbers, started taking doe wives. Normally such radically different beings would never have been able to breed. But the strange magic of the Kentessee backwoods had made it possible, and a whole tribe of centaurian deer indians was born.

He approached the tiny girl and she started in fright to run. But Pat told her he wouldn't hurt her and enticed her forward with some chocolate. The girl already knew how to speak and understood he was going to help her. Since her own father had died a couple of years earlier, she went with the dentist and he adopted her and raised her like his own daughter.

Soon she could read and write as well as speak. She was fiercely intelligent and learned quickly. Pat saw potential and knew she would never be allowed to go to school. So he taught her himself and allowed her to read all his books. She learned dentistry and nursing. Although locals thought she was his assistant, she was actually just as good a dentist as he was. During Pat's Titezium skeleton replacement operation she performed all the surgical procedures. Since she had become such a fixture in Nova Cyrus, the locals came to accept her and even trust her.

When Pat was recovering between the various stages of his operation, Running Deer continued to pull teeth, drill holes and fill cavities to keep the money flowing in. After all he had been through, Pat could no longer bring himself to perform the dental duties.

It was like he'd lost all taste for it.

When Running Deer was old enough, she decided to return home to visit her tribe and let them know what she had achieved. But when she reached the Kentessee backwoods she found her whole tribe was gone, wiped out by a horrible disease called the Red Plague. Affecting only centaurs, it caused their skin to break out in huge bloody blisters. They wept watery tears of blood. They would ooze and cry until there was no more liquid left in their bodies, and die of dehydration.

It was not known where the disease had come from. Perhaps a gypsy trader had brought it from the Old Country. Perhaps it had come from one of the east coast manufactories and run down into the rivers.

But since that day Running Deer had not seen another centaur indian. So she returned to Nova Cyrus, to Pat—the only family she had.

She told him about her awful discovery. He may have been a country dentist, but during his spare time he researched the Red Plague, spent all his hard-earned cash on trying to find a cure. He ordered books and new-fangled equipment from the east to help with his experiments.

"I miss him terribly," Running Deer sighed when she'd finished.

After such a sad tale, Zeke and even Steel felt sorry for the poor deersquaw. Pat may have been a lying, cheating and thoroughly incorrigible cur but he had certainly had a very real soft spot for Running Deer. And now Running Deer had lost a loved one just as Steel had lost Sallianne.

Zeke stared meaningfully at Steel. He knew the tall, skinny gunslinger knew exactly what had happened to Pat. Tell her, he thought.

But Steel dropped his gaze again.

Zeke sighed and took a deep breath. "All right ma'am-"

"Just call me Running Deer," she interrupted softly.

"In that case, you can call me Zeke. And this tall, thin steak of misery is Steel."

"Pleased to meet you." She stuck out a delicate hand. Zeke took her fingers and kissed them, but Steel just shook the digits.

"Here's what I know," Zeke began. "We was camped down on the plains, under this big ol' billius tree. A maracleptops herd had just finished goin' past, and there was a couple o' dead ones left behind. We cut bits off one for a bit of a cookout, but knew they would attract scavengers. So we set watches during the night. Pat took the first while the rest of us slept."

Running Deer stared at him, taking in every word. Steel watched, his face still shadowed beneath his hat. He wondered what Zeke was going to come out with. He knew, if he wanted to keep the spider-man's trust, he would have to tell him his part of the tale. But be damned if he was revealing it to Running Deer.

"Anyway, a few hours later I was woken by this gawd-awful commotion. Snapping, snarling, yowling loud enough to wake the dead. Both Steel and I shot out of bed as Pat's gun went off, and goshamighty, there before us was a sight right outta the bowels of hell itself! It was a whole pack of dogs-o-war."

"Dogs-o-war?" Running Deer gasped. "What are they?"

"Military trained werecoyotes. Bigger, hairier, smarter and faster than normal coyotes. During wartime they're used to hunt down the enemy and deserters. But when the wars are over they're no longer needed and killed. But some managed to escape, makin' the west country even more dangerous than it already is. They come out at night and raid chicken coops and armadillo ranches. And sometimes, if they think they can get away with it, they attack travellers."

"But why attack Pat? Didn't you say there were several of those . . . maracleptops beasts?"

"The pack was two dozen strong—the biggest one I ever seen. They cleaned those mutant bisons down to their bones and hooves and they were still hungry. That's the trouble with werecoyotes. Being as big as they are, with super-fast healing abilities, they're always hungry. They went for Pat, and he blasted several down with his laser-rifle. Thinkin' he was on his own the remainder continued to harass him. When Steel and I appeared with our guns, several of the brutes had managed to get under Pat's guard and . . . they tore him to pieces."

"Zooterkins!" Running Deer clapped a hand over her mouth, tears brimming in her eyes.

"Steel and I started blastin' into them, but a couple managed to sneak around behind us—and they got into the tent where Sallianne Veerhoven, one of our party, was sleepin'. By the time we realised, it was too late. Those brutes killed her too."

"Oh no!"

"Yeah, it was horrible all right. But I never seen anyone fight as bravely as Pat did. We buried both him and Sallianne under the billius tree, and then went on our way. Some time later, Steel wanted to visit Sallianne's grave, so I agreed to go with him. It was then we discovered it had been tampered with. Her remains had been crimped by those nefarious two-headed injuns. We believe they also took Pat's body for trade."

"But who would want long-dead body parts?" cried Running Deer.

"Scienticians to experiment on," Zeke answered.

"We're on our way to find those Duoquois injuns, maybe get their bodies back so we can re-bury them—or at least find out who they sold 'em to."

Running Deer clasped her hands together. "Since we all seek the two-headed indians, might I accompany you?"

Steel pulled a face, but Zeke answered, "Sure—you seem a strong, capable young lady. Way you nearly tore your way outta my web proves that."

She looked up at him solemnly. "Thank you."

"Way you didn't scream at the mere sight of me proves that too," Zeke continued with a grin.

But Running Deer did not smile back. Her big dark eyes remained serious. "I may only be young, but I've already seen a lot. As a giant spider-man you are strange, but certainly not the weirdest thing I've seen."

Steel looked up at the sky. "Time's a wastin'," he growled. "Let's be moseyin' on."

"Yeah, sure," agreed Zeke.

They continued on down the narrow side-trail, following it down the cliff until it rejoined with the main one. Running Deer slipped back to pace along behind them. She preferred to keep a bit of a distance from the pair while she mulled over her own thoughts.

Steel felt uneasy. He could feel that deer woman watching him. Each time he turned to see if she was still following she was wearing a mean scowl on her pretty face and a piercing, accusatory look in her eyes.

"Great horn spoon, you're like a cat on hot bricks, Steel," Zeke growled in a low voice. "You'd better be tellin' me the truth about Pat Davison now, afore I buck you off."

Steel swore under his breath. He was beginning to think joining up with this spider-freak was a bad idea and wondered if he ought to just continue on his own. But then Zeke moved a lot faster than he did, almost as fast as a mechanical horse.

And not only had he revealed that he'd killed and eaten a human or two since becoming a spider, but he also had a life-long habit of chewing on human bones. Thus his eating habits were almost as bad as Steel's own. He had no right to point a finger.

Steel sighed. "All right. I et him."

Zeke almost tripped over one of his own spindly spider legs. "Ya *what?*"

"Pat Davison. I *et* him!"

"Et? As in gobble gobble munch munch?"

"Yeah. I'm a zombie."

140

"Dadgum! So that's why yer so light! Yer dead!" Zeke cursed some more, and Steel thought he was going to buck him off anyway. But he managed to right himself and continue trotting along. "Thought there was something weird about those long, pointy fingernails of yours," Zeke muttered.

Steel glanced over his shoulder at Running Deer, but she was still following at a safe distance, giving no sign that she'd picked up their conversation with her enhanced hearing.

"Dadgum," Zeke said again. "Yer right, you are a freaky bastard. So why'd you eat him? Was you just hungry?"

"Naw. I was a miner up at Mt Boloja, and I'd just found a huge Titezium haul. Worth . . . thousands. Nah, Tens. *Hundreds a thousands.*"

"Uh oh—I think I know where this is goin'."

"Anyway, I was carryin' the metal into town in a big sack when Pat stuck his head out of his surgery and said he had a cart round back I could borrow. So I went to meet him, like the dumb, trusting fool I was. Well, he was waitin' for me all right, but not with a cart. With a shovel. Only I didn't see it 'cause back when I was alive I couldn't see much of anything. I was near blind from an explosion in the mines. So Pat beat the living daylights outta me, killin' me stone cold dead. But he buried me in the beggars' bone orchard, which had a habit of sproutin' zombies during heavy rains. That's where I woke up, still wearin' the wounds he gave me. I was fit to be tied, but I managed to keep my wits about me and plan my revenge. On the way I ran into some o' those two-headed injuns—what'choo call 'em? Duoquois?"

"Yeah."

"They had some slaves, and one of 'em was Sallianne. She'd survived her fall over the edge of the cliff—no thanks to Pat Davison! She had a hold of him—he could have saved her—but he kicked her off and let her fall."

"Holy moly! I never knew that!"

"I rescued Sallianne and we travelled together. I found you when that maracleptops herd was still rumblin' past and hauled Pat outta the tent. He fired his gun, tryin' to kill me—again—and that's what started the stampede. When it was over Sallianne was dead and Pat was tryin' to run. I caught him and I bedded him down. Then I et him and took back my Titezium. I left a few bits of him—maybe a hand or foot—I dunno. I buried them 'fore I buried Sallianne. They mighta bin taken too—I dunno. That's the whole truth of it, Zeke—I swear to Thanatoxotl. Or whoever'n hell listens to zombies."

"Well bugger me sideways," Zeke declared. "Pat told me about that metal skeleton of his. I wonder if Running Deer knows where he really got the Titezium from?"

Steel glanced over his shoulder at the quiet deersquaw. "I dunno, but I'm sure she knows somethin' about what I done. She keeps givin' me the stinkeye somethin' fierce."

"She don't know nuthin'" Zeke snapped. "And we'll neva speak of it again, ya hear?"

"Yeah, I hear ya," Steel answered.

They continued on in uneasy silence. Steel hunched down into the collar of his dusty leather coat. He could feel Running Deer's cold stare raising the hackles on the back of his neck.

# CHAPTER 20

**A**FTER LEAVING THE narrow mountain pass with its numerous hidden trails, the three travellers approached a large, flat rock where some large brown and gold lizards were basking in the noon sunshine. As Zeke drew closer the lizards began to stand up on the hot rocks. The closest opened its mouth to reveal the bright red colour inside, and flipped out a frill around its neck.

"What in tarnation-" Steel began, surprised by the strange creature and its aggressive behaviour.

Then, bizarrely, the frill burst into flames, consuming the frill and then roasting the critter alive. Meanwhile the rest of the troupe scrambled to safety.

Abruptly Zeke stopped, swung his huge spider's backside around and squirted out some sticky threads at the retreating reptiles. Steel nearly slid off his back. "Gotta snare us some of those! They might come in handy."

Zeke managed to lasso a couple of the fleeing lizards before they could open their frills. He tied some silk thread around their bodies and stowed them into his shoulder bag for later. With the frills pressed close to their bodies, they became quiet and docile.

"Well I'll be blowed! I never seen anything like that!" Steel exclaimed as Running Deer joined them.

"Fire-frilled-neck lizards," Zeke explained with a gap-toothed grin. "They spend all day soakin' up the sun, absorbing its heat, so they can do that. Their skin also burns really well, but the little varmints are real hard to catch. They live in little colonies, and when they're threatened the critter closest to the predator sets itself on fire as a diversion. It sacrifices itself so the rest of its family can escape."

"Pat had a matchbox made of fire-frill-neck lizard skin," Running Deer added. "It was excellent for striking lucifers on."

"During wartime, if you could catch these little buggers without 'em firing up on you, you could tie twine around their frill, holding it to their body, and stop them from bursting into flames. Then you could use 'em in an attack."

"How?" asked Running Deer.

"Hold down the frill, pull off the twine, and hurl the lizard at the enemy. It would burst into flames and badly burn whoever you pitched it at!" Zeke chuckled. "I tossed one into a powder magazine once. Whooo-eee! A real hog-killin' time was had by all!" He flung all his arms into the air, mimicking the massive explosion that had ensued. Even Steel managed a smile at that!

But Running Deer was horrified. "That's horrible! Those poor little critters!"

"Come now, little lady—they're bred to burn. That's what they do. And besides, durin' wartime you have to make do with whatever weapon you can get." He peeled the body of the charred lizard from the flat stone slab. "And they come ready cooked for dinner!" He laughed again as he held it up.

Even though it was no longer raw, Steel's stomach still growled. At the moment, a meal was a meal.

Running Deer pulled a disgusted face and stomped off.

Zeke took the cooked critter down into the shade of the big rock ledge and there used his sharp talons to hack it to bits. He handed Steel and Running Deer equal portions. Steel gobbled his down, skin, bones and all, but Running Deer could only pick half-heartedly at hers. Being part deer, she wasn't a big meat eater. Steel eyed it off and she glared at him.

"You can have it," she muttered, and moved a few feet away, settling herself down for a nap. On the other side Zeke also curled up for a quick kip. Steel wanted to keep going, but realised the feast had made his living companions sleepy. Before ten minutes were up both were snoozing. Steel got up and climbed onto the ledge to be the lookout for a couple of hours.

He may have had enhanced undead sight, but his hearing was normal. Neither was he a scout or hunter, and didn't hear the subtle movement behind him until something clicked and there was a soft "shing" sound.

Steel spun around with a snarl to the sight of Running Deer

looming over him. She, on the other hand, *was* a scout and a hunter. Her dark eyes were practically popping from her face with anger, her nostrils flaring. Her mouth was twisted into a scowl with teeth bared.

She had one hoof lifted, pointing at his throat. Steel realised with a jolt of horror that she was wearing shoes made from Titezium, *his* Titezium! They had had switchblades installed, and one razor sharp knife was centimetres from Steel's throat. One flick of that hoof would be enough to decapitate him.

That didn't worry him too much but it would be a damned inconvenience.

"Did you eat his brains too?" she hissed.

How the hell had she figured out he was a zombie? Couldn't he pass for human now? "Wha-? What'n hell are you talkin' about, woman?"

"You wear Pat's eyes in your rotten skull!"

Steel gaped. "H-how do you-"

"The only person I ever met who had eyes that colour—the colour of azure—was Pat." She took a deep, shaking breath. "'As blue as the sea that I've never seen and bright as the sky under which I'll die,' he would always say to me."

Running Deer pushed the blade into Steel's neck, piercing his dry skin. "Those are *Pat's* eyes! You killed him and took them!" Her own dark eyes flashed with the need for vengeance.

Steel blurted out the first thing that popped into his head. "No, I swear, he was a goner. He saw my blindness and with his dying breath he bequeathed me his eyes. He—he was a good man."

She paused in reflection and then a tear escaped down her cheek. "Yes—he was a good man." She whispered in agreement and started to lower her hoof.

Just then several streamers of sticky threads shot out from underneath, tangling around Running Deer's legs. She stumbled a few steps, but was already hog-tied by the thin, strong strands. She crashed to the rocky platform, bleating and thrashing.

Zeke scuttled up onto the stone and stood over her. "There'll be no trouble on my watch, missy," he growled, glaring furiously down at her. "Now, you can come along nice and congenial or we can leave you for the werecoyotes. What's it to be?"

Steel grabbed Zeke's bony shoulder. "No—she won't be no more trouble, Zeke—I guarantee. She's just a bit upset, is all. Here-"

Steel used his long nails to carefully poke the blue eyes from his head. He offered them to Running Deer. His one milky eye popped forward and a maggot squirmed across the lower rim of his other hollow socket. He plucked it off and popped it into his mouth.

"Guess I won't be needing this no more," Steel removed his hat and carefully peeled off an immaculate head mask. Made of the finest silk, crafted and painted at the Watkins manufactories to appear as real as possible, it sat snug as a second skin. "Kinda ruins tha effect without tha eyes."

Zeke and Running Deer gasped as the zombie revealed his true decayed form.

Even though he could see with his one milky eye, he would always appear blind. So after devouring Pat's brains, Steel had plucked out Pat's eyes and popped them into his own rotten skull. They merged with his undead flesh. Then, once settled back at Nova Cyrus he had the exquisite mask fashioned along with his clockworker Salliannes. In this way he was able to join society as a respectable citizen instead of remaining a hunted, undead freak. He passed himself off as the late Steel Hawl's younger brother; Ira.

"Gosh-all-hemlock!" Zeke declared, turning a little green.

Running Deer took a deep breath, "You're a good man, Mr Hawl. There'll be no trouble."

"No more fussin' or feudin'?" Zeke growled.

"No more," Running Deer promised.

"All right then." Zeke cut her free and she took Pat's eyes from Steel. Zeke was about to gobble up his silk when the deersquaw interjected, "Do you think you could use it to make a pouch to keep Pat's eyes safe in?"

"I suppose." Zeke wove a little silk bag to nestle the eyes in. He added a strap so Running Deer could carry it around her neck or slanted across her shoulder with her other satchel.

That way she would always be able to keep a part of Pat close to her heart.

They continued on into the afternoon. Every so often Steel glanced over his shoulder to check on Running Deer. She no longer glared so accusingly, but trotted despondently with her head bowed and sad.

For the first time since exacting his revenge, Steel felt a pang of guilt. He started to talk but Zeke cut him off before he'd said two words. "I said we'll *neva* speak of it again."

# CHAPTER 21

A S THE SUN slid down towards the horizon, the odd little trio finally caught up with their two-headed indian foes. It was Running Deer, with her enhanced hearing, who heard their voices first, coming from some yards up ahead. She hurried up to Zeke and Steel to warn them.

"Let's git off the trail!" Zeke hissed, and carried Steel up a grassy hill towards a cluster of boulders leaning drunkenly together. Looking over her shoulder, Running Deer followed close behind. Quickly they concealed themselves behind the lopsided stones.

"There!" Running Deer pointed a long finger.

A group of the Duoquois indians had gathered by a large boulder just off the main trail. A few battered, but heavily decorated mechanical horses had been parked off to one side, and their latest cluster of slaves was tethered to a gnarly tree. While the Duoquois argued amongst themselves around a small campfire, the slaves were using the opportunity to catch up on some much-needed sleep. Due to their bonds they couldn't go far, and were resting by leaning against each-other.

Steel unslung his massive rifle from his back and powered it up. "Here's what we do. I reckon one good-sized laser ball right in the middle of that group ought to fry most of 'em like chickens. Then we all charge down. I'll shoot my pistol at whoever's still standin'. Zeke, you tie up whoever's left alive, and Running Deer—you free the slaves."

Zeke grabbed him on the shoulder. "Nah, hear me out afore you run in guns a-blazin'. I got a better idea."

The two-headed indians, known in common parlance as the Duoquois, were arguing amongst themselves over the best place to sell their latest batch of slaves. Unlike other local tribes, such as the Blemmyae, who still actively resisted the white men's intrusion, the more unscrupulous Duoquois saw an opportunity and decided to work with them in return for profit. They were prepared to do all the nasty jobs white men would no longer sully their hands with—such as slave-trading. Unscrupulous land owners needed slaves to work their farms, plantations, factories and mills. For a few years the price of slaves soared. But lately it had started dropping and conditions for those unfortunate enough to be caught and enslaved had worsened dramatically. Land owners were no longer prepared to pay a decent price for slaves, as few lasted longer than a few months before dropping dead from the appalling conditions or some horrible new disease.

However, the price for dead slaves was soaring. Scienticians craved corpses for experimentation, but they refused to buy live slaves and kill them. Although the scienticians could conduct the most gruesome of experiments on corpses, their own bizarre code of ethics would not allow them to actually kill.

And the Duoquois had no wish to execute their latest batch and drag their heavy, rotting bodies all the way to the east for sale. Neither did they want to keep feeding them. Thus they continued to quarrel, and were involved in a very heated discussion by the time the indian on scout duty finally noticed the approaching couple. He shouted a warning and the Duoquois snatched up their spears and bows, aiming them at the pair coming out of the setting sun.

A tall, lean white gunslinger in a broad-brimmed hat and long leather coat approached, leading a deersquaw along by a silk lasso round her neck. Although his single white eye reflected the light of their fire, it was obvious he could still see. However, the indians were far more interested in the zombie's slave. They could only gape in amazement. None of them had seen a deersquaw in years. She would fetch a massive sum, dead or alive!

"Hey, don't bother getting up. Jus' lookin' ta trade, is all." Steel drawled, not worried in the slightest by all the pointy implements directed at him. "Gotta rare beauty here. One of a kind. A deersquaw."

The leader of the group rose to his feet, all four of his eyes gleaming with greed. "What you want for deersquaw, dead man?" asked one of his heads. "We got no brains to trade," declared the other.

You sure don't, you dumbasses, Steel thought.

"He's just a stupid zombie," one of the leader's heads sneered in the indian's native tongue, and a few of the others laughed nastily. "Hit him in the head and let's just grab the deersquaw!"

An arrow was fired with deadly accuracy, right through Steel's hat and into his head, piercing his brain. "We take deersquaw now," the leader announced, rising to his feet.

Steel experienced a brief explosion of stars behind his eye, but his senses quickly returned. "Now that wasn't very neighbourly. I came in peace." he drawled.

"Why you not dead?" the Duoquois leader demanded, perplexed that he hadn't fallen down. His followers also started rising, muttering in agitation. Some kept their bows and spears aimed, but the weapons shook in their hands.

Steel smiled thinly. "Oh, but I am dead. It's just not quite as permanent a condition as you'd think." He yanked the arrow from his head and turned it around in his hand. Then, with a flick of his wrist he launched it back at the indian who fired it. Gaping in horror, the Duoquois turned to run. But Steel's massive undead strength ensured the arrow skewered the redskin through both of his heads. He crashed to the ground, dead.

"You evil spirit!" the indian chieftain cried, yanking a tomahawk from his belt.

"Evil? Dunno about that. But right now I'm a mad-as-hell spirit!" Steel pulled off his hat and poked a bony finger through the arrow hole. His forehead bore no sign of the wound that should have been beneath. "That was a brand new hat, dammit!"

He dropped the lasso and Running Deer immediately leapt into action, her Titezium-shod hooves flying and kicking with switchblades flicking out to gut the indians that had surged forward to grab her. A few arrows and spears were loosed in her direction, but all missed. She was too fast. She flung out one arm, blocking a spear and sending it to the ground with a clatter.

While Steel stalled the indians and took up all their attention,

Zeke had climbed to the top of the boulder beside their fire. Now he leapt into the fray, landing on top of two braves who had been about to attack Steel with their tomahawks.

"Thanks buddy!" Steel grabbed one attacker by his two heads and banged them together so hard he shattered both his skulls. The Duoquois Indian slid to the ground, dead.

Running Deer chased after another and trampled him to death under her sharp, deadly hooves.

Zeke's four fists flew like pistons, cracking jaws and breaking noses. He even lifted up onto two of his back legs, kicking out the other set to send a Duoquois flying into one of his fellows. Both ended up in a tangle of arms and legs that Running Deer immediately trampled over, ensuring they wouldn't be getting up again in a hurry.

Steel caught a spear in the guts, but with his enhanced strength he yanked it out and used it to stab his attacker in the chest, piercing his heart.

Steel and Zeke whooped and hollered, having what Zeke would call 'a real hog-killing time', but Running Deer fought silently and with a determined expression on her pretty face. Soon all the Duoquois indians were defeated; either dead or unconscious. Only a handful escaped.

The bound slaves had woken during the commotion. Some had foolishly tried to run and brought down the whole group. They were all huddled together, cowering in fear. Zeke scuttled over to them and cut their ropes with his talons. As soon as they realised they were free they scarpered in all directions.

Only one remained; a gruff Black Rock indian brave. He stayed by the camp while Steel, Zeke and Running Deer hunted through the Duoquois' supplies. They found a large collection of skins and body parts, but nothing from anything human.

"She's not here," Steel muttered.

"No sign of Pat's remains either," Running Deer agreed.

The Blemmya indian stepped up, unafraid. "My name is Bear Foot," he said in heavily accented, but passable English. "I been held by Duoquois for weeks. I can help."

Steel and Running Deer both looked up hopefully. Then they realised that his face was actually in his stomach, and quickly looked down into his numerous eyes. Or rather scarred sockets. He only had one eye left. It was chocolate brown in colour.

"You look for your dead?" he asked.

"Yeah, we're lookin' for the body of a tall blonde lady and a curly black haired fella with a moustache," Steel answered. "Although I dunno how good a condition they'll be in by now. It's been a few years."

"Duoquois indians can't preserve dead. They always trade dead bodies quickly to someone who can keep 'em."

"Who?" asked Steel.

"The Body Snatchers. They keep 'em for potions or take 'em east to sell to medical schools. They can keep bodies for years."

Both Zeke and Running Deer scowled at the mention of the Body Snatchers.

But Steel was more annoyed about what the Duoquois had done to Sallianne. "Heathen bastards, disrespectin' my poor Sallianne like that!" He turned away in a temper and started stomping around the ruined campsite, cussing, kicking sand into the fire and punching the gnarly tree where the slaves had cowered. His bony fist caused the entire growth to quiver, lose leaves and put a good-sized hole in its trunk. Both Running Deer and Bear Foot looked apprehensive.

Zeke scuttled over to the furious zombie. "C'mon now Steel. That ain't gonna do you no good."

Steel said some more choice words and straightened up. When Bear Foot saw that the undead gunslinger was no longer flying off the handle, he cautiously approached Zeke and Steel. "Bear Foot good Blemmya scout. I stay and help track Body Snatchers."

Zeke liked the sound of that, but wasn't this the Black Rock indian's home? "We'd sure love your help, Bear Foot, but what about your people? The . . . er . . . Blemmyae. Don't you wanna go back to them?"

"No. No plan to go home right now. Help you to find your dead. Trade for freeing me from Duoquois. Yes?"

"All right," Zeke agreed, and Steel nodded vigorously. Running Deer joined them, and Zeke told her that there was still a chance of finding the bodies of Sallianne and Pat.

Now their little crew numbered four. Steel could ride Zeke and Running Deer could gallop just as fast, but Bear Foot could only jog at a normal human pace. So they collected the best of the mechanical horses the two-headed indians had abandoned. Even Zeke decided to take one, since it was tiring running all day with a man on his back. But it took him a little while to work out how to sit in the damn saddle. His efforts to get his odd-shaped body comfortable drew sniggers from Steel, Bear Foot and even coaxed a thin smile from Running Deer. In the process he discovered something interesting in one of the saddle-bags. A musty smelling, somewhat singed but mostly intact gown covered with precious gems. It was very familiar and with a jolt he realised where he'd seen it before.

It had briefly adorned the shapely clockworker body of Marilou-Belle Watkins. Zeke wondered how the Duoquois had managed to get hold of it, but then he remembered Emmet T. Billings pulling it from Marilou's headless body. Then, after they rammed a spear through Zeke's body, the Blemmyae pulled Emmet from the coach. Then, some time later, the Duoquois must have picked up Bear Foot, who'd had the dress in his possession.

Zeke glanced at Bear Foot, realising that he must have been the one who'd hauled Emmet from the coach with the grappling hook. What had Emmet done to deserve such treatment? It must have been something pretty serious. But then the easy-going old driver shrugged. Everyone had their secrets.

Zeke wrapped the expensive dress up in a silk package and stowed it back in the saddlebag. All those sparklies would come in mighty handy since none of them had a single Lincoln skin between them, and he doubted Running Deer wanted to part with those purdy but deadly shoes of hers.

# CHAPTER 22

**B**ACK AT STEEL Hawl's Armadillo Ranch and Bordello, his clockworker Salliannes were pacing up and down the hallways. Despite their standard punch-card programming, they were beside themselves with worry. So wrapped up in his own depression, Steel hadn't realised that his clockworkers had slowly become self-aware and started to develop their own personalities. The care and love he had shown them initially had caused this, as clockworkers weren't usually treated with so much respect.

When Steel hadn't returned from checking the armadillos they feared that something awful had happened to him. So they were at a loss. Their job was to maintain the house and bordello, make sure all the customers were served drinks and food on their arrival, and kept entertained.

They rarely, if ever ventured outside. But they knew they couldn't keep worrying. They had to do something.

Three Salliannes, the one in black, the one in red and the one in white, decided enough was enough and it was time to go into Nova Cyrus to hire a gunslinger to track him down.

The Salliannes donned more modest attire; long skirts and jackets to cover their tight leather corsets, and walked the mile into town. The sun, heat and flies did not bother the three clockworkers one bit.

They entered the biggest bar on Main Street, known as the Lucky Miner, and looked around at all the grizzled faces gaping back at them in the smoky gloom. Some of these inebriated farmers and prospectors had availed themselves of their services in the past, but they were all shocked to see the beautiful clockwork ladies out of their natural habitat.

The three Salliannes searched for a likely candidate, but all the men appeared to be drunks and losers. A couple got up to greet them, huge inebriated smiles on their faces, hoping for a freebie or two. But the girls pushed past them and marched right up to the bar. The men's hopeful expressions drained into anger, but they didn't dare push their luck. Those clockworkers looked like they meant business, and they were built to take a pounding.

"Barkeeper, we are looking to hire a gunslinger," declared Red Sally.

"A good one, not one of these lushes," added Black Sally.

"Our boss has gone missing and we'd really like to find him," explained White Sally.

"So we need someone good," Red Sally finished.

The barkeeper put down the glass he was cleaning. "Then you'll be wantin' the Gatling Gunslinger Sisters—they're the best—always get their man."

"Where can we find these Gatlings?" asked Red Sally.

"They's upstairs in their room . . . but they's indisposed right now." The bartender winked. "If you care to wait at a table, I'll send Hank up to fetch 'em fer ya."

"Thank you, kindly." The three Salliannes marched over to a spare spot in a corner and sat down to wait.

Upstairs, in the Lucky Miner's biggest room, the biggest bed in the house was getting one heck of a workout. Springs howled, the bed-head slammed against the wall so hard sawdust pattered from the ceiling and all the sheets and blankets had since been ripped off and strewn all over the floor. On the bed a formidable tangle of arms and legs, belonging to six almost impossibly entwined bodies shuddered to a thundering climax. There was rootin', tootin' and shootin' all round.

"Hoo-wee! Best slapping I ever 'ad in my entire eighteen years on this hot dang earth," one of the men involved in the six-way declared, mopping his blond hair out of his brow.

"Hot diggity dog, whatta romp," agreed a second man, identical to the first.

Carefully, checking whose body part belonged to whom, the

bodies started to untangle. The three men, all spitting images of each other, start to hunt around the mess of bedsheets and blankets for their clothes.

"Yessireebob, gotta agree with you, Silas. Ain't nuthin' like a Siamese sandwich to set the day up right," declared the third man as he dug out his shirt.

"Silas? Did you jus' call him, Silas?" asked one of the Gatling sisters. The three of them were still on the bed, straightening their hair. It had flown all over the place during their wild activities.

"Yes ma'am. We's brothers: Silas, Sterling and I'm Stu. We's the Sixsmiths." Stu pulled his shirt over his head.

"But we know the Sixsmiths as Stiles, Seth and Shane!" protested another sister.

"You do? Well, they's our brothers too." Stu yanked on his trousers.

"You mean there's *six* a you?" gasped the third sister.

"Sure are. We's sextuplets." Stu laughed and his brothers, Silas and Sterling, joined in.

"Emphasis on the *sex*. Heh heh heh!" Silas added.

"Hmm, you do all look alike with your blonde hair and hazel eyes," the second Gatling agreed.

The Sixsmiths were a notorious gang of sheep rustlers who usually carried out their nefarious activities with their cousin John Wayne Wesson. They had come to be known far and wide as the Sixsmiths and Wesson.

The Gatlings had no problem hanging out with criminal types. They knew these types of varmints well. Too well.

As the Gatling sisters pulled on their clothes someone knocked on the door.

"Who is it?"

"It's Hank, ma'ams. There's some . . . er . . . ladies downstairs want to hire your gunslinger services."

"We'll be right down, Hank."

As the Gatlings descended the stairs the barkeep pointed out the three ladies sitting at a table. At first the Gatlings wondered why they weren't staring at them in surprise. But then they realised why.

The three ladies were clockworkers from that big, expensive bordello out of town. Not much fazed them.

The Gatlings took three stools from the bar, spiralled their way gracefully across the room, and sat down at the table.

They introduced themselves to the Salliannes as Geraldine, Ginger and Gertrude Gatling. They were actually Siamese triplets joined at the sides. Their arms were free but on their sides, just behind their arms, from their underarms to the bottom of their ribcages, they were attached by a thick strip of flesh that contained several major blood vessels.

One of those fancy doctors from the east could have separated them, but when they were young, their eccentric but enterprising mother decided they were a blessing from the mysterious goddess Triplexia, a three-headed deity worshipped in the Old Country. With her eloquence and the girls' own natural charm and athleticism, she built up a substantial following amongst locals dissatisfied with conventional religion. And for a while the Cult of Triplexia enjoyed wealth and power.

But then a fanatical but charismatic preacher arrived and denounced the Cult of Triplexia as an evil heathen religion. He called Triplexia a demon and declared that anyone following her would go to hell and burn forever. The ultimately superstitious locals panicked and hounded the family out of town.

In order to keep the dollars rolling in, the Gatling girls turned their unique deformity into an advantage and became sharp-shooters. Over the years they had managed to stretch the skin joining them and learned to move together and perform nearly impossible acrobatic manoeuvres. As adults they could stand or lie in a row shoulder to shoulder to shoulder, but they often formed a horseshoe shape. They could even curl into a circle, back to back to back. By facing in all directions no-one could sneak up behind them. To sleep they learned to sit and lean against each other. This helped one of them stay away and keep a look out for trouble while the others took turns sleeping.

Sometimes they walked in a circular pattern, spiralling round and round like dancers so they could watch in all directions. During

less dangerous times they walked sideways like crabs or simply straight ahead in a row.

They each wore specially designed shirts to fit around their joining—halter tops that tied up around their necks and their waists. They didn't bother with dresses—they were too much effort—and due to the odd way they moved they tended to step on each other's hems. Instead they wore normal trousers with chaps, boots and spurs. Of course each wore a gunbelt with ammo and two sixguns on each hip. And each carried a huge knife in her boot.

During the cold weather they donned thick ponchos. They also had a big one specially made with three holes in it. It did look comical, but no-one ever laughed. No-one dared.

The Gatling sisters had long straight black hair, dusky complexions and celestial eyes. 'Gatling' was not their real name. Their real name was some long fandangled unpronounceable thing from the Old Country. They became known as the Gatlings because when all three were spinning, shooting their six sixguns it was like a Gatling gun firing on all cylinders.

Gertrude stood on the left with Geraldine on the right and Ginger in the middle. Ginger thought she was the leader but all three often squabbled over that position. Gertrude and Geraldine also squabbled over who they really were. All three looked alike, but because Gertrude and Geraldine were on the sides, they actually got confused as to which sister they were. Ginger usually had to mediate when these fights got out of hand. They always stopped when Ginger threatened to get their names tattooed on them.

Neither wanted to be Gertrude.

The Salliannes introduced themselves. Even during their walk into Nova Cyrus they had started to develop their own identities and think of themselves as Red, Black and White Sally.

"Pleased to meet you," answered the Gatlings as one.

"What do you require of us?" asked Ginger, who always used the most hoity toity phrases.

"We need you to find our boss, Mr Hawl," Red Sally explained. "He's gone missing."

"He went out one day last week to check on the armadillos and never came back," explained White Sally.

"We're quite concerned," added Black Sally.

"What's this . . . " Ginger began.

" . . . Mr Hawl character look like?" finished Geraldine.

"Tall and skinny. Pale skin, white hair. Blue eyes," Red Sally began.

"He looks human but he's not," added White Sally.

"He's a zombie," said Black Sally.

"He goes by the name of Ira Hawl these days, but his real name's Steel Hawl," added Red Sally.

All three Gatlings raised their eyebrows in surprise at the clockworker's deadpan descriptions. Still—three clockworkers asking to find a walking dead man wasn't the weirdest job they'd been asked to do. Not by far.

"We miss him terribly," said Black Sally.

"How can you miss him?" asked Gertrude.

"You're clockworkers!" added Ginger.

The three Salliannes exchanged glances, and then they said together, "We love him."

The Gatlings stared again. That, they had not expected. How could machines love? How could they feel anything of any kind? But the Gatlings had learned long ago not to ask questions. There was no money in it.

"Will you help us?" asked Red Sally.

"Can you pay?" asked Ginger.

"We don't do charity," added Gertrude.

At the same time each Sallianne reached down into the bodice of her corset and produced a small purse. Three rolls of notes were deposited on the table.

"That'll be fine!" approved Geraldine.

"For a job this weird we don't take less than three thousand," declared Gertrude.

"We're just going to find the zombie, not kill him, Gertrude!" reproved Ginger.

"I'm Geraldine!" declared Gertrude.

"No, *I'm* Geraldine!" shouted Geraldine.

"Ladies!" Ginger snapped. "This is not the time or place for your silly little feud!"

Both Gertrude and Geraldine sniffed disdainfully. Little feud indeed! Identity was important, dammit!

"One thousand then," Ginger declared.

"Five hundred down payment for your expenses and five hundred upon the safe return of Steel Hawl," Red Sally declared.

"We agree to your terms. Five hundred now and upon the delivery of Steel Hawl to one—er, three—Sallianne Veerhovens we receive five hundred . . . apiece." Ginger glanced at her sisters, and they nodded, for once in agreement.

"A piece?" the Salliannes all said together.

"That's a bit steep, isn't it?" added White Sally.

"Not at all, Ms Veerhovens. After all, being unique as we are, we have special needs," Ginger continued. "And special needs require extra expenses. For instance, our hoss and its saddle had to be specially crafted to sit us three comfortably."

It was indeed a unique construction, allowing Ginger to face forward while Gertrude and Geraldine rode side-saddle.

"All right then," agreed Red Sally. "But Steel must be returned unharmed."

"We understand, ma'ams."

The Gatlings returned upstairs to their room to fetch a fresh contract. Each of them signed and the Salliannes all scribbled their names together. Strangely enough their signatures were all slightly different.

# CHAPTER 23

**B**EAR FOOT THE Blemmya scout followed a trail only he, even with his one single eye, could see. Every now and then he had to stop his mount, jump down and check the tracks more closely. Steel, Zeke and Running Deer followed him at a distance of about thirty feet. The trail led them out of the grassy, relatively fertile Black Rock Hills and into flat, dry scrubland only sparsely populated by vegetation.

For a while everyone was silent, then Steel asked; "Who are the Body Snatchers?"

Both Running Deer and Zeke shivered. "I've heard of 'em, but never seen 'em," Zeke declared. "They operate further east than I normally travel, in the badlands behind the Dragonback Mountains." He looked in that direction, where the scrubland eventually gave way to flat, featureless hills devoid of life.

Bear Foot stopped so they could catch up. "The Body Snatchers—also called the Feratu Noi," he answered softly in case someone was listening. But their surroundings were silent save for the rumbling from their mechanical horses and the eerie moan of the wind. "A secret group from the Old Country that came out about two hundred years ago." He pointed due east. "They all wear black. Long black coats, long black trousers and tall stove-pipe hats with wide brims that shadow faces." He lifted a hand to Zeke's face. "But eyes that glow. I seen them. Scared me to my soul."

"They don't sound so tough," Steel growled. "I'm sure one good laser ball in the face will blow 'em up just like everyone else."

Zeke snorted. He had to agree. But Bear Foot didn't smile. "You already dead." He prodded Steel in the chest. "You no need to fear for your soul. It already gone." With that he turned and walked back to the tracks he was following, the faint marks that only he could see. He climbed back onto his mount and resumed travelling, moving at a relatively slow pace of fifteen miles per hour.

Steel glowered after him. As far as he was concerned, his soul was still inside him. He remembered everything about his life and wasn't under anyone else's control.

"Don't piss off the scout," Zeke growled at Steel as they resumed their journey. "I don't know this country. If he decides to up and leave us, I don't think I could get us back." He glanced at Running Deer.

"Yes, these lands are foreign to me." She sniffed the air. "And they don't smell right."

They continued on in silence, and about an hour later Bear Foot paused beside something on the ground and jumped down from his horse again. The others gathered around him. A barrel lay broken on the dirt. Bear Foot knelt and nudged it with his foot, making sure nothing was camped inside, then knelt down and poked his hand in. He scooped out something and held up a couple of fingers full of something yellow.

"Beeswax. We are on right path. The barrel belonged to Body Snatchers."

"Whatta they need beeswax for?" asked Zeke.

"Preserve the dead?" suggested Steel.

"No," responded Bear Foot. "Body Snatchers keep slaves called Jarboys. They need beeswax to rub on their leathern longjohns to keep them soft. If they don't, they seize up and can't move."

"Leathern *longjohns?*" gasped Zeke. "What'n hell are those? They sound mighty uncomfortable!" He screwed up his craggy face at the thought.

"Explain later. Help gather wax for candles." Bear Foot pulled a leather bag from his belt and started scooping out the rest of the beeswax. The others joined him, quickly clearing out the broken barrel.

It was Running Deer who heard the sound of flapping wings first. She looked up as a large, sabre-winged creature soared past about a hundred yards above. She patted Bear Foot's shoulder and pointed.

"Sky demons!" he hissed. "There is body somewhere out here."

The pterosaurolophus pterosaur joined others circling in the sky. They were diving down on something about two hundred yards distant. Occasionally two would drop at the same time and attack each other with a furious flurry of screeching and clawing.

"Let's go." Bear Foot headed off through the dry bush on foot. The others followed. Steel hadn't had a decent meal since the fire-frill-necked lizard, and even the thought of something that had been dead for a long time made his stomach growl. Better get something soon, he thought.

Presently, the crew found what the pterosaurs were picking at and ripping to pieces. A humanoid body, staked out on the ground.

"Let's get rid of them," Bear Foot growled.

"You don't need to tell me twice! Here, pardner." Steel handed Zeke his pistol and unslung his rifle. "Been itchin' to shoot somethin' for ages!"

While Bear Foot and Running Deer shot at the flock with bows and arrows, it was the laser blasts from Steel's weapons that scattered the opportunistic scavengers. The monsters flapped off in indignation, but they didn't fly too far, and circled around to a safe distance to watch and wait.

The crew approached the body to check if there was any life left in it. But it soon became obvious from the torn wounds in its chest and stomach that it was dead. Very dead. The rank odour of decay disgusted everyone except for Steel, who was still hungry. He would have started drooling had he had any salivary glands.

The body was quite small. It could have belonged to a boy or young teen, and it appeared to have been clad in some sort of full-length leather jumpsuit, now dried and cracked in the harsh desert air. The scavenging pterosaurolophuses had shredded it in places with their sharp teeth to get at the flesh beneath.

"*Those* are leathern longjohns." Bear Foot pointed. "The Body Snatchers stitch you up in 'em tight as drumskin. Then stake you out in open air and pour water all over so leather nice and soft. They leave you. As sun dries you the leather tightens and tightens till it squeezes the breath out of you."

"Golly!" exclaimed Zeke, looking a little green.

Running Deer also appeared queasy. "What an absolutely ghastly way to go."

Even Steel wasn't quite as hungry as he had been. "Wonder what this feller's crime was? Doesn't look much more'n a boy!"

Once again Running Deer's acute hearing detected the approach of a pterosaurolophus that decided to take a chance and dive at the living, far tastier-looking morsels surrounding the corpse. "Look out!" she shouted, and loosed an arrow at the approaching creature. Her shot struck it in the throat but didn't penetrate its leathery hide deep enough. It continued to swoop.

Steel, Zeke and Bear Foot fired their weapons. Steel's swirling, blinding laser ball removed the monster's head, and it crashed to the ground mere yards from where they were standing, charred neck smoking.

Meanwhile the Gatling Gunslinger Sisters were hot on the trail. They rode on their specially-crafted mechanical horse fully-equipped with a platform that elevated them to their seats. Their saddle resembled three chairs with a central back for them to rest against. The horse's "head" also leaned back at an angle so Ginger could reach the controls more easily. Each sister had a belt she could pull across her belly to hold her into her seat.

The horse was specially designed and crafted by the famous mechanologist Sid Chrome. He used to work for the Watkins Corporation as one of their head designers. He was a genius and added a touch of sentience to the clockworkers that previous scienticians had been unable to.

After Sid had a falling out with the Watkins, he headed west and hung up his shingle. He made custom designed horses and other devices without being persecuted for adding his own individual touches to his creations.

The Gatlings' bizarre contraption purred softly along, ejecting small puffs of smoke and the occasional hiss of steam. While Ginger controlled the beast, Gertrude and Geraldine sat in their side-saddles with their rifles ready to fire at the first sign of danger. But as they neared the small, ragged figure trudging along the side of the path they realised he was no threat. He was small and stooped, dressed in rags and covered with scratches and bruises.

The Gatlings slowed down beside him. "You look a little lost and mighty far from home," remarked Geraldine, the closest to him.

He looked up at the bizarre composite creature that was the Gatlings, but was too beaten-down to be surprised. "I'm a freed slave."

"Who freed you?" asked Ginger.

"The weirdest damn trio I ever seen, ma'am . . . ma'ams. There was a big spider fella and a deersquaw, and they was led by a zombie with one white eye."

"One white eye . . . Doesn't the fella we're looking for have blue eyes?" asked Gertrude.

"Yes," answered Ginger. "Can you describe the zombie some more?"

"Yeah, he was real tall and skinny and wearin' a long cowboy coat and hat. And carryin' the biggest damn rifle I'd ever seen."

"Sure sounds like Steel Hawl," declared Gertrude.

"Yeah, how many other zombie gunslingers are there wanderin' these hills?" asked Geraldine.

"We'll keep going," decided Ginger. She handed the freed slave a couple of dollars for his trouble.

Finally his expression brightened. "Thank you, ladies!" He tipped an invisible hat and the Gatlings continued on their way.

Out here in the badlands, where everything was flat and still and the tallest plants were only a few feet high, there wasn't anywhere safe to camp. After the horses had been brought to the campsite, Zeke wove a tent about thirty feet from the fallen pterosaur carcass. Bear Foot plaited some threads of cloth and used them as wicks in the beeswax candles. They burned quickly and stank, but provided enough light to move around the site without stubbing toes or falling into holes.

They built a fire from the dried-out bushes lying around and cooked sections cut from the remains of the pterosaurolophus. Steel gobbled down a large portion of the creature raw, and then ate dessert in the form of the brains of the staked-out man. "Can't let 'em go to waste, now can we?" he asked his disgusted companions through mouthfuls of delicious grey matter. Of course, after all this time there was no life left in it, but it was still soft and nutty and flavoursome.

Bear Foot just shook his head, wondered for a moment how he had fallen in with these freaks, and cleared his broad throat. "Let me tell you more about the Feratu Noi and how they are tended by their slaves, the Jarboys."

Steel settled back down at the campsite, holding his gun across his knees. Since he didn't sleep, it was his job to watch over the camp while the others slept, making sure the numerous desert predators didn't venture too close. Of course, they could worry the dead pterosaurolophus as much as they wanted, but as soon as they approached the silk tent one laser ball from Steel would send them to oblivion.

He didn't mind staying awake if he had the opportunity to shoot things. Killing an enemy would take his mind off Sallianne and dwelling about the awful possibility that she had already been cut up on some scientician's slab, her various internals removed and scrutinised for possible use in their infernal experiments and machines.

"The Jarboys look like lads but are grown men, captive since childhood," the Blemmya scout began in his rich, deep voice. His stilted, halting tone had long since ceased being a problem with his companions. Now they hung onto his every haunting word. "They were snatched from their beds at night by wicked Feratu Noi. They move quickest in the dark. Everyone has Body Snatcher myth. You white folks and redskins alike. All believe in evil spirits who take the young 'uns in their sleep and spirit them away to some evil place for evil work. But these Body Snatchers, the Feratu Noi, are real."

"Yes," Running Deer cast her gaze downward. "When I was young grownups in my tribe would frighten naughty children with tales of the Body Snatchers." She looked a little pale in the light of the flickering fire.

Seated nearby, Steel simply grunted. Having spent his entire life groping around in the mines, he had heard few stories about the mysterious world outside. He felt a little left out of things. But at least now, in a new virtually indestructible body, he could see the world. Was it possible, if he couldn't find Sallianne, that instead of trying to kill himself that he could spend some time exploring, learning all about the strange world he had ignored for far too long?

"As children the Jarboys are sewn into heavy leathern

longjohns with just a small flap front and back for the waste," Bear Foot continued solemnly. "The longjohns never come off and stop Jarboy from growing too big. The kids stay child-sized, but crushed and strange-looking. Their heads and hands and feet, not trapped in longjohns, grow bigger than rest of body. They look funny, like spirits from another world. They also don't get much food to eat. Bones, scraps. Whatever they can find. They stay small. Stunted."

"Between hay an' grass," Zeke mused thoughtfully. Running Deer stared at him curiously.

"Neither man nor boy, half-grown," Zeke explained.

"In old days the Feratu Noi used clay jars instead of leather to hold bodies, only arms, legs and head sticking out. That is why they still called Jarboys," Bear Foot continued. "But that not all."

"What more could those fiends possibly do to those poor boys?" asked Running Deer in horror.

"Feratu Noi stick . . . 'brainwavers' to boys' heads."

"Brain*what?*" asked Steel.

"Things." Bear Foot waved his hands, struggling for words that finally eluded him completely. "Metal things."

"Machines?" suggested Zeke.

"Yes, machines," Bear Foot answered. He bounced up and down where he was sitting, probably what he assumed was equivalent to nodding for someone without a head. "Machines from the east that stop them from . . . thinking their own thoughts. They become . . . easy to command."

"What'n hell kinda machine can do that?" Steel exclaimed.

"Braiwavers . . . sit on top of head or stick to side and have . . . parts . . . stuck into the skull and brain." Bear Foot waved his hands as he struggled to explain science that he didn't really understand. "I seen 'em with my own six eyes," he finished.

"Six? I only count . . . one! What happened to the others?" Zeke demanded.

Bear Foot pointed to the scarred, empty sockets between his pectorals. "The Duoquois plucked 'em out one by one. Made eyeball soup out of 'em." He smacked his lips.

Steel hated to admit it, but that sounded tasty.

Even Zeke didn't look too disgusted.

But Running Deer pulled a face. "The more I'm hearing about these Duoquois, the less I'm liking them."

"Lucky they left you with one," put in Steel.

"Not for my sake. They didn't want trouble of leading blind injun around."

"They're a considerate lot, ain't they?" Zeke growled.

"The Duoquois are a scourge. They been enemy of my people since start of time. They never fought white man. Rolled over and let him scratch belly. They do what they do to survive. Not care about old ways or beliefs. Even forget about old goddess of many heads and say they worship 'man of iron'." Bear Foot gave a wide yawn that revealed the bulge that was the top of his stomach, located just below the mouth in his belly. All three of his companions grimaced at the sight. "Need sleep now. We should rest. Tomorrow will be busy day."

Zeke, Running Deer and Bear Foot crawled into the silk tent for safety. Although the Blemmya would have preferred to sleep on the bare ground under the stars, he understood the need to remain close to the others and under cover while Steel watched over them.

# CHAPTER 24

THE NEXT DAY, at around midday, the Gatling Gunslinger Sisters rolled out into the low, scrubby desert. Some creatures circling in the sky about a mile distant attracted their attention, and they headed in that direction. A few well-aimed shots from Gertrude and Geraldine sent the predators screeching and flapping away. Ginger didn't have to stop or even slow down. When the three could work together, they were a well-oiled machine.

They found what had attracted the pterosaurs' attention; one well picked over staked-out corpse and the mostly eaten carcass of another pterosaurolophus lying nearby. The staked-out corpse piqued their interest and they jumped down to examine it more closely. There wasn't much of it left now; a few scraps of torn leather clinging to bones. The head had been removed and lay nearby. Geraldine nudged it with her foot and it rolled over. It had been cracked open and the brains removed.

"No pterosaur could have done that. They would have just crushed it between their jaws and gotten at the brains that way," Ginger declared. "That was broken open by something else."

"Zombies like brains best of all," agreed Gertrude.

"Steel Hawl's been here. We're definitely on the right track," said Geraldine.

They cast about for tracks and spotted a collection of prints around the corpses; odd claw-footed indentations, cloven-hoof-shaped prints, a perfectly ordinary set of boot shapes and some bare feet marks. These milled about the bodies, and led to a campsite where the group had stopped for the night. Some mechanical horse tracks led away, heading east. "There are four of them travelling together now!" Ginger observed.

"Perhaps they picked up an indian scout?" suggested Geraldine. "This desert's dangerous."

"Possibly. But what kind of injun scout would work with a spider-freak and a zombie?" asked Gertrude.

"Maybe he was one of the freed slaves," suggested Geraldine.

"We know which way they're going. We can talk on the road." Ginger clapped her hands.

They headed back to their mount.

Some miles ahead, still heading east, the crew continued along, each member immersed in his or her own thoughts. Still astride one of the Duoquois mechanical horses, Bear Foot led the way.

Riding thirty feet back, Steel gave a long, wet burp that was loud enough to attract Zeke's attention. He turned in the saddle of his own horse.

"What was that? A belch?" Zeke exclaimed. "What'n hell could possibly give *you* gas?"

"I know I shouldn't of et that werecoyote I caught sniffin' 'round our camp last night." Steel rubbed his belly. "I think it's fast-healin' is playin' hell with my digestive tract."

"It's tryin' to regenerate in your *stomach?*"

"I reckon so." Steel burped again.

"Leapin' lizards! Well, first sign o' one o' those big hairy brutes comes burstin' outta your guts I'm gonna blow it ta hell, you understand?"

Steel nodded. "I understand." He rubbed his stomach. "I feel a bit better now. Definitely not eatin' one o' those again. Least not unless it's cooked."

Zeke could only shake his head. "I don't think even I'd eat a werecoyote. Hairy, stinkin' mongrels."

"He was a bit gamey, but his brains sure tasted nice."

Zeke lifted a hand. "Ugh! Don't wanna hear any more!"

For the crew the next day passed relatively uneventfully. Those who needed water to survive noticed that the Duoquois' waterskins were starting to run low, and soon they would have to forage for fresh fluid. Bear Foot knew how to dig for water in his own region, but not out here in the scrublands.

They ate some chunks of pterosaurolophus meat they had brought with them, and Steel's stomach finally won the battle against the regenerating werecoyote flesh and settled down.

The sun hit the western horizon, and Bear Foot stopped his mount and turned to the rest of the group.

"We going to camp here?" asked Zeke.

"Not yet. Feratu Noi camp up ahead only a mile."

"We're that close?" gasped Steel. "What'n hell we waitin' for!" He pulled on a lever to accelerate his mechanical horse forward. Bear Foot darted in front, lifting his hands. Steel screeched to a halt. His mount's chimney belched out thick, dark smoke.

*"What?"*

"Everyone off horses. We scout ahead on foot. *Quiet,"* he added with emphasis for Steel's benefit.

Making a disappointed face, Steel powered down his horse, grabbed his rifle and slid off the back. Zeke shut down his own mount, scrambled off and Running Deer joined them. Bear Foot pointed to some tracks on the ground, now clear to everyone. Bare feet, boot prints and the tracks of engine-powered caravans.

Bear Foot held a finger to his lips, then turned and started following the tracks. The others walked after him at a respectable distance. The sun set and stars began to sprinkle across the sky. Up ahead they could see lights appear through low scrub. Bear Foot dropped into a crouch and the others did the same. He, Steel and Zeke could move quite easily low to the ground, but Running Deer wasn't built to stalk like that. They had to wait for her to catch up.

All four came up behind some thorny bushes and peered through a gap in the foliage at the Feratu Noi camp.

It consisted of about half-a-dozen black caravans, battered and dusty from the road, parked in a rough circle around the campsite. Through gaps in between the vehicles the crew could see strings of little lights hanging up, giving off an eerie, fluorescent shimmer.

"Glow-worms," Bear Foot whispered. "Feratu Noi nearly blind, but they use sound. Like bats."

A body could just be seen, strung upside down from a wooden frame. Blood from its severed jugular was pattering into a large pottery jar placed beneath. Other Feratu Noi could be seen moving about, dressed in their long black cloaks. They weren't wearing their tall top hats and their heads were bare. They were bald and appeared to have pointy ears. But at the moment all had their backs to where the crew were hiding. They seemed to be working at a long bench. Bones lay beside them. They looked like they were smashing them and grinding them to powder. Others poured the powder into labelled jars.

"Sell to celestials for magic potions," Bear Foot mouthed. Due to the unique position of his face and the size of his mouth, he could make himself understood with hardly a sound at all.

A Jarboy appeared, dressed in one of his leathern longjohns. It appeared to be glued skin-tight to his bony body, showing all of his ribs and protruding hip bones. It glistened with a fresh coating of beeswax. His head, hands and bare feet all appeared comically large.

But no-one was laughing. The poor deformed creature walked with a stoop as he helped his masters to prepare their potions. His eyes looked like dark, sunken pits in his pale, emotionless face. The brainwaver Bear Foot had spoken of was attached to the crown of his head like a tiny metal cap. It was a dull reddish brown in colour and studded with the rivets that had been used to attach it. A needle on a dial in front flickered to show brain-activity, and switches at the back were used to control the device.

Finally, one of the tall, imposing Feratu Noi turned so the watching group could see its face.

It was not human.

It had cruel, thin slits for eyes, with only darkness behind. It also had no nose, just a pair of flared nostrils with spidery veins radiating outwards from it across its cheeks. A pair of sharp, pointy fangs protruded from its mouth over its lower lip.

It was a *vampire*.

"Let's go down there and show 'em what for," Steel hissed, hefting his rifle so he could put a laser-ball right into the creature's face.

Bear Foot grabbed him by an arm. "No, too dangerous. It night now. They very powerful at night. Must wait till light."

"Dangerous, my ass. There's less of 'em than the Duoquois and we kicked their raggedy asses good an' proper."

"No, Bear Foot's right!" Zeke mouthed. "Look at 'em! They ain't people like you or I. They's beasts! Beasts of the night!"

"Soon as they sense danger, they let out high-pitched scream to bust eardrums," Bear Foot added. "Make ears bleed."

"Don't worry me none. In case you hadn't noticed, I'm a zombie. They can't hurt me."

"Well, that's just fine and dandy, Steel, thinking only 'bout yourself," Zeke retorted. "But what about the rest of us? We might be tougher than most humans, but we're still human." He glanced at Running Deer, and she nodded. "We've all got blood in us."

"They weak in daylight," Bear Foot continued. "Humanoid bats with webbed fingers. Their skin burns in sunlight. Why they cover up in long coats and hats. They sleep by day in those caravans. They feast on blood at night."

As though on cue, one of the Feratu Noi removed the full jug from beneath the dangling corpse and quickly replaced it with another. He lifted the big jar to his mouth, but just as he was about to drink another Feratu Noi snatched it from him and hissed at him. The creatures didn't speak, but were obviously communicating somehow, for the one who'd tried to drink before he was allowed hung his head in shame. The second one slapped him across the face and departed, taking the full jug with him.

"I got an idea," Zeke whispered. "Let's back up a bit so I can tell you proper."

The group retreated from the edge of the camp about fifty yards. Zeke explained. Steel liked the sound of it and smiled.

Bear Foot brought out what was left of the beeswax. Everyone took a portion and stuffed it into their ears. Zeke handed everyone a fire-frill-neck lizard, still wrapped with silk. "Now I'm gonna cut my silk—hold the frills down—don't let 'em go off too early." He snipped the bonds from each creature.

Clutching the wriggling lizards close, the group returned to the camp. But this time, when they paused at the bushes they hurled the lizards into the camp. As the creatures flew they realised they were free and opened their frills. They glowed red and burst into flame. They landed in the middle of the camp, on the bench where the Feratu Noi were preparing their potions. Vampires who had been working suddenly found their hands and arms on fire.

Feratu Noi exploded into flames and became easy targets. They released their high-pitched shrieks, and had the crew not packed their ears with beeswax the sound would have burst their eardrums. It was still uncomfortable and caused an instant migraine, but all that did was make the crew angry.

They raced in, Steel firing his laser rifle at a stumbling, blazing vampire and obliterating it completely. Zeke shot Steel's pistol, removing another creature's head. Running Deer unleashed a barrage of arrows and then charged to attack with twin tomahawks. She didn't fancy getting too close to those vile creatures with her Titezium hooves, although she was sure the fine metal would seriously damage such unholy creatures. Bear Foot also came in with twin tomahawks. These small, heavy axes easily smashed in the Feratu Nois' delicate skulls.

For a moment it looked like they would prevail without so much as a scratch. But then an uninjured vampire plunged with a scream onto Running Deer's back. It was skinny and naked, horribly pale and spindly. But its long-clawed fingers enabled it to hang on tight. It opened its mouth wide, unhinging its bottom jaw so it could better sink those monstrous fangs into her throat. Running Deer reared up to flip him off but he held on. She swung her weapons but couldn't attack—he was right behind her!

Then a laser-blast tore a plate-sized hole in the monster's chest. Its heart and lungs fried, the vampire dropped off. Zeke lowered the pistol and tipped his hat at the deersquaw.

She smiled at the spider mutant, and this time it wasn't one of her usual tight-lipped half-smiles, but a full-blown grin of appreciation that showed all her brilliant white teeth. "Thank you, Zeke!"

# CHAPTER 25

**T**HE GATLING GUNSLINGER Sisters had managed to find the only high ground in the area. They set up their camp and while they were cooking their beans, they heard what they first thought was just the moan of the desert. Then an energy blaster went off with a distinctive sizzling, roaring sound.

"That weren't no wind!" declared Gertrude.

All three rose as one and looked in three directions at once.

Ginger spotted the fiery dot, and as the others turned to join her she pulled out her spyglass, with its many dials and lens attachments. She set it to night vision and carefully focussed on the melee. She could see spindly figures, some dressed in black but others naked. All were on fire. They were running about trying to put themselves out and fight their attackers at the same time. She was glad she couldn't hear the Feratu Nois' high-pitched screeching from this distance.

She spotted a deersquaw and spider creature, standing beside the fallen body of one Feratu Noi. She made out a Blemmya Indian, driving his tomahawk into the skull of another flaming monster. It slumped to the ground and the indian decapitated it and kicked its head away.

Then she noticed a tall, thin man in a long cowboy coat and hat grab a Feratu Noi as it charged him, and rip its head clean off its body with his bare hands. He cracked the fragile skull in half like an egg and scooped out a handful of brains. He stuffed them into his mouth, chewed for a moment, and then spat them out in disgust.

It seemed Feratu Noi brains were too revolting even for zombies.

"I've found him!" Ginger exclaimed in excitement. She handed the spyglass to Geraldine.

When all the Feratu Noi were dead, lying dismembered or in unrecognisable smouldering heaps on the ground, Bear Foot signalled it was safe by scooping the beeswax out of his ears. An eerie quiet descended as the others followed suit. "We should search camp, make sure no others hiding," the Blemmya scout declared as he moved cautiously towards the closest of the old black caravans. Up close they really were old and filthy, with rotten panels and broken sections patched with whatever the Feratu Noi could find. They stank of death and decay. The engines also looked old and rusty, fixed with mismatched panels, animal sinew and strange-smelling glue. A weird scent of sulphur surrounded them, like they had been forged in the bowels of hell itself.

In a large black caravan with its windows boarded shut, Bear Foot discovered the rest of the Jarboys, sleeping in a pile like a litter of rats. Bear Foot was wondering why the commotion hadn't woken them when someone tapped him on a shoulder. Still in battle mode, he swung around with his tomahawk upraised, ready to brain whoever had snuck up behind him.

But it was only the Jarboy they had glimpsed before, the one who had been helping the Feratu Noi. He was looking sheepish and brushing desert sand off his leathern longjohns. He must have hidden the moment the attack started. "Can you talk?" demanded Bear Foot.

The Jarboy stared stupidly at him for a few seconds, his big eyes ringed with black from exhaustion. Then he pointed one hand at his ears and the other at his mouth. He did this a couple of times and stared expectantly at the scout, a hopeful look replacing his previous dumb stare.

But Bear Foot was a well-travelled brave, and he understood. During his youth he had mastered the sign language of the desert indians. The Jarboy was a deaf-mute. Slowly, because he hadn't used the language for a while, he signed back: *why are the others still sleeping?*

*All deaf-mute,* the Jarboy answered quickly, appearing delighted that someone could understand him. *Constant screeching of Masters send them all that way after a while.*

The Feratu Noi's cruelty made Bear Foot feel sick. He climbed up into the ancient, creaking caravan and nudged the closest sleeping Jarboy awake. He started to his feet in terror, rousing his companions behind him. But then the other Jarboy clambered in, holding a string of those strange, glowing worms so they would be able to see him. He signalled rapidly with his other hand, speaking so fast that Bear Foot could hardly follow him. He seemed to be telling them that the evil Masters were dead, and they were all free.

One by one he led them out into the open. They were all wearing brainwavers; some wore little caps attached to the tops of their heads while others had smaller discs attached to their temples. One had a steel plate riveted to the back of his skull. All had dials and switches and various cables running into their heads.

"That is horrible," Bear Foot declared out loud. He turned to Running Deer, who had been examining the various potions and chemicals set out on the bench in the middle of the camp. "You . . . know medicine? Can you help?" He gestured towards the machines wired into the little creatures' brains.

She clopped forward to check out the closest Jarboy, the one who had helped Bear Foot. He seemed to be the largest and most knowledgeable, but he had no name. The others just called him One. She examined the technology. "I can try, but I'll need some tools."

Bear Foot signalled to the Jarboys, and they practically fell over themselves to obey. Soon they returned with a large wooden case full of stolen medical equipment from the east; surgical implements, mercury thermometers, syringes, pumps, a blood-pressure cuff and even a defibrillator that was used to bring back the dead. "Yes—I think I can use these!" Running Deer declared, surprised and pleased by the quality of the equipment. Even Pat had not had his own defibrillator machine! "But I'll need an assistant."

"I'll give you a hand, ma'am—got more than enough of 'em." Zeke held all four of them up. She smiled.

While Running Deer and Zeke worked on extracting the Jarboys' brainwavers, Steel and Bear Foot explored the rest of the camp.

With the help of two Jarboys from the back of the queue, one carrying a string of glow-worms for light, they searched another caravan and found a large cache of weaponry, including the grappling hooks the Black Rock indian savages had used. Bear Foot scowled. "They take from my tribe," he growled.

The caravan was very cluttered, filled with cupboards containing numerous jars of ground-up bones to be sold for use in celestial potions. Steel's features darkened as Bear Foot explained. He curled his hands into fists. "Sallianne could be in any one o' these!"

One of the Jarboys stepped forward and signed to Bear Foot. "What's 'e sayin'?" Steel muttered.

Bear Foot turned to Steel. "He says that one dead body they found a while back was sold to travelling circus."

"What body? *What* circus?"

Bear Foot gulped and signalled very rapidly to the Jarboy. He signalled back. "Body of . . . blonde lady. Circus owned by . . . renowned scientician Dr Barton Bigelow," Bear Foot explained as the Jarboy spoke with his long bony fingers. "Body was taken . . . to be used as an exhibit."

"Some travellin' carnival is usin' Sallianne's body in a five-cent *freakshow?*" Steel exploded. "How could anyone do such a thing to her?" He lost his temper and before Bear Foot could react, he had ripped one of the wooden cupboards from the wall, sending it crashing to the floor. All the jars tumbled out, most smashing to the floor to send their fine powders exploding into a fine mist in the air.

Steel grabbed a second cupboard to reef it from the wall with his superior zombie strength. The doors swung open to reveal more jars of pulverised bones, and all these had labels. Bear Foot grabbed Steel's arm. "No!" he warned.

He snatched out one of the jars and showed it to Steel. It was clearly labelled "Bones of Pat Davison."

Steel's temper eased. He stared, his white eye wide. How could this be? "How did they know his name?"

The Jarboy signalled. "Speak with dead," Bear Foot explained— or rather failed to. Steel just shrugged and examined the jar—the last desiccated, crushed and pulverised remains of the dentist who had killed him. Steel slipped it into his coat.

The Jarboy who'd accompanied them decided to bade a hasty exit. Besides, he had just checked the queue outside and realised there were only a few of his fellows left in front. Running Deer had learned quickly how to deactivate the brainwavers. With Zeke's help she removed the rivets attaching them to the Jarboys' heads and carefully drew the wires from the poor creatures' skulls.

Steel managed to calm himself so he could explore the rest of the caravan and its many cupboards of jars, wrapped specimens, tied up bundles of dried skins from various animals, bundles of bones and various trinkets made from teeth, ears and eyeballs.

It was Bear Foot who detected a whisper so soft he wasn't sure he heard it at all. Not with his ears, but in his mind. He paused to try and listen better. "What is it?" asked Steel. "You hear something?"

Bear Foot lifted a hand for silence. Yes! There it was again! A call so soft it was like a feather across the surface of his brain. "You hear that, dead man?'

Steel shook his head. "Didn't hear nothin'."

The call came again. This time Bear Foot fancied he detected the direction it had come from—the far end of the very caravan they stood in. Bear Foot took the glow-worm string and stepped forward, up to the end of the van. What he had initially taken for the back wall of the conveyance was actually a small velvet curtain.

The voice sounded again; a tiny, plaintive call for help.

Bear Foot drew the little curtain aside to reveal a small shelf with a single large jar standing on it, all by itself. Bear Foot grasped the jar—and immediately a voice filled his mind, strong and clear.

*Thank you.*

He drew the thing out into the light of the glow-worm string. The glass jar was larger than the specimen jars, filled with a cloudy liquid in which something could be seen wriggling. It appeared to have several tentacles, some thin gangly limbs, and a pair of large, luminous red eyes that focussed on Bear Foot's surprised belly-face. A tiny pair of hands pressed against the glass and the face drew closer. A lipless mouth revealed sharp fanged teeth.

Bear Foot recoiled in horror and nearly hurled the horrid thing from him.

*No, no!* the creature cried. *Don't drop me!*

"It was you who spoke?" Bear Foot asked out loud for Steel's benefit. Even the zombie looked a little disgusted by the weird mutation in the jar.

*Yes. I'm Jenny Haniver. I'm so glad you found me. I . . . appear to have lost all my connections to the outside world.*

"What connections?" asked Bear Foot.

"What's it sayin'?" asked Steel in confusion.

The strange little thing actually managed to look sheepish. *My telepathic link through the Feratu Noi, and my mechanical links through the Jarboys are disappearing.*

"Feratu Noi are all dead, and Running Deer is . . . releasing Jarboys," Bear Foot growled, once again tempted to toss the freakish thing on the floor.

*Feratu Noi were easy to influence—blood-craving animals, controlled by their need, easily herded to the next blood-source, but Jarboys were stronger. They needed the brainwavers to keep them in line,* Jenny Haniver explained. *Through the devices I could see everything they could, and feel what they felt. Now I feel nothing. I'm just a freak in a jar barely able to reach out when someone touches me.*

"Do not feel sorry for you," muttered Bear Foot. "But you may live for now. You could be useful." He tucked Jenny Haniver under one arm.

"What did it say?" asked Steel again.

Bear Foot looked up at him. "It control whole group. Feratu Noi and Jarboys. You can't hear it?"

"Nope."

Bear Foot handed Jenny Haniver to Steel. "Say something," he ordered it.

*What would you like me to say?*

Out of Bear Foot's hands, the telepathic voice had been softer but still audible. "Yeah . . . I heard it. Just." Steel handed it back. "But it looks like if I want to hear it, I need to be holdin' it."

"Maybe you not hear well 'cause you're dead," Bear Foot muttered.

"Yeah, but I still heard it. I'm not completely immune to mind-speak."

They stepped down from the caravan to the sight of Running Deer and Zeke freeing the last Jarboy. He collapsed to his hands and knees in the dirt, then scrambled to his feet and dusted off his leathern longjohns. With tears pouring down his sunken cheeks, he grasped Running Deer's hands and held them tightly with silent thanks. Then he thanked Zeke for his help and joined the other

Jarboys standing off to one side. They all looked overjoyed to be free and were hugging each other.

"You fellas are free to go now," Zeke told them. "Run back to yer old homes, yer old lives." He made a shooing motion with all four of his hands. When they didn't understand, he pointed towards the west. Bear Foot stepped up and signed to them what the spider-man had said.

The Jarboys' happy expressions faded, and they looked confused. They started shaking their hands. The Jarboy known as One stepped forward and signed back;

*Most of us don't remember where we came from. The brainwavers scrambled our memories. We have nowhere to go. Can we stay here and help you?*

"They want to stay," Bear Foot translated. "They can't remember their homes."

"Oh no—that's horrible," whispered Running Deer.

"We can't take all those weird little fellas with us!" Steel exploded. "We got no room!"

"Actually . . . " Zeke looked around at the half-dozen black caravans with their old steam engines. "We got plenty of room if we take all these caravans with us! They might be ugly and stink a little, but they're actually pretty sturdy."

Steel, Bear Foot and Running Deer exchanged glances. They couldn't see anything wrong with his idea. Even Running Deer was getting tired of trotting alongside the mechanical horses all day without a rest. Bear Foot signalled to the Jarboys.

*You can come. Can you drive the caravans?*

*Yes. We used to drive during the day while the Feratu Noi slept.*

"They can drive," Bear Foot exclaimed.

"Then it's settled." Zeke rubbed his various hands together. "Come on Steel—let's fetch the hosses. Running Deer and Bear Foot—you two and the boys might as well check out the rest of the vans. See if there's any water or vittles inside. We're really startin' to run low."

A few minutes later, Steel and Zeke brought the horses back from where they had left them, drawing the third one on ropes behind them. Bear Foot, followed by One, the Jarboy, came running up with a crumpled poster.

"We found this," Bear Foot unrolled it as Steel and Zeke jumped down from their mounts. It was a garishly coloured flyer, faded and stained with age. At the top it proclaimed in bright red letters: "THE AMAZING RESURRECTIONIST DR BARTON BIGELOW PRESENTS—HIS TRAVELLING CIRCUS OF BORN-AGAIN FREAKS AND CREATIONS!" The poster beneath depicted a red and black circus tent floating on a cloud of steam. Capering in front were various monsters, mutants and weird composite creatures, including a man with the body of a mechanical horse. Dr Bigelow, dressed in a red top hat and coat, was also floating on a steam-cloud with his arms outstretched. He held a cane that looked like a miniature Tesla coil in one hand, and there were lightning-bolts flying from it. "Behold!" the words continued at the bottom. "Barton's Bizarre Bazaar is on the road once more!" Underneath was a long list of towns.

The Jarboy, One, pointed to one of the first names on the list and signalled with his other hand.

"What's 'e sayin'?" demanded Steel.

"He pointed to name where they sold Sallianne to circus," Bear Foot explained. He squinted at the map. "But that was a couple of years ago. Circus would have moved on. A month or two in each place—it would be at end of tour now. Perhaps even at last town by now." He pointed to the name of the last place on the list, but he couldn't read it. He showed it to Steel.

Steel took it off him. "It says Rancid Falls," he said.

"Sounds as good a place as any to start," Zeke declared. "You find anything else useful? Food? Water?"

"No, just some jugs of blood. They smelled really bad. We poured them out," Running Deer answered. "No water at all. Just this." She handed Zeke a bottle of fine Kentessee whiskey.

Zeke grinned from ear to ear. "Oh yeah! That'll come in mighty handy! Who's gonna join me for a little drink?"

# CHAPTER 26

IN THE MORNING the crew started to pack up the camp, but the Jarboys quickly stepped in to do all the work. It was what they had been conditioned to do, and they were happy enough to do it for the people who had shown such kindness towards them. They collected all the specimens that had been left out by the Feratu Noi, unhooking the glow-worm strings and dismantling the wooden rack the decapitated corpse had been hanging from. The body had been put into one of the caravans so predators wouldn't come sniffing, but come morning it was gone.

"You didn't eat it, did you?" Zeke growled in a low voice at Steel.

"Who me?" Somehow the zombie gunslinger managed to look completely innocent.

"Come on—freshly killed body like that, you couldn't let all that meat go to waste!"

Steel looked away. "Awright. I mighta had a little nibble."

Zeke rolled his eyes. "More like an entire midnight feast!"

It only took the Jarboys half an hour to pack the camp. During that time they had fired up all the boilers and the engines were humming, ready to go. Even the mechanical horses had been prepped. Steel, Zeke and Bear Foot took the horses while the Jarboys drove the caravans. Running Deer settled herself in one of the vans with Pat's remains and a collection of old books and notes she had found while exploring. Some were just sales records, but most were interesting recipes for potions and spells. Jenny Haniver accompanied her to provide advice.

The crew now consisted of Zeke the Freak, Steel Hawl, Running Deer, Bear Foot, the Jarboys and Jenny Haniver.

At a little after eight o'clock in the morning, they rolled out in search for Dr Barton Bigelow's Marvellous Travelling Circus.

But first the group had to find water. The skins in the saddlebags had run dry and there were only a few mouthfuls left in the water jugs in the Jarboys' caravan.

The Feratu Noi hadn't cared about any fluids other than blood, so whenever they camped the Jarboys had had to locate their own water. Out in the desert, they learned how to tap water from cacti.

Not long after their departure, one of the Jarboys spotted a patch of shapely saguaros nearby. From the distance they looked exactly like curvaceous women beckoning to them with their outstretched limbs.

The convoy paused so the Jarboys could cut into the stalks of the succulents and drain the moisture from them into their water jugs. The saguaros started to wither and shrink.

One Jarboy ventured a little further afield into the cactus patch to the largest, juiciest saguaro. This one was shaped like a particularly well-built female. It looked like the queen of the crop. He tapped into its stalk and put the jug beneath to catch the precious flow of cool, crystal-clear liquid. Suddenly, the cactus' spiky arms shifted and snapped closed around the Jarboy in a deadly embrace. Its spikes were thick and sharp enough to pierce his tough leathern longjohns and sink into the pallid flesh beneath. Every drop of moisture within the Jarboy was drained from him, leaving a bony, dried-up husk hanging inside the leather longjohns.

The cactus was actually a distant, desert-dwelling relative of the spikypine. After draining the blood they needed, the Feratu Noi used these plants to suck the rest of the moisture from bodies so that they could more easily grind their bones into the powder they sold for magical potions.

It was one of the other Jarboys who noticed the desiccated corpse pinned to the cactus. He grabbed hold of Bear Foot's arm and pointed emphatically. Bear Foot scowled and drew his tomahawk.

"What'n hell's goin' on over there?" asked Steel.

"Cactus plant took Jarboy," growled Bear Foot.

Steel marched back to his horse to fetch an axe and Zeke whipped two tomahawks from his belt, brandishing them in his two upper-most hands. "Let's cut that damn demon-plant down! I for one am so sick of dang-blasted trees that're always tryin' to kill us!" He led the charge into the patch.

Suddenly the big cactus parted its stalk into two legs and took a step back. It dropped the dead Jarboy and held out its arms to stop Zeke from swinging the axe. A pair of eyes blinked petal-lids open on the succulent's "face" and a mouth appeared beneath. It spoke. "I was only protecting myself. "You took our moisture. Killed my kin."

Zeke, Steel and Bear Foot looked around at the withered and dying cacti.

"Only taking back what you took from us," the cactus continued. "We need the water too. We could have spared some, but no—you had to take it all. You killed my daughters."

Zeke lowered his axes and all the fight bled from him. "Well ma'am, we're mighty sorry but we didn't realise you were anything else but a plant."

"I *am* a plant!" it retorted. "And plants have feelings too, not just you animals."

"Hey now, wait a hot-dang minute! Who you calling an animal?" Steel hefted his axe.

Zeke grabbed his arm with a spare hand. "Now hold up there, Steel. We done her wrong and have paid the price. Nuthin' else we can do. Don't want to add insult to injury." He looked up at the cactus-woman. "Don't want no trouble, missy. We'll be getting on our way now."

They quickly gathered up the dead Jarboy, now little more than a bundle of dry sticks wrapped in leather; his bones rattled like maracas. Steel, with his superior strength, dug him a decent grave. Then they loaded up the water they'd stolen and continued on their way.

After a time Steel manoeuvred his mechanical horse up next to Zeke and said to him, "Ya know that cactus girl is followin' us."

Zeke glanced over his shoulder. Sure enough the large saguaro woman was lumbering along about fifty yards behind, kicking up a cloud of dust along the trail. "Are you surprised? Every doggone lost critter we meet wants to tag along. hell, even I did. You must be wearing some real fancypants cologne, Steel, attracting all the bees and buzzards alike."

"Harrumph," growled the zombie gunslinger, and pulled on a lever, accelerating past the snickering Zeke.

Zeke glanced over his shoulder again, hoping the cactus creature wasn't following them because she wanted revenge.

On the way southeast to Rancid Falls they paused at a hill known as Shilloh Peak so they could scatter Pat's powdered remains to the four winds. As the ashes dispersed, Running Deer walked to the edge of the cliff and looked down. During the course of the day they had left the desert and now prairielands stretched ahead. Although the thick, dry brown grass wasn't much of an improvement on the dust and sand and predatory cacti. Those tinder-dry swathes looked like they hadn't seen water in months.

But there was life. Momentarily forgetting Pat, Running Deer gaped in amazement at the sight of a herd of wild brumby centaurs galloping along, lead by a magnificent bay-coloured creature with a mane that flew in long black streamers behind him.

This is the first time Running Deer had seen any of her kind since she was a tiny child in the Kentessee woods. Even though these were horse centaurs rather than deer she still felt a connection to the magnificent beasts. Suddenly there was a painful wrench in her chest and her heart started to race. She experienced an almost overwhelming urge to run down the hill and join the pack below, to thunder across the plains with those wild things, feel the wind comb through her hair and carry the weight of her worries away into the past behind her.

Then the wind shifted and some of the floating ashes blew back into her sensitive nostrils. She blinked, her eyes started to water, and she sneezed. For a moment she was disorientated. When the dizziness passed she realised that the other centaurs had gone, disappeared into a cloud of dust on the western horizon.

She glanced over her shoulder at the Blemmya scout Bear Foot, the bizarre but kindly Zeke Sarandon, the silent, odd little Jarboys and the mysterious but lonely creature Jenny Haniver. Even the tall, surly zombie Steel, who had given her back Pat's eyes.

She realised she couldn't desert them. They were her family now. After all they'd been through she felt they'd developed a camaraderie—an odd kinship.

And she still had Pat's eyes in the silk pouch around her neck. If anyone knew how to bring back Pat, it was the magnificent Dr Barton Bigelow, renowned scientician and Travelling Circus Showman.

Running Deer detected the unique sound of Zeke's four legs thudding into the ground as he walked up behind her. He touched her gently on the shoulder. "Are you all right, Running Deer?" he asked softly.

She looked up into his kindly grey eyes. "Yes." She walked with him as he turned and joined the others. She loosened the little silk bag around her throat and held it up to Steel.

"Mr Hawl, since you took out Pat's eyes they haven't decayed at all. You must have imbued them with some of your special zombie healing magic."

He stared at her in confusion. "Er . . . maybe," he answered cautiously, wondering where she was going with this.

"Well, Dr Barton Bigelow knows how to bring back the dead. Maybe he can figure out how to regrow Pat Davison from his eyes," she continued.

Steel glanced worriedly at Zeke, and the spider-mutant gulped. Steel felt mighty uncomfortable about the suggestion and really hoped Dr Bigelow wasn't knowledgeable enough to bring someone back from just their eyeballs.

"Uh, perhaps, but there ain't no guarantee," Steel said quickly, and dropped his gaze.

"Well, I'm prepared to try," she declared. She looked at Zeke, and the spider-mutant looked down as well.

"Er . . . okay then," the old driver answered. "If that's what'll make yer happy."

"It is." And with that Running Deer tossed her long dark braids back over her shoulders and trotted back down the hill towards the caravans and mechanical horses parked at the bottom. The Jarboys, carrying Jenny Haniver, began to follow, and Bear Foot brought up the rear.

Only Zeke and Steel remained on the windswept hilltop, looking at each other in concern.

"I wish you hadn't of et him," growled Zeke.

"What—you want her to have him brought back so I gotta kill him again?" growled Steel.

"We gotta tell her the truth," retorted Zeke.

"We can't! What happened to 'we'll neva speak of it again'?" demanded Steel.

Zeke opened his mouth to retort, and then closed it. Steel was right. There was no point arguing. Steel had been a zombie hell-bent on revenge. No force in the world could have stopped him from doing what he had done.

"We can't tell her the truth about Pat," Steel continued. "That the man she loved was really a low-down dirty snake-in-the-grass who beat an old blind prospector to death with a shovel and stole his treasure."

Zeke looked away, shaking his grizzled old head. "Yeah, yer right, dammit." He turned and started off down the hill. Steel followed.

They couldn't do anything but follow to see what will happen.

# CHAPTER 27

**T**RAVELLING SLOWED DOWN with so many extras and caravans to haul along. Even though the conveyances had their own engines, they were old and not nearly as well maintained as the machines Zeke was used to. They were too big and unwieldy to travel much faster than twenty-five miles per hour. Every now and then the mechanical horses drew ahead, disappearing into clouds of dust and smoke, only to slow and realise that they had left the caravans far behind. Steel, Zeke and Bear Foot would have to stop and wait, sometimes for more than half-an-hour, for them to catch up.

When they stopped for the night the Jarboys fussed about setting up the camp; cooking, cleaning, doing the only thing they knew.

The only job Zeke had was to spin up a few hammocks for everyone to lounge in.

"I sure could get used to this," he declared as he climbed into one, and stretched out with all his legs dangling over the sides, his bottle of whiskey in one hand. Running Deer had to laugh at the comical image he made. Steel simply sniffed. But he, too, tried out his own hammock, feeling a bit incongruous lazing on the outskirts of the campsite while others worked.

Even Bear Foot climbed into a hammock for a rest.

Running Deer studied her hammock. She was all hooves and couldn't figure out a way to get onboard without flipping herself out and sending herself sprawling on the ground in a very undignified heap. She pushed the hammock with one finger. The hammock swayed precariously from even that one tiny movement. She backed away, shaking her head. No, she couldn't possibly flip herself up into that dangerous contraption.

Zeke noticed her uncertainty from his own berth. "Whassa matter, Miss Deer? Don'tcha like it? Ain'tcha even gonna try it out?"

Running Deer turned to face him and took a deep breath. "Sorry Mr Sarandon, but such raised bedding does not suit my fawnly form. I think I'll just kip down on the ground in the shade of a caravan here." She gestured towards one of the vans.

"You'll do no such thing, li'l lady!" Zeke scrambled out of his hammock with a lot of flailing of his long, spindly legs, and jumped to the ground. He pulled Running Deer's hammock down, gobbled it up, and immediately set to work spinning a large cushion of extra fine silk. When he was finished Zeke scrambled back up to his hammock.

"There yer go. How's that suit ya'?"

Running Deer marvelled at the glowing white cushion. In fact, everyone did. Even Zeke, and he'd spun the darned thing. He couldn't believe how proficient he was getting at making things.

Running Deer stepped onto the cushion and squatted down. She ran her delicate fingers over the silky-smooth material beneath. "Oh my, it's glorious! I've never felt anything so smooth, so silky before in my entire life." She luxuriated into the fabulous pillow and was very soon sucked into a deep slumber.

Steel leaned back in his hammock. "Whoo-ee, who'da thought something so fine coulda come outta yer crusty behind?"

Zeke gave Steel a dirty glare. "I'll have you know, I've spun plenty of fine silk for all the blue-blood royalty in the Old Country."

Steel burst out laughing. In fact he laughed so hard he nearly fell out of his hammock. "Haw, haw, yer ain't fooling nobody with that cockamamie bull story, Spider-boy! Yer ain't been outta that tree since I saved yer from yer own boredom!"

Zeke glared at him. "Saved *me*? I saved *you*."

"Oh let's not get inta that again."

"Well now Steel, you'd be Feratu soup if it weren't fer my ingenuity, or at the very best you'd be traipsing through the wildlands, a lost lamb chasing his own tail."

Steel pushed himself up on his elbows, making his hammock rock alarmingly. "Now see here, I take offence at your insinuations, you grumbly ol' fart!" He tried to swing a punch at Zeke, but rocked his hammock so much he flipped himself out onto the dusty ground.

Zeke hooted with laughter. "My, my, big fancy words coming from such an uncultured git!" He scrambled about on his own hammock setting it in motion, too.

Steel jumped to his feet. "Git, am I? Why I oughta-"

They both ceased their bickering when a strange, rumbling noise reached their ears. They both turned in surprise, searching for the source of the noise.

Loud contented snores were coming from Running Deer's petite mouth.

They gaped at the deersquaw's serene face as she slept peacefully, blissfully unaware of the bickering fools arguing above.

Steel returned to his hammock. "Now that's one contented little lady."

Zeke snickered. "Who'da thought such a little gal could snore so loud, eh?"

"Hey Zeke, don't suppose we's got any a that wax left? I wanna stuff some in my earholes."

Zeke grinned. "Way ahead a yer, pardner. Rolling up some now. Here yer go." Zeke passed two waxy wads to Steel. Steel closed his eyes and for a few hours actually zoned out of the real world—the closest he'd come since his death to actual sleep.

The Jarboys had been busy catching game for dinner, and cooked up a mess of desert snakes and lizards for their fare. After dinner, everyone retired to the caravans for some shut-eye. The journey had been so peaceful, so uneventful, that no-one thought to set watches. They'd assumed that once they left the desert, the biggest dangers would be behind them.

They were wrong.

There were predators in the badlands that couldn't find anything out there to eat, and so decided to venture further afield. At around four o'clock in the morning they came, sniffing around the campsite and the waste left by its occupants. They realised living beings were slumbering inside the wooden conveyances and started nosing around them, searching for a way in. These weren't stupid creatures, and as they clambered up onto the stairs they soon realised the vehicles weren't locked or latched from the inside, but simply closed. They were able to turn the handles with their half-human hands and pull the doors open.

The Jarboys, all sleeping in their usual rat-pile for warmth and comfort, didn't have a chance. Several were yanked from their van and dragged out into the open where the rest of the hungry horde could tear them apart and devour them.

However, other occupants kicked up more of a fuss. Running Deer felt something grip one of her legs and woke instantly. She was able to reach for a tomahawk as she was dragged from her bed. Out in the bright starlight she beheld the large, snarling forms and fangs that glittered like daggers. A powerful stench of animal musk rolled over her.

She drove her axe between the eyes of a very surprised werecoyote.

Bear Foot also woke as soon as he was grabbed, and was able to fight off his werecoyote before he could be pulled from his van.

Zeke wasn't so lucky. One werecoyote managed to haul him out into the open, where his long, spindly spider-limbs made perfect targets. He tried to ensnare them with his webs but a whole group got hold of him and tried to gnaw his limbs off. He was tough, but their powerful jaws managed to crack through the thick chitin covering the lower half of his body.

Although Steel was awake in his caravan, he was daydreaming about being back in the mine on Mt Boloja, and reminiscing about his Titezium discovery. He was halfway through his Clementine song when a werecoyote locked its teeth around his ankle and hauled him down the stairs before he realised what was going on. Then several more were on him, and suddenly he was being pulled apart like a ragdoll!

Pandemonium reigned all around. Skinny, mangy grey figures, each as big as a mountain lion, raced through the camp searching for food. They fought over the scraps of Jarboys and the pieces of Steel. They pawed open the doors of the other caravans and rummaged about inside, knocking specimens to the floor. They lunged at the living with their ferocious jaws, trying to snap hold of exposed limbs and other body parts.

At the edge of the campsite stood a tall, silent figure, waiting for an opportunity. For some reason the ravenous werecoyotes weren't interested in it.

Running Deer managed to kick one of her attackers and sends

him reeling into the mysterious person at the edge of the camp. The figure grabbed it in a deadly embrace. The werecoyote had time for one surprised yelp before all the moisture was drained from its body by deadly cactus spikes. Soon the creature was left, holding a rank fur-covered bag of bones.

The saguaro held the husk close with her spikes dug in deep, making sure the werecoyote's phenomenal regenerative powers couldn't bring it back.

Unfortunately, the crew were in dire danger of being overrun and eaten. Bear Foot fought furiously, but a werecoyote raked at his torso with its vicious talons, tearing his one remaining eye out.

Two of Zeke's legs were torn off and were being used in a furious tug-of-war between rival groups of werecoyotes. Zeke couldn't balance and fell on his belly. Several slavering beasts surrounded him, lunging for the more tender parts of his body—his human head and torso. He attempted to ward them off with swings of his twin tomahawks.

Steel's body parts were dragged the length and breadth of the site. Although there wasn't much meat on him, the werecoyotes still fought over the shrivelled marrow in his bones.

Running Deer found herself surrounded, about to be ravaged and eaten. Can this possibly be the end for us? she thought miserably.

Suddenly a hailstorm of bullets rained down on the marauders. Some exploded into clouds of shrapnel, tearing the monsters' bodies to shreds; others burst into flame, burning the beasts up from the inside. Others were infused with poison that reduced the creatures to desiccated husks, much like the cactus-woman had. Electrically charged bullets also fried the creatures from the inside, filling the cool pre-dawn air with the smell of ozone and the foul stench of burning fur.

Only a few were wise enough to cut their losses and flee.

The Gatling Gunslinger Sisters came spinning into the fray, firing their weapons at lightning speed, sharp-shooting at the retreating werecoyotes. They too were brought down on the outskirts of the camp. The Gatlings knew what kind of monsters they were, and made sure to set fire to every downed body they could see. Even the most mangled, decimated werecoyote corpse could be in the process of regenerating.

They even yanked the one from the cactus and set fire to it.

As they worked Steel pulled his scattered pieces together with a lot of very imaginative curse words. The flesh that had been torn off and swallowed by the werecoyotes regenerated. Zeke thought he'd need to retrieve the limbs that had been torn off, when he realised he could regenerate at least the arachnid part of him. He popped out a couple of leg replacements and managed to lurch drunkenly to his feet.

"Ugh, what a mess," Zeke declared, looking around at all the smouldering corpses. He noticed a large woman with three heads— no, three women who appeared to be stuck together—going about systematically setting all the dead werecoyotes on fire. Had the mysterious group rescued them? Zeke wanted to approach, but at the moment those females looked like they didn't want to be disturbed. He noticed Steel picking himself up—no need to worry about the zombie—and he hurried over to check on Running Deer and Bear Foot.

The five Jarboys left alive began gathering up their dead. When Steel had finished pulling himself together, he helped them to dig a grave.

Running Deer had managed to get out of the fight with only a few scratches. Bear Foot's wounds, however, were more serious and she tended to him.

The Gatlings finished cremating the werecoyotes, and satisfied none of those dogs-o'-war would be returning from the dead, they turned to look for Steel Hawl. He had just finished digging a grave, and was helping to roll the torn, mangled remains of the Jarboys in. He was bare-headed, his wispy white hair lifting in the pre-dawn breeze, and bare-chested. His pale, bony torso seemed to glow in the light of the campfire.

The Gatlings marched up to him. "Mr Hawl? Mr *Steel* Hawl?"

He straightened to look at the three beautiful women who were joined at the sides. His white eye widened. "Whoa. Yes. Who're you?"

"We are the Gatling Gunslinger Sisters; Ginger, Geraldine and Gertrude," Ginger declared, pre-empting the argument by not gesturing to the girls on either side of her. "We've been hired to bring you home."

"What?" Steel gasped. "Who wants me home?"

"Three ladies who all go by the name of Sallianne Veerhoven."

"What—the *clockworkers* want me back?" Steel gasped. "But they's just machines!" Had it really happened? Had his clockworker Salliannes achieved sentience somehow? Were they just as alive as Marilou-Belle Watkins' head had been?

"They were most adamant," Ginger continued. She reached into a belt-pouch and pulled out her copy of the contract. "Now, are you coming with us? Time's a-wasting."

By this stage Zeke had scuttled over to see what was going on.

"But . . . " Steel glanced over his shoulder at Zeke, at Running Deer bandaging Bear Foot's chest, at the Jarboys covering up the grave and all the caravans surrounding the camp. "I can't go yet—I'm on a mission to find the real Sallianne Veerhoven's body and give it a proper burial!"

"The ladies are waiting for you, Mr Hawl. They're quite beside themselves with worry." Ginger told him. Geraldine grabbed hold of one of his arms.

That certainly didn't sound like the behaviour of mindless clockworkers to him. "But . . . but I can't!" Steel spluttered, easily pulling his arm free.

Zeke scuttled unsteadily forward, still unused to his new limbs. "Ladies, ladies—Mr Hawl will be quite happy to go with you—after we finish our job tracking down the real Sallianne Veerhoven's body. We know where it is—it's with Dr Barton Bigelow's circus in Rancid Falls." He rubbed his hands together. "Shouldn't take us long to get there." He glanced at Steel.

The zombie nodded. "All right."

The three Gatlings exchanged glances, and then backed off for a brief, whispered conference.

"We shall accompany them," declared Ginger.

"What? On their damn fool mission to find and bury a body?" scoffed Gertrude.

"Everyone deserves a decent burial, Gertrude," declared Geraldine in a lofty manner very much like Ginger's.

"I'm not Gertrude!" shouted Gertrude. "I'm Geraldine!"

"Enough!" Ginger lifted her hands. "We're going with them. How the hell are we going to hold a zombie who doesn't want to come with us, anyway? You saw him dig that grave—he's ten times stronger than us!"

Gertrude and Geraldine exchanged glances and sighed. Geraldine remembered how easily he'd pulled his arm free from her grip. "All right."

They walked back to Steel and Zeke.

"We agree to your terms," they told them. "We'll even join your crew and help out—like we did tonight."

Zeke smiled. "Why, that sure would be nice o' you, ladies. And thanks for the rescue tonight, by the way. You did a mighty fine job o' skittlin' those werevarmints."

"Yeah," agreed Steel. "If you hadn't o' shown up when you did, I'm sure we all woulda been worm-food."

"Werecoyotes are a scourge that must be destroyed," declared Ginger.

At that moment the first rays of dawn stretched their golden fingers across the horizon. Running Deer did what she could for Bear Foot; washed his wounds so they wouldn't become infected and bandaged the torn socket where his one remaining eye had been. He appreciated her help, but his voice was soft, sad. He knew as a blind scout he would only be a burden on them. It would be best if he simply walked off into the prairie and let fate take him.

Running Deer blinked back tears. She realised there was something she could do that would help him far more than poultices and gauze.

She touched the little silk bag around her neck and drew the perfectly preserved blue eyes from it. "Bear Foot—I can help you," she whispered to him. "Here—take these." She took his hand and pressed the bag into them. "Pat's eyes, imbued with zombie healing magic. If you put them into your empty sockets, they should join with your flesh, help you to see again."

Bear Foot closed his fingers around the bag in amazement. "If . . . if you do this you never get Pat back."

"Yes, I know," she sniffed. "But it's better to do this and help someone than to keep them for my own selfish need."

Bear Foot gulped. "It's a noble sacrifice, Running Deer."

She removed the bloody pad from the scout's last empty eye socket. He took the eyes from the bag and held them up. Carefully he put one in the raw, weeping socket. Then he held his breath, praying to the Great Spirit that it would work. He could feel a prickling in the socket, like pins and needles. The sharp, cutting pain from the wound and the dull, throbbing ache in his brain eased as the eye's enhanced powers infused him. He saw sparks and flashes of light.

"It working!" he gasped in amazement.

"Try the other one," urged Running Deer.

He slipped the second eye into another empty socket. This one had been the last of the wounds caused by the Duoquois to heal. He held it in with the flat of his hand and began to feel more pins and needles. Could it be?

Then he blinked the first eye and blurred images appeared; the campsite illuminated by the early morning sunlight. Slowly everything became clearer, and as he looked around in wonder the other eye started to work too.

Running Deer couldn't stop the tears from coursing down her cheeks as she beheld Pat's eyes come to life in Bear Foot's face, brightening from a dull blue into a brilliant azure that competed with the lightening sky.

The others, standing nearby, marvelled at the miracle.

Bear Foot took Running Deer's hands and squeezed them in gratitude. "Thank you . . . so much," he said.

The bright blue eyes sparkled with delight in the Blemmya's golden brown chest. Running Deer swallowed her sadness and realised that she had made the right decision.

As though in agreement, a beautiful white flower popped open on the cactus girl's head.

# CHAPTER 28

**E**VEN THOUGH FOUR Jarboys had been killed during the night, the crew continued to swell. Now the group consisted of Steel, Zeke, Running Deer, Bear Foot, the Gatling Gunslinger Sisters, the Cactus Girl, five remaining Jarboys and Jenny Haniver. Not enough Jarboys remained to drive all six Feratu Noi caravans, so Zeke took over one of the driver's seats. Not wanting to abandon his Duoquois mechanical horse, which was still in good condition, he roped it to the back of his caravan to pull along behind. The Gatlings rode their own modified horse and the cactus girl continued to follow at a steady lope.

She had proven that she wasn't a hostile last night, when she had helped them with the werecoyotes, but she still wasn't ready to join the group fully. And she certainly wasn't climbing into one of those dark, evil-smelling conveyances where the sun couldn't reach her.

The bizarre convoy rolled slowly through the dry plains, heading southeast. Geraldine was on lookout duty, and armed with the multilens spyglass. During one of her routine examinations of the horizon, she spotted something large and round, floating about a hundred yards above the scrub. "Why, I do believe that's the Watkins Desertboat Zeppelin!" she exclaimed with delight."

"What luck!" cried Ginger. "Who'd have thought our route would take us right across its path!"

Leading the entourage, the Gatlings drew closer. As the zeppelin became more visible, they no longer needed the spyglass to examine it. It floated slowly above the brown grasses and stunted trees, an enormous, magnificent hydrogen filled balloon. A giant propeller spun at the back, in between two slender stacks that puffed out smoke. A large gondola hung underneath its bulbous belly, resembling a paddle steamer of the type that used to ply its trade up and down the mighty Mississip before pollution made it impossible. It had wooden balconies running around it, large glass windows and elaborate scrollwork at the bow and stern. Sounds of music, merriment and laughter issued from the contraption.

Also a hotel, it could cruise for weeks above the ground. It favoured the deserts as waste dropping on towns tended to irritate the locals. As though on cue a set of trapdoors opened in the hull, and a fresh stream of sewage and garbage splattered into the scrub. Some carrion birds that had been following the craft immediately swooped down on the mess.

Ginger Gatling signalled for the caravan to stop.

"What'n hell is that thing?" gasped Steel, his white eye wide with amazement.

"That, my dead friend, is a gambling boat where some very high stakes games of poker are played," Ginger explained.

"We got some unfinished business there," put in Gertrude.

"We know some real low-down snakes and the lowest of the low is Black-Ace McCade," explained Geraldine.

"One of the most dishonourable and nastiest gamblers in all of Westerillo," explained Ginger. "He's a cheat and a liar who uses any excuse to shoot an opponent in the gut."

"I heard o' him," said Zeke.

"Chances are he's on board that Desertboat right now." Ginger pointed. "It tours every few months or so, and McCade always makes sure he gets a berth."

"And we have a score to settle with him," growled Gertrude.

"Why?" asked Steel.

"We had an uncle—Samuel Simkins."

"Hey, he was one o' my last passengers!" cried Zeke. "Poor bastard got himself et by a huge Kissing Orchid in Duoquois country."

The Gatlings stared intently at him. "Is that how he died?" asked Ginger. "We didn't know the details."

Zeke reddened and looked away. "Sorry ladies—didn't mean to be so tactless. He died tryin' to save a little boy named Billy."

Ginger's expression softened. "He was our mother's older brother." She quickly detailed the time Samuel had almost beaten McCade with a row of aces, and finished with "He survived to live another day, but because he'd put everything he owned on the table, he also lost the family farm," Ginger continued.

"Our poor mother hadn't been the same after that preacher destroyed her Triplexia cult," said Geraldine.

"And when creditors took the farm she fell into a deep depression," added Geraldine.

"A bottomless well!" finished Ginger with a humourless laugh.

"Will you help us to get McCade?" asked Ginger.

Zeke, Steel, Running Deer and Bear Foot all exchanged glances. They all nodded.

"Yeah, sure," answered Zeke. "You did a fine job on those werecoyotes."

"Excellent," said Ginger, rubbing her hands together. "What's the best way to bring down a gambler like McCade?"

"We make him lose," answered Geraldine.

"Big time," said Gertrude. "We're gonna need that telepathic critter you got there." She pointed to Jenny Haniver, which Running Deer had taken to carrying around.

*I will help as much as I can,* Jenny Haniver answered, *but my range is limited.*

"We'll put it on the table and tell everyone it's our lucky charm," Ginger explained. "We'll need it to fight McCade's *own* lucky charm!"

"What lucky charm?" asked Zeke worriedly.

"He has a slinky new friend. Calls her Anna Conda," explained Geraldine.

"She's a big ol' boa constrictor snake with the sweet face of a woman and lots of thick curly hair," put in Gertrude. "She wears a cute li'l hat perched on top. She flickers a forked snake tongue and wraps herself around Black-Ace McCade's shoulders. She's his lady luck. But she is more than just luck, she helps him cheat."

"She is a real charmer. A snake charmer," said Ginger. "She speaks in dulcet tones and compliments people. There's a mesmerising quality to her charming voice that literally hypnotises people. Players at the table go into a trancelike state and that's when she slithers around to check out their cards. Then she slinks back around to McCade and flashes the information to him."

"Flashes? Whaddaya mean by that? She some sort o' mind-reader too?" asked Steel.

"No. She has the scaly skin of a snake but her skin is special. It contains coloured cells like a cuttlefish's. Anna is able to form her colours into the numbers and suits of the opponents' cards. She does this where only McCade can see them. In this way McCade always knows what cards his opponents are holding. No need to play with a marked deck like he used to."

"Dad-sizzle!" exclaimed Zeke. "I neva knew that about cuttlefish!"

Steel looked puzzled, "What's a cuttlefish?"

"I do a lot of reading," Ginger declared, ignoring Steel's confusion. "While my two sisters here are drinking and flirting with boys, I'm trying to expand my mind."

Geraldine and Gertrude scowled at her. "We's at least havin' some fun!" growled Gertrude.

"I'm wonderin' how you can read while they're havin' fun, bein' so . . . close together," Zeke asked.

Ginger glared at him. "I've had years to practise. Besides, I know how to have fun too! I just don't do it all the time like some people! Now, as I was saying—cuttlefish skin can combine basic colours to form more complex hues and moving patterns. One cuttlefish has maybe ten million little colour cells in its skin, and it can control every single one. If you turn some on, but leave others switched off, you can create patterns."

"Enough with the scientic lesson. We need to get started." Steel pointed at the zeppelin, which had already moved some way ahead.

Ginger rolled her eyes. "Yes, my dead friend. But first we need some way of getting into that thing."

Bear Foot lifted a hand. "I know a way." He ran over to the Feratu Noi caravan that contained the cache of stolen weapons. He retrieved the grappling hook and raced after the slowly moving blimp. He was well versed in the hook's use and whirled it in one fist as he ran. He hurled it with all his might at the passing zeppelin and it caught and locked around the lowest balcony's rear railing. There were some people out and about, but fortunately none at the rear.

Steel made sure his hat was sure, tucked Jenny Haniver into his coat and leapt onto the rope, climbing quickly hand over hand up to the railing. The Gatlings clung to Zeke as he scrambled up the rope with the adept skill of an arachnizoid. At the top they clambered over the wooden rail and were able to slip into the Desertboat Zeppelin's gambling hall without being observed.

The main hall was thickly carpeted and lit by electric lights. A small band was playing in one corner and barmaids in tight corsets and pantaloons were scurrying about, taking orders for drinks. They moved quickly and jerkily—Steel had now seen enough clockworkers to realise that they were robots too. And so was the man behind the bar. Even the band members in the corner were clockworkers, programmed to repeat a certain sequence of tunes. They all had smooth silk skin, serene, expressionless faces and perfect doll bodies. Not one single shiny hair was out of place.

"How come no-one seems to care that we've just dropped in?" asked Zeke as another barmaid hurried past him without even looking at him. She was carrying at least a dozen beers in each hand and not spilling a drop.

"Everyone's too busy gambling." Ginger gestured around at the crowded tables where a number of different games were in progress. "And the staff don't really care who gets on board so long as they bring plenty of cash. Losers are literally tossed out over the sides, regardless of where the zeppelin is. IOUs aren't accepted or even tolerated. And yes—all the staff members are Watkins clockworkers. They're much better at enforcing the rules than humans."

"The machines don't care if players trance out at McCade's table so long as the House gets its cut," added Geraldine.

"Now let's watch for a bit," suggested Ginger, and they sauntered closer.

McCade, being such a famous rogue, had a small crowd gathered around his table. Some were just watching, while others were waiting to get into the game. All appeared to be mesmerised. Black-Ace McCade was a tall, very well-built fellow in a black coat, expensive-looking shirt and silkshot waist-coat. He was wearing a bowler hat and had a cigar stuck in one corner of his mouth. He looked every part the high-class crook with his numerous glittering diamond rings, golden cuff-links, pocket watch and a long thin curled moustache. The snake woman, Anna Conda, was undulating behind him, her lovely face hovering above the table. Her scaly skin was indeed flickering with interesting colours and patterns.

Still hidden inside Steel's long leather coat, Jenny Haniver tuned into the players' thoughts and telepathically informed Zeke, Steel and the Gatlings what was really going on.

"Damn cheater! I told ya he was a cur, a cad and a no-good scoundrel," growled Gertrude Gatling under her breath.

"Shhh!" hissed Geraldine.

"How we gonna get into the game?" asked Zeke. "I dunno about you, but I ain't got two Lincoln-skins to rub together!" Then he remembered the dress in his saddlebags and reddened. A couple of those expensive gems would have sufficed.

Steel felt around inside his coat and then checked his pockets. "Dang it, I had some, but I must of left it down below."

Ginger rolled her eyes at the pair's lack of preparation. "Lucky for you lads I have this." She produced the five hundred dollars she'd gotten from the Salliannes. "Next question—who'll be our player?"

"I got plenty of hands!" Zeke lifted them all up with a laugh.

Ginger rolled her eyes again while her sisters snickered. "McCade's a gut-shooter. Looks like a bullet in the belly might still hurt you, spider-boy."

"I ain't too worried 'bout that." Zeke replied, "But tryin' to fit this big ol' spider's behind in one a them little wooden chairs might be a bit of a problem."

Gertrude and Geraldine snickered again.

"He can shoot me in the guts till I shit bullets but it won't bother me none," Steel offered, patting his stomach.

"In that case—you're our player." Ginger handed him the money.

Zeke grabbed Steel's arm. "Afore you go in." The spider-man stuffed a bit of chewing tabackie into his mouth and softened it up. Then he gave the mushy wad to Steel. "So that snake strumpet can't put the whammy on ya."

Steel stuffed it into his ears.

Although the Vykings lost the Transdimensional War of 1808, there were some who said they got in the last shot in the form of some awful, irreversible curse, blasted from the hammer of Thor himself. Just after the last of the Vykings' steam-powered longboats was sent to the bottom of the ocean, a strange tornado started up in New

Haven and made its way inland across the countryside, ripping up towns and leaving mass destruction in its wake.

Since that day it had not stopped. Each time the tornado trashed a village or tore up a farm, people tried to claim they were the victims of a new, different storm. But it wasn't. It was the same tempest. And it had been blowing for seventy-two years!

It stayed mainly in the Mighty Desert, slowly moving in a random route around the area. It was believed to be the reason why the region was largely desert and prairie, with only the hardiest plants surviving its constant rampage. Only the toughest of people dared to eke out a living along the fringes of the storm's hunting grounds. Nomadic peoples who could pack up and move in a hurry.

Occasionally, it swirled out to other parts, even as far as crossing the mighty Mississip, drawing up water and all sorts of fish into its hungry core. But lately the mighty Mississip didn't contain so much water as poisonous run-off from all the machine-powered plantations that now lined the river's shores. This effluent had killed all the fish and mutated all the alligators into huge mutant man-eating freaks with far too many limbs and multiple rows of fangs like kitchen knives.

The tornado sucked up the polluted water and enormous gators and twirled them high in the sky as it continued along its endless and deadly path of destruction.

# CHAPTER 29

S TEEL EASED HIS way through the captivated crowd surrounding the game and bought his way into McCade's game with the five hundred he'd been given. Black-Ace beamed at the large wad of notes and invited him to sit. The zombie slid into his chair at the table while the others gathered behind him. Steel reached into his coat and placed the Jenny Haniver jar on the side of the card table.

"What'n hell's that?" McCade sneered. "That is ugly enough to bluff a buzzard off a meat wagon!"

"It's his lucky charm." Zeke answered for him, since Steel was practically deaf with the tabackie blocking his ears.

"Must be *damn* lucky fer him ta keep such an ornery looking varmint like that!" McCade scoffed. "Although, him being a zombie, he couldn't 'ave been too lucky in life! Hahaha!" McCade hooted with laughter as he tugged on one end of his long black moustache. He let it go and it sprang back into a curl.

"Hey, no need ta get all uppity and insulting. We came to play a friendly game, is all," Zeke put in.

Steel realised he was being insulted, but he still couldn't hear a thing with the chewing tabackie stuffed in his ears. *What's he sayin'?* he laboriously sent to Jenny Haniver.

*You don't want to know,* the telepathic creature whispered back. *It will only make you angry. Best to stay calm and focused on what you're doing.*

McCade gave a brilliant smile, displaying a lot of even white teeth, some capped with gold. "And friendly I shall be. When I take all yer money! Hahaha!" He stroked the ornate pocket watch dangling from his chest, the same watch that had once belonged to Samuel Simkins.

All the Gatlings, standing behind Steel, gritted their teeth in fury.

Their fingers itched to draw their sixguns. Oh, how they all wanted to shoot an ace right between McCade's eyes.

The game began.

A few hands later and McCade was winning easily against all the other suckers who kept trancing out due to Anna's sweet siren sounds and hypnotic movements. The fact she kept snaking around the table and sliding up behind them, purring sweet nothings in their ears, didn't seem to bother them. Her scales continued to glitter and shift colours, making patterns that were almost as entrancing as her soft, melodic voice.

Steel followed their lead and started to act out of it. This was easy, since no-one knew where'n hell his single weird white eye was looking anyway. He played conservatively, not losing much but waiting for the opportunity of a big kill. He was actually looking forward to delivering the coup de grâce, and was more excited than he had been for a long time. Perhaps, if they couldn't find Sallianne's body, he could continue "living".

Once again he wondered if he could continue on, exploring the world he had surely neglected during his life. During the short period he had pursued Pat south, and the last few weeks he had spent searching for Sallianne, he had seen far more of the world than he had during his entire life in the Mt Boloja mine.

On the prairie below, those who'd remained behind roped up the horses to the caravans and kept the procession moving slowly after the drifting Desertboat Zeppelin. Running Deer and Bear Foot were able to keep an easy pace with the convoy. But as the day progressed into afternoon, they noticed the sky start to darken with thick, black clouds billowing in. The winds kicked up, bringing with it colder weather. Tumbleweeds started to wheel and race across the ground.

"Dust-devil!" Bear Foot exclaimed in horror.

The crew could do nothing but watch and wait in fear. They realised as the blimp picked up speed and started to move away that they wouldn't be able to continue following it. Trapped on the ground, they would have to find shelter. Bear Foot pointed to a rocky outcrop, and they directed the Jarboy drivers to make with all speed for the dark, secluded space underneath. As they hunkered down they hoped their people in the zeppelin would be all right.

Finally, an opportunity arrived. Jenny Haniver whispered in Steel's mind that he could beat McCade. Steel pushed all his chips into the middle of the table. It was a decent pile. He had been accruing them slowly during the course of the game.

McCade stared at the large pile and frowned. He wasn't playing with his moustache or watch or laughing any more. Jenny Haniver whispered to Steel that Anna had not been able to read his cards because he was playing too close to his ribcage. The snake woman also realised that he had only been faking trancing out because none of her tricks had incurred him to lower his hands even a little. She had transmitted her concerns to McCade, and he was starting to become antsy.

With a flourish, the zombie cowboy laid all his cards on the table. They made a royal flush. "Beat that!" he declared with a triumphant grin.

Steel hauled in the pot. But McCade had one more ace up his sleeve: his six shooter aimed at Steel's gut. He fired, blasting Steel's gizzards out through his back and splashing them all over his chair. But Steel quickly sucked them back into his body.

"What tha-?" McCade exclaimed as he rose to his feet in a temper, bringing his pistol out from under the table. But before he could fire at Steel's head, the window behind him smashed into a million shards. Something massive flew through it into the room.

Despite the best efforts of the clockworker crew to pilot the Desertboat Zeppelin out of the path of the perpetual tornado, it still managed to cross the blimp's path. The twister's two-hundred mile per hour winds catapulted an extremely ornery mutated gator right into the gondola. The massive creature, measuring twenty feet from nose to tail and possessing six legs, landed in the gambling hall amidst a glittering shower of glass and immediately went on a

BASED ON AN ILLUSTRATION BY TANYA NICHOLLS

rampage. On seeing a table of soft, juicy humans right in front of it, it immediately snapped its enormous fang-filled jaws down on the closest victim and swallowed it whole. Fearless clockworkers, programmed to preserve the source of the Desertboat's income, rushed in to help and were catapulted by the berserk creature's thick thrashing tail. One or two were even sent flying out the windows.

The Gatlings were trained warriors and didn't even flinch. They immediately opened fire on the monster and made mince-meat of it.

But they reacted just a tad too late for Black-Ace McCade. It was he the massive beast had managed to gobble up whole before the Gatlings' exploding bullets ripped into its thick, leathery hide.

At last he had no more aces up his sleeve.

The zeppelin creaked and strained as it struggled to avoid the approaching tornado. But it seemed no matter which direction it took, the whirlwind unerringly followed. The blimp was inexorably drawn up into the ferocious winds and spun around at a furious pace, far too quickly for its fragile infrastructure or its struggling steam engines. Whole sections of the wooden gondola were torn away and blasted to shrapnel as it was whirled around the outside of the tornado and then sent flying, nose-diving towards the ground. Anna Conda was sucked out of a smashed window and whipped into a knot by the ferocious gales. The winds flung her high in the sky and hurled her many miles away.

The Gatlings raced toward the dead gator, each gleefully wielding a huge knife.

Zeke scuttled forward on his four legs. "Quickly now! Everybody, jump aboard!"

Steel snatched up Jenny Haniver from the table and jumped onto Zeke's back. He stuffed the jar back into his coat and wrapped his arms around Zeke's wiry torso.

"This ain't the time to be making yerselves gator-skin boots!' Zeke yelled at the Gatlings as they tore into the massive dead creature with their blades. "Get aboard afore this thing crashes and we's all dead!"

The Gatlings dived across the room and grabbed a hold of Zeke.

Zeke shot across the room and launched himself out of the broken window. He leapt onto the splintered balcony outside and spun himself around. Balancing precariously on the disintegrating wood, he shot a parachute of silk from his spinnerets that the wind immediately caught hold of. He released the railing and was able to float safely to Earth.

Scarcely had Zeke soared off into the maelstrom when the Desertboat Zeppelin caught fire and crashed into the ground. It went up in a massive ball of fire. Tiny black dots that resembled people and robots could be seen diving overboard and fleeing from the conflagration.

"Oh, the machinery!" declared Steel as he scrambled down from Zeke's back. "That musta bin worth a fortune." Suddenly realising that he had failed, he turned to the Gatling Gunslinger Sisters, who were also dismounting from Zeke's abdomen. "Sorry ma'ams, but I didn't get a chance to collect my winnings afore we dived." Steel spread his hands. "It was all I could do to grab Jenny Haniver."

Geraldine, the closest, looked up at him and gave him a wan smile. "S'all right, dead man. T'was worth it to see the look on that black-hearted cur's face when you pulled yer guts back into yer belly!" She laughed.

"Then he got himself et by that smiling gator!" Gertrude laughed.

Ginger turned. "I would have paid twice the price of admission for that show."

Steel managed a smile back, glad he hadn't messed up too badly.

Ginger slipped a hand into one pocket of her jeans. "Besides, we got what we were looking for. Uncle Samuel's pocket-watch. It's been in the family for generations." She held it up. It was beautifully crafted, with several faces and numerous hands that told the time, the day, the month and even the year. It had a solid gold casing with elaborate scrollwork carved into it.

The perpetual tornado roared off across the landscape, ripping up more towns, sparing some, destroying others. Debris included robot parts from the zeppelin's staff. Bear Foot pointed to shattered and scattered rubble as the caravans continued their journey across the plains. The storm appeared to be continuing in the direction they wanted, so they decided to follow in its destructive wake in case they discovered something useful.

The trail took them almost directly towards the large country town of Rancid Falls, at the foothills of the Dragonback Mountains. The famous town had been almost obliterated by the ferocious twister. Only a few of the hardier stone dwellings still remained, but their shutters were broken and their windows were gone. All signs had been blown away and papers fluttered and danced across the deserted town streets. Where the circus had been erected, on a common south of the establishment, only detritus remained.

This was the first time since 1808 the perpetual tornado had travelled this far east.

The tornado had done its work well. Dr Barton Bigelow's Bizarre Bazaar was gone. Only shreds of red and black cloth from his big top remained, along with some broken wooden poles, some carved panels and wheels from various caravans. A couple of posters fluttered in the wind like forgotten birds.

The circus had been destroyed.

Thinking it was a new carnival, locals came out to greet the crew's convoy as it rolled into town, but they couldn't say what had become of Dr Bigelow's circus, only that it was gone. All its members appeared to have been whisked away by the deadly tornado, never to be seen again.

Steel wandered miserably around the decimated site, struggling to come to terms with what had happened. He had thought he would be all right with the concept of failure. During the past few days he had actually started to enjoy "living" again. He had even begun thinking about all the things he could do if he didn't find Sallianne's body.

But now, staring at the flattened grass, torn up sods and rubbish, he felt his dead heart sink down into his chest, as though the tendons that had been holding it up had been severed. He wanted to sink into the ground, fall into blackness, and forget this entire episode had happened. He slumped, staring down at the toes of his scuffed old boots.

# CHAPTER 30

**O**NLY ZEKE HAD the courage to approach the depressed zombie standing in the middle of the ravaged circus. He scuttled cautiously over to him and placed a taloned hand onto one of his shoulders. "We can still go on," he said in a low voice.

Slowly Steel turned his head to look at the scarred face of Zeke behind him. "What?" he asked softly.

Zeke pointed at the shattered remains of tents and caravans, a few coloured paper streamers still drifting in the breeze. The trail led off in a south-westerly direction. "We can follow the trash. We still might find somethin'."

"Doubt it."

"C'mon Steel—Dr Bigelow was a great scientician! He knew how to bring back the dead and could create the weirdest of freaks. You don't think he would've had some way of survivin' a storm like this?"

Steel stared despondently, but then Zeke's words finally managed to worm themselves into his brain. There was still a chance. Why was he giving up so quickly? Hadn't he just started to enjoy his new journey? Why couldn't he keep going? "Awright," he answered softly. Slowly he straightened up. "Let's git outta here."

The crew climbed back onto their mounts and into their caravans and followed the path of destruction through the ragged foothills of the Dragonback Mountains. Not long after Bear Foot spotted, with his keen new eyes, a large dead cottonwood tree with something odd tangled in its broken branches. He ordered the entourage to stop so they could check it out.

He jumped down, followed by Steel, Zeke and Running Deer. With their weapons drawn, they approached the strange thing, which appeared to be writhing, spitting and rapidly changing colours.

Bear Foot and Running Deer hadn't seen this creature before, and they both brandished their tomahawks in preparation to bash its brains in. But Zeke, and surprisingly Steel, stayed their hands.

"It's Anna Conda!" exclaimed Zeke in amazement. "Black-Ace McCade's snake companion!"

The enormous boa constrictor was all knotted up and dishevelled and wrapped around the branches of the tall rotten old tree, so entwined she couldn't escape. She twisted and struggled, but couldn't break free from the clutching branches. She was stuck fast.

Zeke was about to scramble up the tree to try and cut her out, but Steel caught his arm. "She's a goner, buddy. My way's quicker."

He hefted his axe.

Zeke stared at him in horror. "Surely, ya not gonna kill her?" he gasped.

"No, you fool!" Steel used his axe to chop down the entire dead tree. "Now everyone can help to release her."

Bear Foot, Running Deer and the remaining Jarboys hurried forward to free Anna from the gnarly branches and unknot her. "What? You thought I was gonna eat her brains?"

"Er—yeah!"

Steel rolled his white eye at him. "She mighta bin tasty, but I don't wanna eat everyone I meet!"

Anna Conda was badly injured from the fall and suffering from bruises and deep cuts from the rough, jagged bark. Running Deer tended to her wounds and then stretched her out in the relatively empty caravan that had been used as the Jarboys' barracks. Anna lifted her head to look up into Running Deer's kind doe eyes, unable to believe the generosity of these people—the same ones whom she and Black-Ace had tried to cheat and kill. "Thank you," she whispered.

They hit the road again, continuing their search for Dr Bigelow's Circus.

The trail led them deeper into the Dragonback Mountain Foothills. The area was close to where Running Deer had grown up, so many years ago, and it brought back memories of her early childhood. She wondered if any of her kind had survived the Red Plague. Then she wondered if the disease was still lurking in these dark, misty forests, waiting for one more centaur to infect so it could start its evil reign once more. She shuddered and put the black thoughts from her mind.

The perpetual tornado's path of destruction was easy to follow here; uprooted trees, torn up dirt, planks of wood from circus caravans, shreds of canvas—and there, around a bend in the road—three rather battered looking steam-driven wagons, their once bright sides scratched and splattered with mud. But some effort had been made to clean the sign on one, and the words "Dr Barton Bigelow's Bizarre Bazaar" were clearly legible.

"It's here!' cried Steel as he brought his mechanical horse to a stop. He jumped down, and the others followed his lead.

But as Steel approached the bedraggled little collection of caravans, a tall, lean figure dressed completely in black glided out from seemingly nowhere to block their path. It wore a long black coat and a wide-brimmed hat shadowed its face, but did nothing to hide its horrific features or the long, webbed hands folded in front of its chest. Pointy front fangs protruded from its pasty purple lips and its pale, translucent skin was networked by spidery red and blue veins.

It was a Feratu Noi, looking mean and evil as a werecoyote.

The Gatling Gunslinger Sisters had their pistols out and pointed at the creature's head within the blink of an eye. Steel had his rifle whipped out and aimed at the creature's chest within one second. Zeke, Running Deer and Bear Foot reacted next, brandishing various pistols, axes and tomahawks.

Suddenly another figure appeared and stepped out in front with its arms upraised. "It's all right, it's all right! He's harmless. Made sure of it myself."

The newcomer was dressed all in red. A red top hat, a red coat, waistcoat and trousers. Even red gloves. His waistcoat was embroidered all over with glittering gems and stones. And in one hand he held a staff with the miniature Tesla coil on top, although it wasn't spitting sparks right now. He had curly grey hair that poked out behind his ears and was wearing a pair of half-moon spectacles on the end of his long, pointy nose.

Dr Barton Bigelow whipped the stovepipe hat from the Feratu Noi's head, bearing the creature's bald skull. There was a brainwaver attached, larger and more advanced-looking than the ones that had been used to control the Jarboys. It had several dials and attachments, more switches, and a number of wires disappearing beneath the vampire's pallid skin. One of the protuberances looked like a camera.

"Edmond here's my right hand man." Dr Bigelow patted the creature's bony shoulder. "He helps me run the show . . . what's left of it, which ain't much now." The doctor laughed humourlessly. "Plus he's a top exhibit in his own right. Puts the fear into the womenfolk especially."

He stepped forward to pinch Running Deer's cheek with his gloved fingers. It was then everyone noticed that he had an extra finger on that hand. "Ain't that right, little lady?"

Running Deer lunged at his fingers to bite them off and he only just managed to snatch them back. "Whoah! She almost took one off just then! I would've ended up with five instead of six!" He wiggled his hand. "Feisty one, ain't she?"

"You betcha," Zeke agreed with a grin. Running Deer continued to glare, clearly not amused.

Dr Bigelow sized up the crew and rubbed his hands together. He had an extra finger on the other hand too. "So what can I do for you fine folks?"

"Did you buy the body of a woman from some Feratu Noi in the desert a few years back?" asked Steel coldly.

Dr Bigelow looked up at him. "Are you askin' about the body of Sallianne Veerhoven?"

"That's the one. Do you still have it?" Steel insisted. "I want it back. I wanna give her a decent burial."

Dr Bigelow patted Steel on one arm. "Relax, my dead friend. I can do better than that." He hurried over to one of his dilapidated vans and knocked on the door. It creaked open and a familiar figure stepped into the doorway, blinking in the late afternoon sunlight.

Steel could not believe his eyes. His one milky eye nearly popped out of his skull.

Dr Bigelow had resurrected Sallianne Veerhoven as a zombie. Oh, she was a little worse for wear, having lost some of her thick blonde curls and one of her eyes had sunken in and rolled back in her head, but Steel didn't care. She was still the most beautiful thing he had ever seen! And now she was back from the dead, to stay with him forever and ever!

Steel's face broke into a huge grin, the biggest smile his friends had ever seen. Only Dr Barton Bigelow had the know how to perform such miracles.

"Sallianne!" he croaked.

She smiled back at him. She was missing some teeth too. He raced across the distance separating them and caught her up in a huge embrace, swinging her around and around. Dr Bigelow was also grinning from ear to ear.

But at that point the Gatlings moved up, all business. Gertrude placed a hand on Steel's shoulder, but he was too caught up in a kiss with Sallianne to notice. "Mr Hawl, if you could stop trying to eat her face for a moment, a word."

Steel tore himself away and released Sallianne, annoyed at the disturbance to his wonderful reunion. The zombie Sallianne also looked annoyed, and folded her arms. "Who are you three?" she asked in a soft, raspy voice like Steel's.

"You do remember our agreement, don't you?" Ginger asked.

"What agreement?" Sallianne growled.

"You must now come back with us to Nova Cyrus," said Gertrude.

"You've gotta be delivered to Sallianne Veerhoven so we can get paid," added Geraldine. "We have a contract."

Steel held out a hand. "Lemme see that there contract."

Ginger extracted it from one pocket and handed it to him.

Steel unrolled it and looked it up and down then handed it to Zeke. "What's it say?"

Zeke scrutinised the document. "Don't say nothin' 'bout goin' back to Nova Cyrus. Just says you gotta be returned to Sallianne Veerhoven."

"Well, here is Sallianne Veerhoven in the rotting flesh." Steel gestured towards her with pride, and she smiled in triumph. "You ladies've completed your job. Your services are no longer required."

"Not so fast, Mr Hawl," snapped Ginger, not looking amused. In fact, none of the Gatlings looked amused. "There's the matter of our money."

"Well, technically I still own the armadillo ranch and the bordello, so the money's not a problem." Steel spread his hands.

"Mr Hawl, if we don't get paid right now we'll take you a hollerin' and a kickin' back to Nova Cyrus and get our money there!" shouted Gertrude.

"Take me back a-hollerin' and a-kickin'? I'd sure like to see you ladies try!" growled Steel.

Geraldine wagged a finger in his face. "Mr Hawl, I'm sure we could blow you into a couple of small, manageable pieces, separate them into bags, and take you back like that!"

Dr Barton Bigelow hurriedly stepped into the rapidly escalating argument. "Please, please, *please!* Let's not be a-fussin' and a-feudin' on what's supposed to be a happy occasion!" He was smiling, but the Tesla-coil head of his staff was glowing and a rising hum could be heard coming from the coils of wire wrapped around the shaft. Those flying sparks in the picture on the poster had been a real representation of what it could do. The Gatlings and Steel wisely backed apart. "I may have lost my circus but I aim to rebuild," the twelve-fingered showman continued. "This motley crew that's just rolled in is just what I need to get started. They can all stay and become part of my new troupe of sideshow performers." He turned to Steel, dipping his other hand into the pocket of his elaborate red waist-coat. "Mr . . . Hawl, is it? Here." He held out a large wad of notes. "Fifteen hundred if you and your crew will help to rebuild my travelling circus."

Steel stared down at it. He could either return to Nova Cyrus to a luxurious brothel full of mechanical Salliannes all willing to do his every bidding, or stay here with a dilapidated circus and the real zombie Sallianne. He didn't even pause before taking the money and handing it straight to the Gatlings. "I'm stayin'." With that he walked back over to the real Sallianne and slipped an arm around her bony shoulders.

"You fine ladies are also welcome to stay," Dr Bigelow invited the Gatlings. "I'm sure your . . . unique stature will draw in crowds from all around."

None of the Gatlings looked amused. "We don't perform like trained animals, Doctor," Ginger declared.

"We have better things to do," Gertrude added.

"Our paths will cross again one day, we're sure," said Geraldine. Then they turned to walk back to their horse.

Steel realised he was still holding the contract. "Wait!" he shouted, running after them.

"You changed your mind? You want to come back with us?" Ginger asked in surprise.

"Naw. I had me an idea. Anyone got somethin' to write with?"

Dr Bigelow produced a strange-looking pen that appeared to have ink inside it. "Will this do? It's my own invention. I call it a self-inker."

"Thanks." Steel dictated to Zeke, who flattened the contract out on the side of one of the caravans and scrawled on the back. Steel signed it with a flourish. His name being the only thing he knew to write.

"Here ya go." He handed it to Ginger Gatling. "It says 'I, Steel Ira Hawl, am hereby handin' complete ownership of my armadillo ranch and bordello over to all the clockworker Sallianne Veerhovens'. Can ya make sure they get it?"

"Clockworkers? Owning property? I don't think the locals will be happy about that, but who are we to argue?" Ginger rolled the paper up and tucked it into her jeans pocket.

With that the Gatlings hopped aboard their horse and chugged off into the sunset.

"Toodles!" shouted Zeke, giving a cheery wave.

Steel turned back to the zombie Sallianne. "I got no more use for that place. There's only one thing I want more than anything else in the world."

Steel Hawl went down on one knee. "Sallianne Veerhoven, will you marry me?"

"Of course, I will!" answered Sallianne.

Those who had gathered around the outside to watch cheered, clapped and whooped. He got up and hugged her again. This time he could kiss her undisturbed. It lasted for over a minute.

When Steel released her, he glanced around at the grinning audience, realising that not only had he gathered an instant circus but an entire family. "Zeke," he walked over to the old coach-driver, "will you be my best man?"

"Of course! Cripes, I never bin anyone's best man before!" He clapped Steel across the shoulder. "In fact, I got the perfect weddin' dress right here! Found it in the bags of my hoss." He raced over to his mount and rummaged around inside. With a whoop he yanked out a silk package. "It's a little burned, but I think that'll just make it look even better!"

Sallianne unwrapped the glittering bejewelled gown that had belonged to Marilou-Belle Watkins. It was indeed a little worse for wear, having been last worn by an exploding clockworker, but it looked perfect on the zombie woman. "I love it!" she gasped. "It's magnificent!" She flung her arms around Zeke's shoulders and kissed him on the cheek. "Ya know Mr Sarandon, I don't remember you havin' quite that many legs!"

Pleased with the new addition to his circus, Dr Barton Bigelow began inspecting the dilapidated steam-driven caravans. Inside one of the wagons he discovered the snake woman sleeping soundly. As he peered down at her, she stirred from her slumber. Blinking, she looked up at him.

A broad grin spread across his face. "Welcome home . . . Anna."

Anna Conda stared blankly at the tall man resplendently dressed all in red. Then she smiled and flickered her fork tongue.

# CHAPTER 31

**T**HE SHOW HAD to go on!

The travelling circus, now consisting of the three dilapidated wagons Dr Bigelow had managed to salvage from the storm, and the six Feratu Noi caravans from the desert, rolled into Mojo County, down a ways from Rancid Falls. The perpetual tornado had spared it.

The crazy procession of freaks travelled slowly down Main Street of Mojo Town handing out flyers to everyone they met. Performers darted out to stick posters onto walls and windows. All proclaimed that Dr Barton Bigelow's Bizarre Bazaar would be performing this very night in a common field on the outskirts of town. The townsfolk cheered and clapped, mesmerised by the strange, brightly-clad figures capering about on the street and on top of the caravans. They had heard tales of this mysterious travelling show, but they had never seen it appear in their quiet little backwater.

On a common field just outside of town, the circus set up a camp. Although Dr Bigelow had lost everything in the tornado, Zeke's special web spinning skills provided them with a massive new silk tent. It took a lot out of him, and he needed to eat nearly a whole cow to recover, but by the time nightfall arrived, he was nearly back to his old self. Strings of the Feratu Noi's glow-worms were strung up around the tent's entrance and lit it up like festive decorations. More were hung inside to provide illumination.

Over the entrance of the big tent was stretched out the skin of the werecoyote that had been desiccated by the cactus woman. It was a little singed, but had been cured and tanned by Bear Foot.

Everyone worked hard setting up makeshift displays and entertainments to provide amusement until the big show. Some of Dr Bigelow's sideshow entertainments had survived, and there were a few games to amuse the locals; a ring-toss, some knock 'em down pins, a shooting gallery and test your strength booth.

But it didn't take Steel's crew long to figure out that one Jarboy was missing. They went through the Feratu Noi caravans looking for him, but found only Anna Conda fast asleep in their caravan, all her wounds miraculously healed and gone. All her multicoloured scales glittered like jewels, but only a few patterns shifted slowly across her body; dreams acting out on her skin. There was a suspicious bulge in the middle of her snake belly, and they realised that she must have swallowed the Jarboy whole.

So now there were only four of the poor little fellows left.

While everyone was working outside, Dr Barton Bigelow had been hiding out in his trailer. His caravan was full of strange fandangled equipment—everything he had managed to grab just before that accursed tornado hit. Shelves reached from the floor to the ceiling, crammed with boxes of equipment. A portable version of his amazing electro-resurrector machine took up the wall at the back, all glowing columns of light flanking a wooden cabinet studded with heavy brass rivets. Large brass dials flickered constantly. Several two-pronged switches were at the moment in the "down" position. A drawer at the centre of the device stuck out with a few wires dangling from it, as though something had recently been removed. A few tendrils of steam were still issuing from it. Dr Bigelow stood nearby, grinning and rubbing his gloved, six-fingered hands together. He turned to the tall, sallow-faced Feratu Noi standing beside him.

"It worked, Edmond, it worked! My first experiment with my new temporary set up!"

*Those moon crystals must have had sufficient power,* his vampire assistant sent via his souped-up brainwaver.

"You know what this means, Edmond? My experiments can continue while we're on the road! There's no end to what I could accomplish!"

*Yes, of course, sir,* came the droll reply, *but you are still restricted to the size of your device.*

"Oh, that's not a problem, Edmond. The money this new batch

will pull in will surely enable me to buy a much bigger, better caravan!" He rubbed his hands together again. "Now let's get this party started!"

*Yes sir.*

Outside, excited people of all ages, from all walks of life, were starting to line up outside the main tent for the first show. Edmond appeared suddenly, dressed in his long black cloak and broad-brimmed hat, pale-faced with his spidery veins standing starkly out on his cheeks. He raised his arms, darted forward and hissed, baring his deadly fangs.

Gasps and squeals of fright rippled through the assembled crowd. Some people jumped and darted back a few steps. A small child dropped his peanuts and howled. A woman groaned and swooned into the arms of her startled husband.

"Oh my goodness, is that one of those awful Body Snatchers?" someone exclaimed.

"It'll kill us all!" someone else cried.

But then Edmond slipped back into the shadows, as suddenly as he had appeared, only to reappear down the line a-ways to scare more customers.

There were more shrieks, this time of both fright and delight as people realised the creature wasn't trying to hurt them.

He did this a couple more times, providing scary entertainment until the curtain covering the entrance was lifted, and people were allowed to file in.

Edmond vanished as mysteriously as he had arrived.

Inside Zeke's huge silk tent, it was standing room only. Yes, this was because all of Mojo County had shown up to see the show, but also because there weren't any chairs. Dr Barton Bigelow appeared in a pool of light in the middle of the ring, his staff upraised and humming. With a crackle of electricity, it sparked into life and shot lightning-bolts in all directions.

*"I am Dr Barton Bigelow!"* he thundered, as though his voice had been enhanced somehow. Everyone in the crowded tent clearly heard him, despite the conversation and noise. "I was recently laid low by the God of Storms, but I've returned, bigger and better than ever! Providence saw fit to practically drop into my lap a whole new troupe of the most amazing performers I've ever seen, and the opportunity to practise my art once more!"

He paused dramatically. "May I present . . . drumroll if you please . . . *Jenny Haniver!*"

There was a drumroll—no-one knew where the hell it was coming from—and on the ring appeared an entirely new creature. The ugly mutant in the jar had been transformed into a full-grown sexy mermaid creature. It stood about six-feet tall, with long silvery tendrils for hair, a curvaceous female body clad in a fish-scale corset, and four long sinuous arms. Instead of legs it had a fish's body, but at the bottom, instead of a tail, was a mess of tentacles that it used to move around on. The tentacles writhed like a pile of worms as it glided forward, lifting all four arms in the air to thunderous applause.

"She used to reside in a tiny jar," Dr Bigelow proclaimed, removing the vessel from inside his red coat with an extravagant flourish. "But she no longer needs it. Isn't she magnificent?" He waved his gloved hands at her. "But there is more to her than meets the eye! She isn't just a pretty face." He lowered his voice dramatically. "She can also read minds!"

The audience drew in shocked gasps.

"In fact, she can read your thoughts right now!" Bigelow made a show of pressing one hand against his forehead. Then he pointed his glowing, crackling staff at a large woman in the front row. "She is telling me what you, my dear lady, are thinking right now—'did I lock my front door?'" The woman gasped, and he pointed out a tall, thin man in the row behind. "And she tells me that you are thinking about your broken down horse, and hoping that it will be fixed all right!" The man's jaw dropped. "But more of the amazing Jenny Haniver later! Right now I would like to introduce the rest of my marvellous new troupe!"

Jenny Haniver slithered off into the shadows, disappearing from sight, and a new freak appeared, scuttling forward into the light of

Dr Bigelow's staff, and the more diffuse glow coming from the ball of worms overhead. "Preee-senting—Zeke the arachnizoid!" the doctor yelled. "Once a mere mortal like the rest of us, a chance encounter with a monstrous spider caused him to change into a half-human, half-arachnid!"

Zeke "the Freak" Sarandon scuttled forward on all four of his long, thin spider legs. He swept off his battered old hat and bowed low. Then he proceeded to stun and amaze by climbing quickly and nimbly up one of the circus tent poles and spinning a very large web across the ring. He dropped to the floor to thunderous applause and bowed low. Dr Bigelow clapped along with everyone else as Zeke hurried off.

"And now, an exceptionally rare creature—only once in all my travels have I actually encountered one—a *deersquaw!* Meet Running Deer!"

The deer centaur came thundering out on her Titezium hooves, rearing magnificently for the audience to display her shiny metallic feet. She looked breathtaking beneath the glow-worm lights, her jet-black hair shining, her golden skin gleaming with life and excitement. Still standing on her back feet, she flicked razor-sharp Titezium blades from her fore-hooves. The audience gasped and clapped. "Later on she will throw some blades for your entertainment!"

Running Deer darted off, and Bear Foot walked out, Pat's blue eyes gleaming in his chest. There were more cries of surprise from locals who had never seen such a being before. "Allow me to introduce Bear Foot the Blemmya scout, who possesses the ability of 'third sight'!" Dr Bigelow tucked his staff under one arm and clapped his hands. "He can see the truth that lies in your very soul! You can ask him anything, but think very carefully before you do—he is brutally honest! He will be doing readings after this show in a tent of his own!"

Bear Foot gave a bow and walked off.

"Now allow me to introduce a lady I have named Sagara—a beautiful desert bloom from the badlands who lost her colony and became a wanderer looking for a new home! A succulent, a Cactus Girl!" He waved his hands and the large, shapely cactus woman appeared, over ten feet tall and covered with spikes. She drew more gasps and murmurs of amazement. "She has the strength of a tree and can drain all the liquid from an object in the blink of an eye!"

Sagara spread her enormous arms. The spikes covering her body started to grow and lengthen, becoming a truly formidable skin of lethality covering her body. Then she retracted them back to a couple of inches, gave a bow, and walked off to the sound of applause.

"Now I would like you meet another lovely creature who will be performing in our show—Anna Conda, the hypnotic snake mistress!" Dr Bigelow waved his hands and the late Black-Ace McCade's partner in crime slithered forward into the light, her scales glittering as though possessing lights of their own. She made all sorts of amazing patterns appear on her scales as she undulated forward in a sort of sexy, sinuous dance.

"If you think she's enthralling now, just wait until she sings! She can make angels weep, my friends." The doctor clapped his hands, and Anna Conda slid off as silently and gracefully as she had arrived. "But that's for a later time."

"Now allow me to introduce these delightful little fellows!" Dr Bigelow waved his hands, and the remaining Jarboys, led by One, came running out. They leapt, tumbled and fell over each other, ending up in horrible tangles of arms and legs. They got in each other's way, staged mock fights and generally clowned around, much to the amusement of the onlookers. Everyone cheered, applauding the antics of the stunted creatures who had until recently known only misery and suffering. Dr Bigelow had cut open their leathern longjohns, allowing them the freedom to feel the air and sun on their skin, and wash for the first time. However, the Jarboys had soon returned to their suits, feeling too naked and uncomfortable out of them. So the doctor had arranged to dye and style the leather suits into new, colourful outfits. Now they resembled small harlequins instead of slaves.

Dr Bigelow clapped his hands at the capering Jarboys. "Come on now, lads! Enough skylarking! You have a job to do! Bring out my Fabulous Flotilla of Freaks!"

The Jarboys untangled themselves, bowed and scurried off. From the shadows came a loud creaking noise, and soon they reappeared pushing a large black cart containing a set of shelves. Carefully arranged on them were jars of various pickled specimens;

deformed human foetuses, mutant fish, amphibians, reptiles and mammals, and some bizarre composite creatures that looked like they had been stitched together by a mad necromancer.

"Behold! My first collection! Some genuine specimens of true monstrosity, some I created myself when I was still searching for the secret of reanimation. These will also be on display in a separate tent for you to peruse more closely at your leisure! I also have a large collection of weird and wonderful badlands plants for you to marvel upon, including a deadly spikypine and the Kissing Orchid, but you must wait to see them. They are not quite ready. Sagara is still nursing them from seedlings." He waved his hands at the Jarboys, and they trundled the cart back into the darkness.

The glow-worms hanging in strings above suddenly started moving of their own accord, coalescing into a large ball directly above Dr Bigelow's head. He was bathed in their strange, diffuse light, looking almost otherworldly with his hat shadowing his face and his eyes seeming to glow beneath. He lifted his staff and sent more electricity crackling around his head. "And I must not forget to mention myself. I am a scientician, once an eminent doctor from the east, driven from my hospital by the closed, conservative minds of my class to exile here in the hinterlands. But it is here in this amazing wilderness that I was able to follow my true calling! The scientic art of ressurrectionism!" He sent the electricity blasting around the tent, taking care not to touch the silk sides and set them on fire. "I will be developing new and varied creatures for your pleasure and amusement! I will be performing miracles above and beyond the scope of your imagination! *I will be bringing the dead back to life!*" He paused for effect, scanned the awestruck faces of the audience.

There were more gasps and whispers and finally claps and cheers. He waited for them to die down before continuing. "Now, I trust, you have all heard the phrase 'till death do you part'? Well, I would like to turn that phrase on its head. Among my many and varied qualifications, I am also a fully licensed minister in the Church of the Resurrection! Tonight, I will marry two people whose love has transcended life itself! Allow me to introduce Steel Hawl and Sallianne Veerhoven!" He clapped his hands again and the two zombies stepped out into the ball of light.

Steel was dressed in his usual long leather coat, now clean and with all the rips and holes stitched up. His hat had also been cleaned and repaired. He had on a clean shirt and neckerchief. His spurs had also been polished and glinted in the light. There were gasps at the sight of his empty eye socket and the single white eye that seemed to be looking everywhere at once.

Sallianne's wispy blonde hair had been carefully curled and piled high onto her head to hide her bald patches. Her one eye also seemed to be examining the entire audience. She was wearing Marilou-Belle Watkins's jewel-encrusted crinoline, also clean and the collar stitched up. It had been altered to reveal her midriff, where a new clock with several faces showed the time, date, season and phase of the moon.

"Yes, zombies the pair of them!" the doctor boomed. "I knew Sallianne when she was alive, and when I heard of her unfortunate demise, I arranged to buy her body from some Feratu Noi who had been planning to sell her on the east coast. Then Mr Hawl arrived looking for her. He said he had been searching all over the badlands for her. He had tangled with spikypines and Kissing Orchids for her. He crossed the Demon Flats for her. He fought Duoquois, Sabre-Wings and Feratu Noi for her. Now, if that's not love, *I don't know what is!* By the powers vested in me by the Church of the Resurrection, I pronounce thee, Husband and Wife—*till life do you part!*"

Steel and Sallianne took hands to the sound of thunderous applause. He drew her into his arms and kissed her as the sinuous shape of Anna Conda slithered back out of the darkness. She started to shift back and forth, her coloured scales flickering and forming beautiful patterns. Then she opened her rosebud mouth and started to sing.

As Dr Bigelow had predicted, it was so lovely it brought tears to everyone's eyes. Her voice was gentle but powerful, soft but penetrating, reaching all corners of the tent with equal clarity. The song was like nothing anyone had ever heard before, and caused even the hardest heart to melt. Suddenly everyone in the tent was connected through Anna Conda's song into one giant, loving family.

Steel released Sallianne and looked down at her. She smiled up at him.

By joining Dr Bigelow's travelling circus, Steel not only found his true love, but the friendship, companionship and acceptance he'd never experienced in life.

# ABOUT THE TEAM

**Carter Rydyr (a.k.a. SCAR) are:**
**Antoinette Rydyr—Original Concept and Writer**
**Steve Carter—Writer and Illustrator**

Their strange and bizarre works incorporates anything from sci-fi and horror fantasy to surrealism and weird satire. All of it has a strong element of the fantastic and a healthy dose of experimentalism. They create in a variety of mediums—prose fiction, illustration, comic books, screenplays and even music.

Their original screenplay *"Curse of the Swampies"*, a horror sci-fi film, won "Best Feature Film Screenplay" at the A Night of Horror International Film Festival 2010 and they have recently published several graphic novels, including *"Phantastique"*, *"Savage Bitch"*, *"Femonsters"*, *"Weird Worlds"* and *"Weird Sex Fantasy"*.

More grotesque delights can be viewed on their website: www.weirdwildart.com

**Ethan Somerville—Writer**

Ethan is a prolific Australian author with over 60 books published, and many more to come. These novels cover many different genres, including romance, historical, children's and young adult fiction. However Ethan's favourite genres have always been science fiction and fantasy. Ethan has also collaborated with other Australian authors and artists, and is best known for the popular *"Nocturnal Academy"* series, *"The Eridon Chronicles"* series and *"The Circus Infinitus"* series.

Visit the website: www.stormpublishing.net
Visit Ethan's facebook page at:
   http:/www.facebook.com/Ethan.Somerville.writer

**Dave Heinrich—Cover Artist**

Dave Heinrich is an illustrator and graphic designer based in Adelaide, well known for his work internationally in publishing, particularly comicbook art, cartoons and caricatures, but he has also worked extensively as an artist in advertising, game design and webcam animation. His publishing credits include *Batman: Legends of the Dark Knight* (DC), *The Phantom* (Marvel), *Elvira: Mistress of the Dark* (Claypool Comics) *The Eternal Warrior* (Valiant) and *Conan the Barbarian* (Marvel).

## Boiled Americans by Michael Allen Rose

Boiled Americans is a puzzle box in book form, inspired by the violence of living in urban America and exploding the tendency to forget or ignore.

## Great American Slasher by David C. Hayes

Baseball, apple pie . . . and murder.

## The Bohemian Guide to Monogamy
## by Andrew Armacost

Here, a strange labyrinth of interlinked short fiction assembles itself into a darkly moving novella that deftly explores the bottomless pain and pleasure of love and commitment, the hinterland between youth and adulthood.

## Surreal Worlds edited by Sean Leonard

An anthology of surrealistic compositions created by some of the finest names in genre fiction. A showcase of international talent undaunted by the conventions of language and common narrative structures. Here is timelessness. Here is Surreal Worlds

## How to Succesfully Kidnap Strangers
## by Max Booth III

Do not respond to bad reviews. If you must respond to bad reviews, please do not kidnap the reviewer.

## ADHD Vampire by Matthew Vaughn

He came, he conquered, he was distracted a lot

## Notes from the Guts of a Hippo
## by Grant Wamack

A rugged journalist travels to Brazil in search of a missing hippo researcher and the notes left behind lead to something earth shatteringly revelatory.

# All Art is Junk by R. A. Harris

Lana Rivers, a girl with paintbrush hair, is missing and it's up to Lancelot, her cyborg knight, and his bionic conjoined twin, Cilia, to find her before her evil father, a disrespected artist turned mad-scientist, performs a terrible experiment on her.

# Cherub by David C. Hayes

Cherub wasn't like the other boys—too slow, too rough— but he didn't deserve what that hospital did to him, and now he will make them pay.

# Skinners by Adam Millard

Los Angeles, the City of Angels. At least, that's what the brochure says. What it fails to mention is the earthquakes. Oh, and the flesh-eating creatures lying dormant beneath the concrete, waiting for the chance to surface once again. Their wait is over . . .

# The After-Life Story of Pork Knuckles Malone by MP Johnson

What's a farm boy to do when his pet pig becomes an evil, decaying hunk of ham with slime-spewing psychic powers?

# A Lightbulb's Lament by Grant Wamack

A gentleman with a lightbulb for head wakes up in a world full of darkness, hooks up with a beautiful ex-prostitute, and an old man who can heal people; he travels down south to find the mysterious Creator.

# The Horror Show by Vincenzo Bilof

A poetry novel—a narcoleptic, amnesiac Nobel Prize-winning poet becomes the subject of an experiment to cure madness.

# Beyond by Jordan Krall

From Jerusalem to Mars, psychiatry and the unraveling of the universe

## Gravity Comics Massacre
## by Vincenzo Bilof

An absolutely shitty novella involving comic books, aliens, a serial killer, teenagers in an abandoned town, horror-trope dream sequences, and an ending you're going to hate.

## Glue by Scott Lange

Sticky bowels and sticky situations.

## Ascent by Matthew Bialer

Is the 8 foot tall creature haunting a small town in Iowa in the fall of the year 1903 the product of a hoax and collective imagination or was it one of the first documented paranormal event in America? This epic poem grapples with these questions.

## Elusive Plato by Rhys Hughes

The last in a long decadent line of piratical Spanish eccentrics, Bartleby Cadiz grows up in isolation to be as mad, bad and metaphysical as his ancestors. But he feels there is something different about him. What can it be?

## The Fairy Princess of Trains
## by Christopher Boyle

Danny's mediocre life turns upside-down when his couch starts whispering to him. Then he's charged with a supernatural mission: Rescue the Fairy Princess of Trains.

## Terence, Mephisto & Viscera Eyes
## by Chris Kelso

9 new science fiction stories from Chris Kelso

## Industrial Carpet Drag by Bruce Taylor

Chemicals make you do great things!

# Bizarro Bizarro: An Anthology

The finest bizarro short stories from 2013.

# Necrosaurus Rex by Nicolas Day

Necrosaurus Rex tells the tale of Martin, a simple janitor, who takes an unfortunate trip through time, becomes a violent mutant, and the father of us all. There's 14 billion years crushed inside these pages, and most of them are pretty nasty.

# Day of the Milkman by S. T. Cartledge

In a world dominated by the milk industry, only one milk-man survives after a terrible storm sinks all the ships and throws the Great White Sea out of balance.

# Moosejaw Frontier by Chris Kelso

An unapologetic disaster of metafiction

# The Boy Who Loved Death by Hal Duncan

From blackest humour to bleakest horror, with twisted relish, Hal Duncan's eighteen tales dig into death—and the life that goes with it.

# X's for Eyes by Laird Barron

Between the machinations of the disciples of black gods and good old corporate skullduggery, it's winding up to be of a hell of a summer vacation for the Tooms Brothers.

# Omega Grey by Seb Doubinsky

When professor Todd Bailer embarked on a psychedelics quest to discover if the land of the Dead really existed, he had no idea he would threaten the cosmic balance of the universe by triggering a real-estate conquest of the new Frontier.

## Berzerkoids by MP Johnson

The first short story collection from Wonderland Book Award-winning author MP Johnson

## Retch by David Bernstein

What would you do if you were cursed to puke right before you reached orgasm? You'd do anything, right? (You know you would.) Find out what one wealthy, good-looking, playboy will do to try to end his abhorrent curse.

## Static/Orgone by Jamie Grefe

A double-novella of literary grindhouse nightmares and theoretical post-apocalyptic vengeance.

## Wonder Weavers by Matthew Bialer

An epic poem about a mysterious sighting in 1896.

## Battering the Stem by Bob Freville

A darkly comic urban crime novella. What would it take to make you beg?

## Cartoons in the Suicide Forest
## by Leza Cantoral

When we're dead
You know she'll adore us

www.ingramcontent.com/pod-product-compliance
Lightning Source LLC
Chambersburg PA
CBHW070818180626
46818CB00001B/314